I'LL NEVER TELL

I'LL NEVER TELL

ABIGAIL HAAS

Previously titled *Dangerous Girls*

Simon Pulse

New York   London   Toronto   Sydney   New Delhi

SIMON PULSE

An imprint of Simon & Schuster Children's Publishing Division

1230 Avenue of the Americas, New York, New York 10020

This Simon Pulse hardcover edition June 2019

Text copyright © 2013 by Abigail McDonald

Previously titled *Dangerous Girls*

Jacket photograph copyright © 2019 by Sonia Neisha/Arcangel Images

All rights reserved, including the right of reproduction in whole or in part in any form.

SIMON PULSE and colophon are registered trademarks of Simon & Schuster, Inc.

For information about special discounts for bulk purchases, please contact
Simon & Schuster Special Sales at 1-866-506-1949 or business@simonandschuster.com.

The Simon & Schuster Speakers Bureau can bring authors to your live event.

For more information or to book an event contact the Simon & Schuster
Speakers Bureau at 1-866-248-3049 or visit our website at www.simonspeakers.com.

Jacket designed by Tiara Iandiorio

Interior designed by Mike Rosamilia

The text of this book was set in Adobe Caslon Pro.

Manufactured in the United States of America

2 4 6 8 10 9 7 5 3 1

Library of Congress Control Number 2019935872

ISBN 978-1-5344-4509-3 (hc)

ISBN 978-1-4424-8661-4 (eBook)

The truth is rarely pure and never simple.

—Oscar Wilde

I'LL NEVER TELL

ARUBA EMERGENCY SERVICES
911 TRANSCRIPT—8:45 p.m.

DISPATCHER: **Hallo, hoe gaat het ermee?**

FEMALE 1: **Hello? Hello?**

DISPATCHER: **What is your emergency?**

FEMALE 1: **We can't find our friend. . . . We haven't heard from her all day; she's not picking up her phone.**

DISPATCHER: **How long has she been missing?**

FEMALE 1: **No, she's not missing, but her door's locked and—**

(background) FEMALE 2: **Tell her . . . the blood.**

FEMALE 1: (muffled) **. . . you shut up!** (louder) **We think . . . It looks like there's blood on the floor. Can you send someone?**

DISPATCHER: **I'll have a patrol come by. What's your address?**

FEMALE 1: **We're in one of the houses, on Paradise Beach.** (muffled) **AK, what's the address?** (background)

MALE 1: (unintelligible)

DISPATCHER: **Miss? Are you there?**

FEMALE 1: **Max says her balcony door's smashed. . . . He's going around the back.** (muffled) **Chels, try her phone again.**

FEMALE 2: She's not picking up.

MALE 1: Wait, I can hear . . . Can you . . . ?

(unintelligible)

DISPATCHER: Miss, tell me where you are.

FEMALE 1: Max is climbing up. (muffled) Max? Is she there?

(pause)

FEMALE 2: (crying) I don't like this. She wouldn't just leave her phone. You know she . . .

(scream)

FEMALE 1: Oh my God, is that Max? What's going on? Max, is she in there?

MALE 1: Max, open the door! Max!

(sound of movement)

(screams)

FEMALE 2: Oh my God!

FEMALE 1: Elise! No, no . . .

(more screams)

DISPATCHER: Miss, tell me what you see.

FEMALE 1: I can't. . . . (sobbing) Blood. There's blood everywhere!

DISPATCHER: Who's bleeding? Are they okay?

MALE 2: She's not breathing!

FEMALE 1: (unintelligible) I can't. . . . She won't. . . .

FEMALE 2: Help her!

MALE 1: **Tate, Get them out of here!**

(sounds of a struggle)

FEMALE 1: **No! Let me go!**

(pause)

DISPATCHER: **Miss? Are you there? Miss?**

FEMALE 1: **(sobbing) She's dead. There's a knife, and . . .**

Oh God, I can't. . . . She's dead!

THE BOSTON GLOBE

An American teenager has been found dead in Aruba, authorities there have confirmed. The girl, who has yet to be named, was on a weeklong vacation with friends in the resort town of Oranjestad. The group contacted police Tuesday night after the victim failed to answer her cell phone. Investigators discovered the body that night at the luxury beach house owned by the father of one of the teens.

Local police have refused to comment, but investigating judge Klaus Dekker confirmed to our reporter that the death was suspicious, and a murder investigation has been opened.

BEFORE

"Shots! Shots! Shots!"

We yell it together, slamming our hands on the sticky wooden table. The dreadlocked waiter pours a row of something lurid, neon blue. It's our first night on the island, and the music is almost too loud for me to think—some European dance-pop thing that shakes the crowded beach club, making the glasses quiver and the blood vibrate in my chest.

"Aruba, bitches!" Elise raises her shot in a toast, lights splintering off the glass, golden in her hair.

"Spring break!" The group whoops, and then I'm gulping down the drink, shuddering at the sickly bittersweet taste and the familiar burn that snakes down my throat. Melanie screws her face up, gagging; Max and AK pump the air and howl, but

Elise is already reaching for another, plain tequila this time, with a side of salt and lime.

"Easy, girl," Tate says, and laughs to Elise, one arm slung around my shoulder.

She ignores him, turning to me with a wicked smile. "Bottoms up, babe." Elise grins, but instead of shaking the salt out on her hand, she sprinkles it on my neck, leaning in to lick up along my collarbone before downing the shot.

I shiver at the touch and playfully shove her away. "You're drunk."

"And you need to loosen up!" Elise shimmies, blond hair flying out around her bare shoulders. "We're on vacation. Time to party!"

She grabs Mel and Chelsea and heads for the dance floor, her hips already moving to the thunder of bass. They dance and whirl, swallowed up into the tight press of sweaty bodies.

I search for the rest of our group. Chelsea's twin brother, Max, is already off bro-ing it up with AK by the bar, trying their luck with a pair of Swedish-looking blondes. Max's fair hair and AK's black curls are bent close, to hear the girls or check out their cleavage, I don't even have to guess. Lamar sprawls on the other side of the booth, the lights hitting blue and deep indigo against his black skin. He peels the label from his beer bottle as Chelsea, who left the dance floor, tries to tempt him out. She grinds above him like a lap dancer, laughing, until he finally catches her around the waist and follows her into the dark, one hand draped possessively across her shoulder.

I'm left alone in the corner with Tate. I slide closer, kissing him until I feel the tension in his shoulders. "What's wrong?"

"Nothing." He shakes it off. "I guess I'm still stressed from finals. Everyone said Yale would get back to me before—"

"They will," I tell him firmly. His blond hair is mussed, so I reach up to push it out of his eyes. I let my hand stay there, resting against his cheek. "They have to take you." I grin, teasing, "You're the chosen one. I mean, if you don't get in, what hope is there for the rest of us? I'll be sweeping floors at community college." I laugh, but Tate still looks distracted. "It'll be fine," I reassure him again. "And even if it's not, there's nothing you can do now. You might as well have fun."

Tate exhales, finally smiling. "You're right. I'm sorry." He leans to drop a kiss on my forehead. "I guess I just need to de-stress."

"Lucky for you, we're in the right place for that." I lace my fingers in his. "A whole week, no parents, no rules . . ." I reach up to kiss him, and this time, there's no tension, just a familiar low heat building, and Tate's hands sliding along the edge of my shirt—

Arms suddenly encircle me from behind, dragging me away. Elise. She squeezes tighter, kissing my cheek.

"What are you sitting around for?" She yanks me to my feet. "Come! Dance!" Elise grabs Tate with her other hand; we exchange a look as she drags us deeper into the crowd.

The music shifts to some dirty hip-hop beats, and soon I'm surrounded by skin and sweat and heat, a mass of bodies moving in a slow, grinding pulse. Elise keeps hold of me, dancing and posing, pulling me into it, until my self-consciousness drifts away and I'm as lost in the music as she is. Every party, every dance floor, every illegal warehouse rave is the same: once I'm past that first, awkward moment, once Elise has dragged me into it—out of myself—it's like nothing else. I'm not Anna, I'm not me anymore; I'm something beyond, my heart racing as the songs melt into each other, and all that matters is the beat and their bodies, and that bass, pounding on.

Breathless, I let my body go, let it move and sway, caught up. Tate brings me tight against him, and then it's the three of us, me and Elise dancing up close to him and spinning away; green strobe lights cutting through the dark. Tate laughs between us, his hands lingering on Elise's waist as she grinds against him. The spotlights strobe across his face, the beautiful angles of his jaw, and suddenly I want him with a fierce ache in my chest. *Mine.* I grab his hand away from her, pulling him wordlessly to the edge of the dance floor, my back finding some solid surface, his hands finding the curve of my hips, his lips finding mine.

He leans in to kiss me, pushing me hard up against the wall. I wrap my arms around his neck, pulling him down, locking him against me as our mouths hungrily roam over lips and skin and shoulders. I wish I could stay like this forever—the tightrope wire between drunk and sober, between flesh-and-blood and *free*. Then the music changes again, something pulsating and euphoric, and we're back on the floor, dancing. I don't know how long we've been out there when Elise yanks me away. "Bathroom break!" she orders, collecting Chelsea and Mel from their spot by the DJ booth.

We girls spill into the tiny bathroom, scattering lip gloss and mascara on the countertop, crowding around the cracked mirror. "So, who's in for some skinny-dipping?" Elise hops up by the sink and swings her heels against the cabinet. She fixes me with a mischievous grin. "What do you say, like that time in Walden Pond?"

I laugh. "Yeah, and we nearly died of hypothermia."

Elise shrugs, unconcerned. "So it's a good thing we're in the Caribbean now."

"You're not serious?" Mel blinks from under her blunt-cut black bangs. "It's pitch-black out there; you'd drown."

"Maybe I'll find a cute Aruba lifeguard to come protect me." Elise carefully pouts, applying another layer of pink lip stain.

"Or cut you into tiny pieces and feed you to the sharks," Mel mutters. She tugs at the hem of the skirt we had to talk her into, trying in vain to yank it an extra inch down over her pale thighs. I feel a stab of irritation at her whining. Typical Mel—always acting like a chaperone even when the rest of us are having fun. Straight A's, future med student: she wants everything to run on a strict plan. Her plan.

"Lighten up." I sigh. "You're not still pissed about the room thing?"

"It's not a room," Mel complains. "It's, like, a closet with a pullout bed."

"You could share with AK and my brother," Chelsea calls from inside the tiny cubicle. There's a flush, and she emerges, finger-combing her long, salt-bleached hair. She barely glances at her reflection, barefaced with her dusting of freckles. But then, she doesn't need to. Chelsea has that whole natural, beach beauty thing down cold. Even during icy Boston winters, she always manages to look like she just strolled in from a surfing session in the sun. "Although," she adds with a smirk, "you'll have to deal with all their gross boy underwear lying around."

"That's not the only thing they're trying to lay," I quip. Elise laughs, and high-fives me.

"Maybe they'll let you watch," she adds to Mel. "You might learn something."

"La, la, la!" Chelsea protests, covering her ears. "What's the rule?"

"No talking about your brother and his sex life." Elise sighs.

"Or his lack of one." I grin, but Mel is still sulking. She turns to Elise.

"I don't know why I can't just share with you."

"Because I plan on having fun." Elise smiles. "Like with that blond guy, the one in the VIP booth."

"They have a VIP booth here?" Chelsea laughs, trying to rinse her hands under the sputtering tap. Her wrists are full of knotted yarn bracelets and exotic beads, fraying until they're barely hanging on. "They don't even have running water."

Elise just applies a coat of gloss red lip balm. "He's cute, I'm telling you. I think I'll have him come back to see the house. The view from my bedroom . . ." She winks.

"Elise!" Mel protests, like clockwork, "You don't even know him. He could be a rapist, or murderer, or—"

"Stop with all the buzzkill," I interrupt.

"You need a drink," Elise agrees. She hops down and links her arm with Mel's, giving me an exasperated look over her head. "Two drinks. And a hot, sweaty local guy."

"I'm not—"

"Interested, we know." Elise steers her out, back into the club.

We chorus in unison, "You're not that kind of girl."

Melanie pouts. "You say it like it's a bad thing."

Elise rolls her eyes. "No, we say it like it's a dull thing."

Back on the floor, Elise points out her target for the night.

He's lounging with some buddies in the corner: he's handsome, in his early twenties maybe, with a bored nonchalance that just screams *rich kid*.

"Cute, right?" She grinds against me, flashing flirtatious looks over at the guy, pulling me in to nuzzle at my neck.

I laugh. "He looks like trouble."

She grins back. "Just the way I like them." And then she's gone, ducking through the crowd toward the guy. I watch her go. Within seconds, she's smiling and laughing with the group, that one guy giving her an approving grin.

Tate reappears next to me. "Where's Elise?" he yells to be heard.

I shrug vaguely, but Tate looks across the floor to where she's already angled, cross-legged in the booth with them, leaning in to talk to her prospective conquest. Her hair glows purple and red under the lights, tanned legs long and bare under her skirt. I smile, watching her at work. She's gorgeous; no man would stand a chance of resisting.

"I don't like this. We should stick together," he yells again, frowning.

"Relax!" I slide my arms around him, pulling his lips down to mine. "Elise is a big girl. She can take care of herself."

THE HEARING

"I didn't do it!"

I leap up, the words flying from my lips the moment the lawyer steps into the holding room. "I didn't do it," I say again, gripping my hands together as if I can save myself from drowning. "This is all a mistake."

Even as I say it, I can hear how cliché it sounds, like I'm stuck in the nightmare of one of those trashy soaps I would watch with my mom as a kid. I swallow back the hysterics, try to sound calm and collected. "You believe me, don't you? You have to make them see."

The lawyer's name is Ellingham, and he's all jowls and receding hairline, an international law specialist Tate's dad flew in from New York. He doesn't speak until the guard closes the door behind him and we're alone in the small room. Then he places his briefcase on the table they've bolted to the floor and finally looks at me.

"That doesn't matter, not today."

I stare back in disbelief. "Of course it matters! They're saying . . . They say . . ." My voice breaks.

"Today is a simple bail hearing," he explains, unclicking the stays on the briefcase. It's leather, expensive. Everything about him is expensive: the crisp shirt, the designer linen suit, the heavy fountain pen he uses to sign the top sheet of the papers. In the prison, they have me wearing an itchy canvas jumpsuit, but my dad brought clean clothes for the hearing. I've never been so happy to wear a simple white tank top in my life: the cotton soft against my skin, smelling like our old detergent. Like home.

"This hearing isn't to argue your case," Ellingham warns me. "You'll go sit, state your name, and then enter your plea. Sign here." He offers the pen.

I sign, awkward in handcuffs. "Can you get them to take these off?" I ask hopefully. My wrists are ringed with red and bruises now, but I'm lucky: the first court appearances had me in leg shackles too, and I flushed with shame to stumble across the room like a drunk freshman trying to walk in heels.

He shakes his head. "Not right now, but once the judge grants bail, you'll be released."

"Then we can go home." I feel a sob of sheer relief at the prospect, and fight to swallow it back. I can't be the girl weeping in the courtroom, I know. I have to be strong.

"You mustn't leave the island." Ellingham looks at me as if I should know all this already. "It'll be a term of your bail. You have to stay until the trial."

I nod eagerly. Anything to get me out of jail. They've kept me in isolation since the arrest, five long days when I've seen nobody but unfriendly guards and the distant sight of other prisoners as they march me between the exercise pen and my cell. It's too hot to sleep, and I spend every night huddled on my bunk on the thin wool blanket, counting cracks on the ceiling and waiting to wake up and find this is all a dream.

But it isn't.

The guard knocks, then enters, gesturing for us to go.

"Is Tate okay?" I demand, following Ellingham down the windowless hallway. The guard matches me, step for step, as if I'm about to break free and run. "Will he be there?"

"You'll be processed together." He's already checking his phone, done with me. "Don't speak to him, or anyone, until you're out of there. Just your name and plea."

I nod again. I used to give the lawyer messages to pass along, words of love, little in-jokes, but he never brought any word back from Tate, so I quit even trying. I was so used to texting back and forth with him every hour I was awake, I still hear phantom rings; a low buzz that makes me leap up, searching around the cell for the phone. But of course, there are none in there, even if Tate were free to call. He's been locked up, like me, somewhere on the other side of this sprawling compound. The longest we've been apart in five months.

It's the longest I've been apart from Elise, too, but I can't think about that.

They transport me in the back of an unmarked van, with another two guards sitting on each side as if I'm still planning an escape. I want to laugh and tell them I can't even make it through cross-country trials in phys ed, let alone flee police custody. Besides, where would I go? The island is less than seventy square miles: nothing but beaches and high-rise hotels and cacti growing wild in the dusty swathes of land not overtaken by fast-food outlets and Caribbean beach bars. *Paradise*, all the tourism websites called it. Ellingham is traveling separately in his rented luxury sedan. The driver up front in the van plays a local Aruba radio station, the DJ babbling in Dutch between American pop and rap hits. I remember that first night on the island. Elise and Melanie and Chelsea and me, dancing together in the club. We took photos on our cell phones, uploading them to all our profiles right away with the title "Best Spring Break Ever." We tagged and commented and reposted, just to make sure everybody back home would see it and know what a fabulous time we were all having. Know that they weren't invited.

I wonder how long it'll take the tabloids to find the photos. Or maybe they already have, and they're printed on some front page somewhere.

A cautionary tale.

"Tate!"

I know what the lawyer said, but I can't help it—he's already sitting at the defendant's table when the guard leads me in, his head bowed and staring at the floor. "Tate!" I all but sprint down the aisle toward him.

"Miss!" The guard yanks me to a stop, "No running. Don't make me get the leg shackles."

I stop. "No, please, I'm sorry. I wasn't thinking."

He glares at me for a moment, then loosens his grip on my arm and shoves me toward one of the empty chairs.

I sink into it, my eyes still on Tate. He doesn't look up, just sits there, head bowed beside me. "Hey," I can't resist whispering. "Are you okay?"

The lawyer hushes me, but I don't care. "Tate?" I whisper again. "Look at me."

He does, and the defeated expression on his face moves me more than the blunt metal on my wrists, or the bruise on my ribs from where an unseen passerby shoved me on my first night in jail. His blue eyes are glazed; red from crying, and everything about him seems hunched and broken down.

Tate, the golden one; future president, king of Hillcrest Prep. Tate, who was always so confident, safe in his world of privilege and success, who could charm even our principal's cranky secretary into smiling submission. Tate, my boyfriend, my love, looking like a lost boy: scared and alone, his right leg trembling uncontrollably.

"What did they do to you?" I gasp, my own sleepless nights forgotten. His eyes just slide away from me, back to the floor.

I feel a hand on my shoulder, and turn to see my father. He reaches out, as if to touch me, but that's against the rules, and when the lawyer quickly clears his throat, my dad's hands drop to his lap. "Everything's going to be okay," he tells me in a voice that almost makes me believe he's right. But his face is pale, and there are dark shadows smudged under his eyes. He forces a smile, placing one hand on my shoulder. "Don't worry, sweetheart. This'll all be straightened out."

"Mr. Chevalier." Ellingham's tone is a warning. Dad pulls his hand away.

"Of course. I'm sorry." He smiles at me again: forced and so upbeat, I have to match it with my own.

"Thanks, Dad," I murmur back as he takes his seat again.

Tate's parents are sitting in the row behind us too: poker-faced and immaculate in tailored suits and carefully styled hair. There are others with them, their heads bent in whispered consultation, brandishing briefcases and notepads and frowns of careful concern. More lawyers, local advisors, assistants, maybe. Mr. Dempsey runs a hedge fund back home, and Mrs. Dempsey runs the Boston social scene; whenever I saw either of them, it was always with some secretary or junior associate scurrying along behind. Now, the numbers make me calm, just a little. I'm not alone in this. They'll make sure this is okay.

"Rise for the Honorable Judge von Koppel."

Ellingham stands in place between us, and we line up to watch the judge walk in. The room isn't a chambers or courthouse, just a regular conference room in a squat, whitewashed building, with tables and folding chairs set out, like the kind you find in hotels for business conventions. Our table is on one side, with our parents and their entourage behind, and the police investigators sit at another table across the aisle. In front, the judge takes a seat behind her table and stares through her wire-rimmed glasses at the papers already waiting for her. She's in her forties maybe, a cool blonde in a navy suit.

"State your names and plea for the record," she tells us. Her Dutch accent is lilting, almost sing song. Tate and I do it in turn. Tate Dempsey. Anna Chevalier. Not guilty. Not guilty.

The judge scribbles something. "You are seeking bail for the defendants?"

Ellingham leaps up. "Yes, Your Honor. Given that both are minors, and have been held on only circumstantial evidence—"

"Objection!" There's a cry from the other table. Ellingham doesn't pause.

"We ask that the courts release them into the custody of their parents as they await trial."

The judge looks curiously at both me and Tate in turn. I stare back, unblinking, trying to show her I have nothing to hide. She looks away, toward the prosecution.

"And you object?"

"Yes, your honor." The police investigator is a short brute of a man, lights gleaming off his bald head. I've spent hours locked in small rooms with that reflection, as he yelled and cajoled and yelled some more, demanding a confession to crimes too awful to contemplate.

I hate him.

"Given the serious nature of the crime, and the defendants' status as foreign nationals, we urge the court to remand them into custody and avoid a flight situation. These people are a risk to the public." He turns to glare at me, and again, I try to stare him down, unflinching.

"Do you have anything to counter these concerns?" The judge asks Ellingham.

One of the associates from behind us leans forward, and he and Ellingham confer, their voices low. After a moment, Ellingham pulls away. "May I approach?"

She nods, and Ellingham and the police investigator move forward to talk with her at the front of the room.

"Hey," I whisper again, using the distraction to reach over to Tate. I touch his arm lightly, and he flinches. "Tay, are you okay?"

He looks up and swallows. "I will be," he replies softly, his eyes on mine. "When we get out of here."

"Everything's going to be okay." I repeat what my dad told me. He nods. "We just have to be strong, and stick together."

Tate manages a faint smile, and my panic ebbs. We'll be okay. We have to be.

Ellingham finishes talking up front, and returns to stand between us. The judge shuffles some papers around.

"I've been informed that the Dempsey family has rented a house on the island and will be remaining here with their son until trial. Given those assurances, I am setting Mr. Dempsey's bond at five million dollars, and releasing him to the custody of his parents."

Tate deflates in a great gasp of relief, and there's a sob from his mother behind us. My heartbeat thunders. Thank God.

"However, my concern for Miss Chevalier remains." The judge peers at me, her eyes like ice. "Her family can offer no such assurances, and so I agree with the investigator. The defendant is a flight risk, charged with a violent crime of the highest degree, and will therefore be remanded to the Aruba Correctional Institute awaiting trial for the murder of Elise Warren. Hearing adjourned." She bangs her gavel.

I don't understand.

As the guard pulls me to my feet again, Tate is embraced by his parents. He doesn't turn, not once, as I'm led away, stunned. I catch a glimpse of my father's face staring after me, hollow and slack-jawed.

I open my mouth to call for him, but I can't make a sound.

THE BEGINNING

I meet Elise three weeks into spring semester, junior year. Dad's company is taking off—new clients flooding in, and talks of buyouts and share offerings—so he moves me from the local public high school to Hillcrest Prep, across the bay. If you've ever been the new kid, you know: the meat-market looks and razor-quick judgments are bad enough that first day in September; switching midyear is so much worse. I beg to stay where I am, or wait until senior year, but Dad doesn't listen. He talks about the new opportunities for me: art, and dance, and drama, and how if I switch now, I'm practically guaranteed an Ivy League spot when I apply to colleges, but we both know the move is as much for his benefit as mine. Hillcrest is the home of Boston's elite, and Dad's eyes are fixed on their investment funds. They aren't the parents of my future friends, they're potential clients.

So I switch. And for two weeks, I stay blissfully unnoticed in the crowds of garnet blazers, preppy boys, and perfect girls. I keep my head down, answer only when called on, and eat my lunch alone in the solitude of a study carrel, stationed between Ancient Latin and Anthropology in the huge, wood-beamed library. Nobody notices me, nobody cares.

Not that I mind. The less high school bullshit I have to deal with, the better: the endless popularity contests, the inane gossip. I don't know what happened—if I was out that one time in elementary school, when everyone learned how to talk about nothing all day and think that it matters, or at least, fake that way—but somehow I never learned the trick. The girls are the worst, acting like empires will rise and fall because someone wore last year's colored denim, or someone else hooked up with a guy behind his girlfriend's back. I want to tell them all: the world is bigger than high school.

Sometimes, I get this strange urge, a fierce scream bubbling in my chest; I fantasize about pushing back my chair and howling until my lungs ache and every head turns in my direction. Just to cut through the babble of white noise.

But of course, I never do, and for those first weeks at Hillcrest, I make it my mission to blend in to the background. Better unnoticed than the center of all their curious stares, I decide. I have my routine, my escape routes, my nondescript A–/B+ average, and soon, it looks like I can make it to the end of the year without anyone even noticing I'm there at all.

Until I open my gym locker Monday morning and find a heap of rancid clothing.

"Eww!" "Gross!" The cries go up from the locker room as I lift out my shirt, dripping with what looks like curdled milkshake. It's been left to sit and mold for two days at least, over the weekend, and the smell is sour even through the fog of scented body sprays and pink-flowered deodorant. "What is that?" The other girls shriek, gagging and retching like it's the plague.

My cheeks burn as I search the crowd for the loudest voice; the most wide-eyed look of disgust. There. Lindsay Shaw. I should have guessed. Of all the Hillcrest girls with their perfect ponytails and straight-A grades and sharklike stares, Lindsay's is the most perfect, straightest. Deadly. I'd been called on to debate her in civics the previous week, and had reluctantly offered my arguments as if I was facing a mountain lion: Don't look it in the eye, no sudden movements, and keep your body language submissive.

Clearly I wasn't submissive enough.

Lindsay holds my gaze a moment, smug. "You should get that cleaned up," she tells me in a fake-helpful tone. "Coach Keller is really big on hygiene."

"Thanks," I manage. For a moment, I feel that scream bubble up, but I would have to be crazy to take Lindsay on—in front of everyone this time—so I swallow back my anger and the hot flush of shame, and set about cleaning the mess into the trash with damp paper towels so that by the time Coach arrives to usher us off to volleyball, there's no sign of my ruined gym clothes.

"You." Coach finds me skulking at the back of the crowd, still in my regular uniform. "What's your name?"

"Anna," I mutter, my eyes fixed on the blue linoleum. "Anna Chevalier."

Coach looks me up and down. "Is there a reason you're not dressed yet?"

I look around, catching Lindsay's eye. The challenge in her expression is clear. "I . . . forgot my clothes," I say, my shoulders hunched in defeat.

Coach tuts impatiently. "Don't think you're getting a free study pass. I want an essay on the importance of preparation on my desk by the end of the period."

I nod, trying to ignore Lindsay's victorious grin as the rest of the girls file out, leaving me alone in the locker room with a faintly rancid scent in the air.

The essay is easy enough. I settle into a plastic chair in the Coach's office down the hall, and soon I'm back to scribbling lyrics in my battered red journal and wondering what other fresh hells Lindsay has in store for me this semester.

"Hey."

I turn. A blond girl is in the doorway, pressed and precise in her polo shirt and sports skirt. Elise, I remember from French class. She looks around cautiously at the mess of lacrosse sticks and yoga mats. "Are we supposed to wait in here till the end of class?"

I nod, quickly tucking my notebook away. Not quickly enough.

"'You want a revelation'...That's Florence and the Machine, right?" Elise asks, seeing the lyrics scribbled on the cover.

I don't answer. She's friends with Lindsay, or at least part of that clique—I've seen them around school, their ponytails swishing in unison. Elise is one of the quiet ones. She didn't join their teasing in the locker room before, but she didn't stand up for me either.

"She played a show here last month, but nobody else likes them, and my parents wouldn't let me go alone." Elise looks rueful.

"I went," I tell her, remembering the night I snuck out for hours and nobody even noticed I was gone. "She played two hours, it was amazing."

"No way!" Elise's reply is the sound of pure longing. She wanders closer. "You're Anna, right? Did you just move here?"

"No," I answer, still careful. "Transferred. From Quincy."

"Oh." Elise looks at me curiously, and I feel myself tense up, waiting for a cutting remark or some bitchy fake advice, but instead she looks almost sympathetic. "You're lucky," she finally offers. "A girl last year, Lindsay, used tuna fish. Stunk out the whole place. Guys were saying . . . Well, you know." Elise shrugs. "I think she transferred in the end."

"Sure," I agree, sarcastic. "I'm lucky."

"Seriously, don't worry about it." Elise looks quickly toward the door before adding, "She's a bitch."

I don't take the bait. I know how this works: anything I say now could be used against me later, spun and filtered through the high school gossip chain until I'm the one attacking poor, innocent Lindsay.

"It's okay," Elise adds, as if reading my mind. "We're not friends. I mean, we hang out, but . . . you know."

I give another vague shrug. "What about you?" I change the subject. "Why are you sitting out?"

"I have a midterm after lunch." Elise wanders restlessly over to the window. She pulls herself up to sit on the wide ledge, looking out over the neat lawn. "I figured, if I lay the groundwork now, it looks more convincing when I get out sick."

"Smart."

She shrugs, swinging her legs to tap out a staccato rhythm against the wall. "If I don't get an A, my parents will send me back into tutoring." She sighs, looking out the window again. "Because a B in American lit will really wreck my entire life."

I don't reply, and pull out my math textbook, but after a few moments, I can still feel Elise's stare burning into me. I look up. "What?"

"Nothing, I just . . ." Elise bites her lip and glances again toward the door before asking, "You want to get out of here?"

"Where to?"

"Downtown, maybe? We could take the T, get a coffee. We'd be back by the end of lunch."

"I thought only seniors were allowed off campus."

"We wouldn't get caught," Elise promises, her eyes bright now. "Everyone does it."

"Have you?" I ask.

There's a pause, then she shakes her head. "Not yet. But that's only because they won't go with me," she adds quickly. "Lindsay never breaks the rules. Except, you know, the ones about being a decent human being," she says with a slight grin.

"I don't know. . . ." I'm still suspicious, looking for her angle, but Elise hops down from the window ledge.

"Come on, it'll be fun. And if they ask where you were, just say you were helping me. The teachers here love me, I never do anything wrong." Her voice twists on the last words, something almost like regret, and the familiar sound is enough to make me pause. I never do anything wrong either—I've never taken the chance. Other girls skip out for shopping trips, and birthdays at the beach, loudly planning their exploits right beside my locker without a second glance. But me? I'm too careful for that. I've never skipped so much as a study period in my life.

I'm still wavering when another girl bursts in, breathless and flushed. "Elise, oh my god, are you okay? Coach wouldn't let me check on you until we'd run laps."

Elise laughs. "Relax, Mel, I'm fine. It's nothing."

"Are you sure?" Melanie's eyes are wide with concern. She's petite, with glossy dark hair and delicate features, and she reaches up to test Elise's temperature. Elise ducks away.

"Mel, I'm fine! I was just faking to get out of the lit test."

"Oh." Melanie pauses. "Right!"

"Me and Anna are going to ditch, go get a coffee downtown," Elise tells her before I can object. "Want to come?"

For the first time, Melanie's gaze slides over to me. She blinks, as if trying to place me, even though we've had at least six classes together since I arrived. "But we're not allowed."

"So?" Elise beams.

"But we'll get in trouble!" Melanie whines.

"Then stay here." Elise scoops up her bag. "Cover for us, okay?" She turns back to me. "Coming, Anna?"

NOW

The chaplain in prison loves to talk about turning points. The moment we chose the wrong path, the point of no return. It's supposed to help us, to take us back to the place it all started. We're supposed to know better now, you see, understand the error of our ways. So, we pick over our past, tracking back crimes and consequences through our short lives until we find the linchpin. That one decision that could have changed everything.

This was mine.

I can see it as clear as the moment I was standing there myself: the three of us in the jumbled athletics office, midday sun through the windows, and the sounds of the lacrosse match drifting in from outside. An invitation. An adventure.

Elise's eyes, bright with friendship and possibility. Melanie's round face guarded with jealousy. And me, wavering there between them.

If I'd said no that would have been the end of it. Elise would have gone back to hovering quietly in the folds of her shiny, perfect clique, and I'd have eaten lunch alone in the library, been tormented by Lindsay until graduation. Our worlds would probably never have collided again, merely passed in the hallways and spun off on our different orbits, to college and first jobs, white-confetti weddings, and babies nestled, safe and gurgling on our hips.

She'd be alive. I wouldn't be accused of her murder.

CUSTODY

My cell is ten feet by twelve. It has bare concrete floors, and chalky whitewashed walls, and orange paint peeling from the bars.

I've been here twenty-two days.

There are two hard bunk beds set with thin mattresses, and a metal toilet in the corner bolted to the wall that makes me ill with the smell. Everything's bolted down, smooth, too; no sharp edges to catch accidentally against our clothing or wrists. I have a thin blanket, and sheets that make me itch, but it's still too hot and I still can't sleep, surrounded by the strange, ragged pace of other people's breathing.

Their names are Keely and Freja and Divonne. They're older, or maybe just look that way, and after the first stare-down, have paid me little attention at all. They strut around the place with their shirts tied high and contraband lipstick on their faces, bumping fists and calling to cellmates across the aisle. They've been here a while, and will be for some time, bantering and laughing with one another in their foreign tongue. I don't understand a thing except the bitter note in their voices, and the suspicious looks they send my way when they're talking about me and my many terrible crimes.

I never thought I'd miss the pounding silence of isolation, but some nights, I do.

They wake us at six for bed-check, then herd us to showers, and then the dining hall. We line up for trays of flavorless oatmeal and bruised fruit, eat at long metal tables. "Like school," the young assistant from the American consulate told me during our weekly visit, trying to sound cheerful. Not mine. Hillcrest had salad bars and off-campus privileges; my group would gather at the far right table in the cafeteria, reigning over for all to see.

I've lost at least ten pounds. There was a time I'd think that was an achievement.

After breakfast is free time, then lines in the dining hall again for lunch, and dinner—so many lines, I half expect us all to join hands, like in nursery school, snaking across the playground. I've been told I'm lucky there's no work duty, just long days I fill by watching TV, reading the dog-eared paperback books in the makeshift library, and trying not to catch someone's eye in the rec room. I walk for hours in the yellowed grass of the exercise pen, trying to memorize the sprawl of blue sky to take back inside the cell at night. The prison is set on the edge of a cliff: the stretch of blue ocean beyond the walls on one side, an expanse of barren earth separating us from the rest of the island on the other. But we can see neither, of course, just the solid walls and barbed wire penning us in, and the guard towers stationed, always watching.

I can make calls from three to three thirty p.m., but I have nobody to talk to. Dad is back in Boston, trying to remortgage the house and keep a lawyer paid. My friends were swept home by their parents the moment the police allowed them to leave; now they talk to reporters and newscasters, spilling stories and theories about the three of us, Elise and Tate and me. Lamar sent me letters the first couple of weeks, but even those have stopped now—the only time I see his face is scowling in the back of paparazzi shots, his hand blocking the camera as he enters the school gates. He and Chelsea broke up; her and Max's parents are talking about moving them back to California, away from everything.

And then there's Tate. He's somewhere across the island now, in the safe cocoon of his parents' money: waking up alone behind a door he can lock, taking showers behind the privacy of frosted glass, eating cereal straight from the box before he wanders out onto an ocean-view balcony, and meeting with his five assorted lawyers to plot his defense.

He hasn't come to visit me. I don't know if I would see him if he did. I can't forgive him for what he did—for leaving me to face this all alone.

They say the trial will begin in four months. Three, if I'm lucky. Every day, I wonder how I'm going to make it that long.

But of course, I don't have a choice.

THE TRIAL

The photo clicks up on the display projector overhead. Although everyone must have seen it a dozen times over, I still hear the gasps of shock ripple through the court-room.

"Objection!" My lawyer leaps to his feet. The judge sighs, staring over her thin wire-rimmed glasses. "Your objections have been noted, Counselor. Many times."

I sit silently in the witness box. They've been trying to bring up the photos for weeks now, and for weeks, my lawyer has been fighting. They're unrelated. Out of context. Prejudicial. If there was a jury, then maybe he would have won, but here in Aruba, there's no jury deciding my fate. It's just Judge von Koppel, and as she's told him every time, she's already seen them. Hell, everyone has. From the day some journalist browsed our profile pages and hit the tawdry jackpot, those photos have been printed and reprinted, emblazoned across every newspaper front page in the world.

"Miss Chevalier, if you could look at the first photo ..." He clicks again, making it larger this time. "Can you tell us, when was this taken?"

"Halloween," I reply reluctantly. "Last year."

"And that's you in the photograph?"

"Yes."

"With who?"

"Tate," I say quietly, picking at the skin around my left thumbnail. They said I'm supposed to keep my hands folded, unmoving, but I can't help it. Every nail is bloodied by now, scabbed and torn.

He's still waiting, so I take a breath. "And Elise."

"The victim," he announces, as if they didn't know. "And what are your costumes, here?"

"Vampire cheerleaders."

It sounds so stupid, out loud in court, but that's what Halloween is for, right? Slutty nurses and zombie cats; guys with fake limbs and girls in trashy fairy-tale costumes. It doesn't mean anything; it's all just a game. It's not supposed to be blown up as evidence on a display screen one day, like you planned it out from the start.

"Elise and I were vampire cheerleaders," I say again, "and Tate was . . . a bootlegger, I guess. Something from the twenties. He wanted to wear the suspenders and hat."

"And these photographs were taken at . . . the Newport residence?"

I nod. "I mean, yes. We were going to a party, but we all met at the twins', Max and Chelsea's, to get dressed, and take photos and stuff."

He hasn't put the other photos up from that night: Max in his zombie football player uniform; Chelsea as Princess Leia with her hair caught up in fat braided whorls; Lamar as Black Jesus, with the robes and a blinged-out cross; Melanie in her usual slutty cat outfit, whining that she didn't know Elise and I were going to match. We must have taken hundreds of photos that night—dressing up, and posing, and later, at the party— but of course, nobody wants the rest of them. Not when they have the ones they need right there: four pictures, saying everything they want to see.

"And the blood—"

"Fake blood," I interrupt.

"Yes." He gives me a patronizing smile. "Whose idea was that?"

"I don't know. We found it, online," I explain. "The same place we got the costumes."

"We. That's you and Miss Warren."

"Yes."

She had been so excited, showing me the website. Proper horror costumes, like the kind they use for movies and music videos. Blood and scars and fake wounds oozing pus. We'd scrolled through the options, laughing and crying out with disgust. Alien baby. Zombie spinster. Not that we picked any of them in the end. We wanted to look hot, too. Hot with an edge.

"And the knife, whose idea was that?"

I feel my cheeks flush. "I don't know."

"You don't know? But that's you holding it, isn't it?" He clicks the photo even bigger.

"Yes. I mean, I don't remember. There was a lot going on. It's not mine," I add, remembering my lawyer's instructions not to seem sullen or withdrawn. I force a polite smile. "Someone got it from the kitchen, for the photos."

"Somebody." He drags the word out, sounding skeptical. "But you don't remember who?"

"No." My voice is small.

"And you were drinking that night." It doesn't sound like a question, so I don't reply. "You drank often?"

"Objection!"

He turns to the judge. "I'm merely trying to establish Miss Chevalier's normal partying routine."

"I'll allow it." She nods. He turns back to me.

"The drinking," he prompts.

"We all drank." I protest. "Just some wine, or vodka with mixers, you know? The guys had beer. AK always smoked—"

"That's not relevant." He interrupts me quickly. "You and Miss Warren, and Mr. Dempsey. You drank together." He clicks to the next photo, to answer his own question, and there we are: Tate pouring vodka into both of our mouths.

"Yes," I admit. I know what comes next; my lawyer's warned me well enough. He'll ask about the weed and the pills. About my mom's Xanax, and the times Elise tried her dad's Percocet. About the cocaine Melanie saw Elise try over Christmas break, and the liquid X Niklas tried to feed her in the club that night. It sounds so bad, all run together like that, but there's no way around it, save lying, and too many people saw too many things to get away with that. Besides, they told me over and over again: just tell the truth.

I take a breath, bracing myself, but instead the lawyer clicks again, to the next photo. "Can you tell me about the necklaces?"

I stop. "What?"

"A necklace was ripped from the victim's neck that night, and there's a possibility it was the one she's wearing here, in the photograph. You have a matching item. Where did they come from?"

"I . . . me. I got them." I look over at my lawyer, but he looks just as confused as I am.

"With the costumes?"

"No, this was before then."

"When?"

"Uh, over the summer, I think." I pause. "Yes, summer. We were up in Northampton, there's this jewelry store there . . ." I wait, still lost.

"Why did you buy them?"

"I . . . don't know." It's a trap, I know, it has to be, but I can't figure out why or what for. "It was just a gift," I explain. "We would do that: buy two of something, so the other had one. So we matched."

"Why this necklace in particular?"

"It was pretty." I shrug. "It looked cute."

"And can you describe to me the shape of these necklaces?"

My lawyer's face changes to something like panic, but I still don't know why, so I shrug again and answer. "It's geometric. You know, like a—"

I stop. I can see it now. This was his plan all along, and it's worse than we ever thought, but the word is hanging in the air waiting to be spoken.

"Like what, Miss Chevalier?" His voice gets louder, booming in the courtroom. "What was the necklace you bought for Elise?"

I close my eyes a moment.

"A pentagram," I whisper.

"Speak clearly, Miss Chevalier."

I say it again. Another murmur ripples through the courtroom: shock, speculation.

"Wait," I add quickly. "It's not like that. I didn't mean—"

"That's enough." He cuts me off. "No further questions."

"But you can't!" I leap up. "It wasn't like that!"

"Miss Chevalier," the judge interrupts me. "That's enough! Do I need to return you to custody?"

I sink back into the witness chair. He's left the photos up on display. Elise and Tate and me, covered in fake blood. Me holding the knife to her throat. Tate's shirt open, his arms draped around us both. Elise and me licking strawberry syrup off the blade. The close-up of the pentagram necklaces.

They say a picture is worth a thousand words, but these only have one:

Guilty.

BEFORE

I spend that afternoon with Elise cloistered in a coffee shop downtown, talking and laughing and pouring tiny packets of sugar into bitter espresso drinks as we gaze longingly at the ruffle-haired college boys brooding over their laptops. It's new for me: I've never been one of those girls linked arm-in-arm in the street, head bent over a magazine, friendship bracelets falling, frayed, off a wrist. I'm wary at first, still waiting for the sharp comment, the mean-girl backlash, but none comes. Instead, away from her clique, Elise unfurls, hair slipping from her neat ponytail, waistband folded over another daring inch. She gets brighter, louder, almost breathless with gossip, as if she's been keeping this part of herself back for years and can't help but spill over in a torrent of bitching and wishful thinking and plans of traveling in Europe before college, and the California campuses far, far away from her parents.

I'm swept up in her exuberance too, in the tiny space of warmth and easy friendship, like a square of sunshine falling on the cold winter floor. As we sip our coffees and hum along to the indie rock songs on the café stereo, I find myself beginning to hope that maybe, just maybe, things could be different after all. I look at Elise's animated expression, her arms flung wide to illustrate her story, and see an alternate version of my life unfold for the first time: the version where I have a place to sit at lunch, a partner in the lab, after-school plans that count for something more than curling in our living room, alone, eating take-out pizza to the lonely sound of the TV.

And then we slip back into school in time for fifth period, and Elise is gone. Back to Lindsay, and her old clique, back to following them down the hallway—walking half a step behind; her eyes down when she passes me by my locker. Back to the lesser girl she was pretending to be.

And I go back to being nobody at all.

I know I shouldn't be surprised. What was she going to do? Tell her friends to go fuck themselves, cast herself out of their world, all alone?

Of all the many sins of high school, this is the worst. Better to be a sneak, or a slut, or a narc, or a bully, than *alone*. The rest, you can laugh off, turn away from, and pretend it's not true, but when you're alone, you have no one to turn to. You need them: to sit with at lunch, to save you a place in line, to wait with for the bus outside the gates after school. To stand alone says you're an outsider. Different.

I don't blame her. Hell, if it was me in her place, I'd probably do the same, but that doesn't stop the sharp sting in my chest whenever her gaze slides past me and her group explodes in a chorus of giggles. I go back to spending lunch periods in my library carrel, ignoring the whispers and the not-so-subtle way the jock boys sniff the air around me— the legacy of the milkshake prank. The week passes, and turns into the next, and one after that, too, and soon it feels like our stolen afternoon was a dream, some out-of-body experience.

Until Elise finds me weeping in the second-floor girls' bathroom one afternoon, three days before spring break.

"Anna?"

I jolt at the voice, spinning around in panic. I got a hall pass from French because I couldn't make it to final bell. Did someone follow me out?

"Hey, it's okay, it's only me." Elise shuts the door behind her and moves closer. She looks just the same, with her neat ponytail and blazer decorated with merit pins. I back away instinctively. "Anna? Anna, what's wrong?"

I still can't speak, the tears I've held back all day forcing themselves from my body in great noisy sobs. These aren't delicate tears; these are wretched and angry, and it's all I can do to fall against the wall and slide to the ground, my shoulders heaving, my whole torso racked with pain.

Elise crouches on the floor beside me and tries to take my hands, but I shrink away. I hate that she's seeing this. I hate that I fell apart at all.

"Please," I manage, my voice hoarse and cracked. "Just go!"

"Shhh." She gets up, and for a moment I think she's going to leave, but it's only to grab a handful of tissue from one of the stalls. She sits back down beside me on the hard tile floor. "Was it Lindsay? Did she do something? I told her not to, but . . ."

Lindsay? I try to laugh, but it comes out as a garbled squawk through my tears. I shake my head. "No, it's not . . . it's not that."

Elise waits, rubbing my back in slow, soothing circles, and eventually—long minutes later—my sobs fade away, leaving nothing but exhaustion and the familiar dull throb of a headache in their place.

"Here." She wets a paper towel and dabs at my face. I try to duck away again, but she rolls her eyes. "Trust me. That mascara isn't waterproof." I quit struggling and let her pull me back together: blotting my red eyes, smoothing back my tangled hair, until there's nothing left to do, just silence between us in the empty bathroom.

"I'm sorry," Elise offers finally. Her voice is soft, fearful. "I know I shouldn't have ditched you like that, but—"

"You think this is about you?" I have to laugh again, harsher this time. "You're not . . ." I stop, trying to find the words, but there are none. "The world is bigger than high school," I bite out at last.

She waits.

"You can go back now." I take a deep breath, willing my pulse to slow. "I'm fine."

Elise doesn't move.

"I mean it." I wipe my face again, blow my nose. "I'm good, see?" I force a smile. "It's nothing."

"Bullshit." Elise's voice is low but clear. "Come on, Anna. Talk to me."

She takes my hands again, forcing me to meet her gaze. I take another breath, ready to brush away her concern with some flippant comment or sarcastic crack, but instead, the words slip out of my mouth, unbidden.

"The cancer's back. My mom . . ." And then my voice breaks, and I collapse into tears again.

"Oh, Anna . . ." Elise pulls me closer. "I'm so sorry, I didn't think—"

The bell goes off, but we don't move until the door swings

open and a rush of sound slips in from outside. "You can't even ask him." A familiar voice is midsentence. "I mean, he was—" The voice stops. "Um, hello?"

We look up to find Lindsay and a cluster of other girls in the doorway, looking down at us with matching expressions of disdain. "Elise?" Lindsay frowns. "What are you doing?"

"Find another bathroom, okay?" Elise doesn't loosen her grip on me. "We're busy."

"I can see." Lindsay's voice drips with sarcasm. "You guys sure look cozy."

Elise turns away from her, and back to me. "You think you can get up?"

I nod, wordless.

"Aww, did someone hurt your feelings?" Lindsay crows. I ignore her, taking Elise's hand and letting her pull me to my feet. "Or did we, like, interrupt something?" She laughs. "Maybe that was the reason you wouldn't go out with Carter, huh, Elise?"

"Oh, fuck off." Elise glares at her. There are gasps from the chorus, more of delight than shock. Lindsay's face changes.

"What did you say?"

"You heard me. And get the hell out of our way." Elise pushes me toward them, to the door, and I stumble forward, too drained to do anything but go where she points me.

The group parts, all except for Lindsay, who stands firm,

blocking our path. "You want to think about this," she tells Elise, her voice low and furious.

"No, I don't." Elise's hand is on my back, steering me, but I stop. She shouldn't have to do this, throw everything away because I couldn't keep it together.

"Don't worry," I tell Lindsay quietly. "She was just . . . taking pity on me. She's not . . . we're not friends."

"Anna—" Elise starts, but I cut her off.

"It's okay," I tell her. "Really. I get it."

I head for the door. This time, Lindsay moves aside.

"See you in gym," Lindsay calls after me as I make it to the hallway and start walking away, my head bent in defeat. As I go, I hear her turn on Elise. "This is so not acceptable, do you even know—"

"What?" Elise's voice echoes after me. "That you're a skanky bitch with no soul?"

I stumble in surprise. She didn't . . . ?

But she did. And she isn't finished. "Sorry to break it to you"—Elise's voice is loud enough to get the attention of even the students passing in the hall—"but pretty much everyone knows by now! And FYI, we *are* friends."

I hear hurried footsteps, and a moment later, Elise falls into step beside me.

"You didn't have to do that," I say softly, tears welling in my throat again.

"Yes, I did." Elise links her arm through mine. "Now, tell me everything."

So I do.

I thought it would be hard, but I've spent so long holding it back that it's easy this time. A relief. We head downtown again, and the words tumble out as I tell her about what happened last time around. The scans and abnormal tissue samples, and the hours spent waiting on hard plastic chairs in fluorescent-lit hospital corridors. Chemicals and radiation, hair clogging up the bathroom sink in long, curling strands. We tried to make a game of it, with DVDs and trashy magazines, and Popsicle Fridays, sucking ice treats by her bedside during chemo as her skin got paler, and everyone talked too loudly about "the fight" and "her journey" and being a "survivor." But it was worth it, that's what they all said. She got better, the tests came back clear, and it was over.

Until now.

"The worst part is, it's like I've already lost her." The words feel like a betrayal, but I need to get them out. "She faded so fast during treatment last time." I explain. "Most days she could barely stay awake. And that was okay. I mean, it wasn't, but I understood. She was sick. And I did everything—I sat with her, and fed her, and stayed up all night. . . . I forgot about everything else. It was like I could make her better just by trying hard enough, you know?"

Elise nods.

"I figured it would be okay. It had to be okay. She'd get better and go back to being my mom again. But, even when it was over, she wasn't the same." I stop walking. The streets are dark now, crowded with commuters shoving past, but I don't move.

"She got . . . obsessed," I continue, "with health foods, and meditation, and these support groups with other survivors. It's taken over her whole life. She spends every day off at retreats and the yoga studio. She doesn't even notice me anymore."

Elise puts her hand on mine; a dark leather glove over my red mittens.

"I don't think I can go through this again." My voice twists. "It was like I lost myself, trying to make her better, and I never got me back. I can't do that again, I don't even know who I am anymore."

Other girls would speak up now; reassure me that my mom does notice me, love me. That everything will be okay. But Elise doesn't.

"Then we should do something," she tells me at last. "Just for you. So you can remember yourself this time."

"Like what?"

Elise slowly smiles. "Do you trust me?"

I shrug.

"Come on, Anna. Do you trust me?"

I want to laugh it off, but there's something in her expression that keeps me standing there in the middle of the busy sidewalk: determination. Enough to make me believe what she's saying, that I don't have to be lost again. And God, I want it so, so much.

I can't go through that again.

So I nod.

"I trust you."

The pink streak is two inches wide, hidden behind my ear on the left-hand side. Elise had one done too, matching, in deep peacock blue. They're invisible, until we pull our hair back, and then there they are: bold, bright. Brave.

You wouldn't think a lock of dyed hair could make a difference, but it does. I look at it every night at home, as the chemo gets under way and my mom fades back into that pale stranger, drinking juice through a sippy cup and sleeping through my days. I stare in the mirror, and remind myself: I'm here, I exist.

I'll be okay.

NOW

Everyone is trying to make like it's my fault. Prosecutors, her parents, reporters, TV. They say I led Elise astray; that I took a sweet, innocent straight-As girl and dragged her down to my level. That I coerced her into skipping school, and staying out too late, and drinking dollar shots in dive bars until she screwed strange guys in the bathrooms of clubs that should never have let us in.

That I made her this way.

It sounds bad, I know, but the truth is, we made each other, like we learned about in science class. Symbiosis. I was the partner-in-crime she'd been waiting for: a hand to hold as she ran, laughing, away from the ivy-covered gates she'd been gazing over her entire life. And Elise . . . She was my catalyst.

The glint in my eye, the giddy thrill in my stomach, the voice urging me to be louder, bolder, to blend in to the background no more.

We were both responsible for what we became, which I guess means we both have to share the blame. If Elise is the cause of everything that's happened to me, then I'm to blame for her fate too. It's both of our faults, equally.

Except she's gone, and I'm all alone again. And so the blame—the great weight of it, the months of media specula-tion and fury and bitter, seething outrage—falls entirely on me. Some days, it's like I'm drowning in it, like I'll never see the surface again. She was always the one to pull me up, my hand to hold when it felt like I was going under. She saved me, and now she's gone.

How am I supposed to get by on my own?

THE NIGHT

The first round of questioning is simple: "When did you last see Elise?" "What were you doing that day?" "Did you see anyone suspicious near the house?"

They take us one by one into the interview room, while the rest of the group slouches, tired and weepy on yellow plastic chairs in the lobby of the police station as people mill about us in a state of barely disguised panic. We've called our parents, stuttered through the terrible news, and now there's nothing left to do but wait. Chelsea's eyes are red and tired. She sits, frozen, clutching Lamar's hand with both of hers, staring at the bloodstains on her jeans. Melanie huddles her small body into a ball, her arms hugging her knees, her voice raw from sobbing. I can hardly bear to look at them. Every part of my body feels wired with a terrible rush of shock and adrenaline, as if my atoms are about to break apart and spin out into the world.

I leap up. "Mel, you got any quarters?"

She blinks at me from behind straight black bangs.

"The machine, I need a soda." I nod to the vending machine. Melanie slowly rummages in her purse, like she's moving underwater, and passes me some change.

I go try the machine in the corner by the reception desk. The precinct staff look as shocked as I feel; over and over again we've been told this doesn't happen here. This is a safe island. Some robbery, a few drunken traffic violations, but murder? The first patrol to arrive at the house didn't know what the hell to do. One of them just stood there, staring blankly at the blood, while the other vomited in the hallway and stumbled back outside. It took another half hour for more police to arrive, and longer still for anyone to even approach the body. They trampled in and out of the room all night, and it was almost five in the morning before they finally bundled her up onto the stretcher and drove away.

I've been feeding the money in over and over before I see that the prices are listed in euros, not dollars. It doesn't take American currency. I search my pockets, but there's nothing. After everything, it's the can of Coke that breaks me, out of reach behind the glass. I slam my hand against the machine and swear, loud in the silence of the room. Everyone looks over.

"Sorry," I mutter, sliding back into my seat. Tate is sitting on the floor in front of me, his legs outstretched. I put a hand on his head, twisting my fingers in his hair. He turns and gives me a faint ghost of a smile, but it's enough to calm me. It always is.

"He's been in there forever." Chelsea can't keep her eyes from the interview room door. It's Max's turn now, and Chelsea pulls her sweatshirt around her, looking anxious for her brother. "Why are they keeping him so long?"

Silence.

"He was first, to see the body," I offer. "He saw the room before we all came in. The open balcony door."

"I still say we shouldn't be talking to them." Tate's foot twitches again. "Not without a lawyer." He looks to Akshay. "Didn't your dad say he was finding someone?"

Silence.

"AK?" Chelsea nudges him gently. AK flinches. "Your dad, the lawyer?"

AK shrugs. He has a distant look in his dark eyes, like he doesn't see any of us at all. Usually he's the one with a joke and a quip, but now he looks wrung out. Detached.

"We're minors, too," Tate adds. "We shouldn't be alone in there."

"They need to find out what happened," I tell him gently. "So they can find the guy who did this."

"What if he's still out there?" Melanie turns to us, wide-eyed. "What if he comes back to the house?"

There's a long pause. For the first time, I stop thinking about what has happened and look ahead, to what still may be to come.

"We'll go to a hotel," Lamar speaks up, his voice the only steady one. "We'll stick together."

"But he could be after us!" Melanie's voice cracks. "We don't know why he came for her. It could be anything; it could be—"

"Mel," I warn her. "Calm down."

"How can you . . . ?" The tears are coming now, fast down her cheeks. "You saw—you saw what he did to her! She must have been so scared, and nobody was there, and . . ." She collapses into hysterics, hiccupping for air. "I can't . . . I can't . . ."

"Melanie." Chelsea tries to reach for her, but Mel ducks away. She's gasping, doubled over, hyperventilating. "Mel!"

"Get a paper bag." I leap up. "That's what we're supposed to do, right? A paper bag?"

I get blank faces. AK is still spaced out, Tate looks lost, and Chelsea is helplessly searching through her purse for something. "Guys!" Melanie's face is red; she's wheezing desperately, her whole body shaking, so I cross the waiting area and slap her once across the face, hard.

She stops, gaping at me. Her breathing goes back to normal.

"It's okay," I tell her quietly. "But you need to calm down. There'll be time for that later. We have to stay strong. For Elise."

Melanie nods wordlessly, but she scooches her knees up to her chest and hugs them again, turning her face away from me. I exhale.

"Sorry," I tell her quietly. She doesn't reply.

The main precinct doors swing open, and another serious-looking man strides through. He was part of the crowd back at the house too: squat and bulky and balding on top. Although he's not in uniform, people quickly move out of his way as he steams across the floor toward us.

"Has something happened?" I ask. "Did you find something?"

He looks at us all for a moment without speaking, then turns and enters the interview room, the door slamming shut behind him.

I swallow. "Maybe you're right," I say softly to Tate. "Maybe we should have a lawyer."

When Max is done, the bald guy calls Tate back in for another hour. Chelsea and Mel try to get some sleep; stretched on the bank of chairs with sweatshirts draped over their faces to block out the strip lighting overhead. I can't even try. Every time I close my eyes, Elise is staring back at me, empty and lifeless, so I keep them open—playing Tetris and Super Mario on my phone until my whole world shrinks to the lines of tiny colored blocks and there's no room even to think. It's bliss. As long as I keep my mind filled with jumps and moves and left/right commands, I can pretend I'm anywhere—waiting for a ride or killing time in study hall. Anywhere but here, for any reason but this.

"Anna?"

I don't register the voice at first, I'm so focused on the tiny screen.

"Anna." Lamar's voice is sharper. "Judge Dekker needs to talk to you." I look up to find the bald guy waiting, his face blank. Tate emerges from the interview room behind him, looking drained, his tall frame slouching.

"I already went," I tell them.

The Dekker guy gestures for me. "Just a few more questions."

I don't want to go back in and talk them through it again. The phone, and the door, and the blood. "I'm tired," I say, a plaintive note creeping in my voice. "Can't we do this tomorrow?"

But he's unmoved. "Miss Chevalier."

I pull myself upright and stumble toward the room, catching AK's eye as I go. He looks so freaked, I lean in as I pass.

"It better not take long," I tell him, managing a weak smile. "I'm so hungry, I could slaughter a goat."

THE TRIAL

"She said that?" Dekker pauses for effect, a note of horror in his voice. "'Slaughter?'"

"Yup." AK is sitting confidently on the witness chair like he's slouched on the front steps before class, watching cheerleading practice across the lawn. The dazed confusion and thousand-yard stare from that night are long since gone: this is the AK who has a weekly commentator's spot on the *Clara Rose Show*, offering his valuable opinions on news, crime, and—of course—this case. Last week he closed his million-dollar book deal. Today, he's wearing a designer shirt and a signature red pocket square in his blazer, all the better to pop for the cameras.

He hasn't looked at me once during his testimony.

"And what was her mood like that night?" Dekker asks.

My lawyer leaps up. "Objection."

Dekker sends him a crocodile smile. "Let me rephrase. How was the defendant acting? She must have been very emotional. After all, you'd been through such a terrible trauma."

I can feel my lawyer tense beside me, like he wants to object again, but he doesn't.

"She was . . . normal," AK told him. "That was the weird thing. I mean, we were a wreck. Mel was crying, and Chelsea . . . Max could barely keep it together. But Anna was totally calm. Like nothing had happened."

"She didn't cry?" Dekker sounds shocked again, but after the theatrics he's put on this week, I'm not even surprised. The guy could step into a Broadway production any time he liked.

"Never." AK shrugs. "Not that I saw, anyway, and I was with her all that night. She didn't cry when we found the body, or when the police came. She didn't do anything, except . . ."

"Yes?"

"She hit the vending machine, at the police station. She just exploded, swearing and everything."

"A violent outburst?" Dekker turns to the room, to drive his point home. It's packed with reporters, Elise's family, my former friends lined up to watch the show. I just have my dad with me now, and my lawyer here, trying the best he can.

"It was weird. It freaked us out." AK nods. "It was just, like, this flash of rage. She looked possessed. And then she hit Melanie."

"Objection!"

Dekker smirks. "The defense counsel objects to the witness testimony? I wonder why."

My lawyer glares. "It's on the record—a slap; Miss Chan was hyperventilating."

The judge nods impatiently. "So noted, continue."

Dekker pauses a moment. "No further questions."

Judge von Koppel makes a note, icy blond and steely eyed at her table. "Any follow-up?"

I scribble a note to my lawyer. He glances over, then stands. "Mr. Kundra, that slaughter line, it was a running joke in your group, wasn't it?"

AK coughs. "Uh, yeah."

"You would remark on your hunger by using bigger and bigger animals," he explains for the sake of the room. "'I'm so hungry, I could slaughter a pig, or a cow, or an elephant.' Isn't that right?"

"Yes, but—"

"In fact, you said it yourself, on many occasions." He holds a piece of paper. "March eighteenth, your status update. 'So hungry, could murder a fucking rhino.'"

"Yeah, but that's a joke!" AK exclaims.

"Right. And that's what Miss Chevalier was doing, wasn't it? Joking?"

AK slumps, his self-righteousness gone.

"Mr. Kundra, answer the question."

"Yeah, she was joking."

My lawyer turns, giving me a smile, but AK hasn't finished.

"But who does that?" he asks, his voice loud in the silent courtroom. "Elise was dead. Someone hacked her apart. We still had blood on us, and she's joking around? Who does that?"

"No further questions," my lawyer says hurriedly, but it's too late. There are murmurs of agreement from the crowd as AK heads back to his seat.

The damage is done.

NOW

Would it have made a difference if I had cried? I've had long enough to think about it, but even now, I can't know for sure. If I'd fallen apart, and wept, and screamed. If I'd curled up, shaking, into a ball in the corner of the police station and refused to speak. Would they have believed me then? Or would they have just found another way to spin it: that my grief was remorse, for the terrible thing I'd done. That my outbursts were too fevered, too public, too much for show. An act, to cover my tracks.

The truth is, once Dekker got it in his head that the break-in was staged and one of us killed her, there was nothing I could do. He was coming for me, and every little detail of my life was evidence, if you held it up to the light and looked at it just right.

He was coming for me.

FIRST
INTERROGATION

VOICE: **This is Officer Carlsson speaking, also present is Investigating Judge Dekker. Record of the first questioning of Anna Chevalier, 5:52 a.m.**

ANNA: **Second.**

CARLSSON: **What?**

ANNA: **It's the second time I've talked to you. You already interviewed me, before.**

CARLSSON: **Yes, but this is on the record now. And Judge Dekker has some questions too.**

ANNA: **A judge? But—this isn't court.**

CARLSSON: **In Aruba, a judge leads the investigation. Just think of him like another detective.**

ANNA: I'm tired. Can we do this tomorrow? I haven't slept. . . . I haven't slept all night.

CARLSSON: This won't take long. Now, when did you see Elise last?

ANNA: Should we have a lawyer?

CARLSSON: I . . .

DEKKER: You haven't been arrested. These are simple questions.

ANNA: But Tate said . . .

DEKKER: Don't you want to help find the person who did this? We need you to talk to us if we're going to find them.

ANNA: I guess . . . Okay. Can I get something to drink? Water or something?

DEKKER: Later.

ANNA: I'm tired, okay? I need something to drink.

DEKKER: When you've answered our questions.

CARLSSON: But sir, we shouldn't—

DEKKER: Fine. Get her the water. Interview paused, 5:56 a.m.

(pause)

DEKKER: Interview resumed. So, when did you last see Miss Warren?

ANNA: Last night. Monday night, I mean. We all went out, to dinner, and the bars along the main strip.

DEKKER: And then?

ANNA: Then we all came home and crashed. About two a.m., maybe. That was the last time I saw her.

DEKKER: She wasn't there in the morning?

ANNA: No. (pause) I mean, we thought she was, but I didn't see her. I went to find her, but her door was locked. So we figured she was crashed out.

DEKKER: What time was this?

ANNA: Nine, maybe. We were all booked to go on a dive trip, so the others left around ten. We texted Elise, but she didn't reply, so we figured she was still asleep.

DEKKER: Her door was locked. You didn't find that unusual?

ANNA: No. I mean, she liked her privacy, and . . . she'd been with Niklas the other night.

DEKKER: Had she been drinking?

(pause)

DEKKER: Miss Chevalier?

ANNA: Yes. We all had. It's legal here.

DEKKER: I'm aware.

(pause)

DEKKER: Why didn't you go on the dive trip with your friends?

ANNA: Me and Tate stayed back. We were . . . tired. Hungover. We figured we'd just hang out on the beach.

DEKKER: What time was that?

ANNA: I don't know. We left the house around twelve thirty, I think. We chilled on the beach most of the day.

DEKKER: And you were together all the time?

ANNA: Yes.

DEKKER: You didn't once part? To browse some shops, or use the bathroom?

ANNA: No.

DEKKER: You didn't use the bathroom?

ANNA: No. I mean, yes.

DEKKER: So you weren't together.

ANNA: For, like, two minutes! We were at the café, way down the beach. We used the bathroom there. We bought sodas. You can check. And . . .

DEKKER: Yes?

ANNA: Nothing.

(pause)

DEKKER: Do you keep a diary?

ANNA: What?

DEKKER: A journal, some record of the day?

ANNA: No. No diary.

DEKKER: Very well. What time did you return to the house?

ANNA: Six, maybe? We hung out for a while, showered, and went out to dinner. . . . This pizza place, just down the street. The others had just gotten home from diving when we got back. That's when we started to worry and called the cops. Look, I've told you all of this already. Can I please just go?

DEKKER: You were back at the house between six and seven. There was no sign of Elise then?

ANNA: No. Her door was still closed.

(pause)

ANNA: I texted to see if she wanted to come eat, but there was no reply. We figured she'd gone out.

DEKKER: And you didn't check her room?

ANNA: No. I mean, we were, you know, busy. If she had been there, she would have come out and talked to us. I went and knocked on her door, but, nothing.

DEKKER: You didn't hear anything from her room?"

ANNA: She was on the other side of the house from us. Me and Tate were by the main doors. And we were busy, so . . .

DEKKER: Busy doing what?

ANNA: You know, just hanging out.

DEKKER: Be specific. What exactly did you do, from the moment you returned home?

ANNA: I . . . We went to our room, and put some music on.

DEKKER: The police responder first to the scene says there was blood in the hallway; you didn't see it?

ANNA: No, it wasn't there.

DEKKER: What do you mean?

ANNA: When we came in, the blood wasn't there. It was there later. The blood must have been on our shoes or something, after we found . . . after we found her.

DEKKER: What happened next, after you and Mr. Dempsey returned to your room? You turned on music and . . .

ANNA: I can't remember.

DEKKER: Try. Did you make any calls? Watch TV, perhaps?

ANNA: I don't know. . . . I took a shower, I remember that.

DEKKER: Where was Mr. Dempsey while you showered?

ANNA: In the bedroom.

DEKKER: But you were in the bathroom; you wouldn't have been able to see him.

ANNA: Well, no, but it was right off the bedroom. . . . He was right there.

DEKKER: Was the bathroom door open or closed while you were in the shower?

ANNA: Open, I think.

DEKKER: You think, or you know?

ANNA: I don't know. Open. Yes. Open. He was right there, on his computer. Why are you asking all this?

What does it have to do with anything?

DEKKER: I'm just trying to get all the facts. You said music was on. Was it loud?

ANNA: Not really, no.

DEKKER: Were you and Mr. Dempsey making much noise?

ANNA: I don't . . . I don't understand.

DEKKER: You are a couple, no? You were alone in his room for almost an hour. Were you engaged in intercourse?

ANNA: I . . . You can't ask me that.

DEKKER: I can ask anything I like. Answer the question, please.

CARLSSON: Sir, I don't know—

DEKKER: The question, Miss Chavalier.

(pause)

ANNA: No. No, I'm not talking to you anymore.

DEKKER: I'm just trying to ascertain the level of noise in the house, and—

ANNA: No! I won't say anything else without a lawyer. You can't talk to me like that!

(pause)

CARLSSON: Interview terminated, 6:20 a.m.

THE NEXT DAY

It's morning by the time we check in to one of the high-rise hotels along the beach. Tate's family chartered a jet for our parents; they'll be landing by noon, but for now, I can think of nothing but sleep. The adrenaline is gone from my system; I'm more tired than I've ever been in my life.

"Don't wake me until my dad's here," I tell the others, in the gray carpeted hallway. Even swiping my key card takes almost more energy than I can bear. They must feel the same, because I get nothing but dull nods in reply before they stumble into their rooms.

Inside, I take five steps and fall face-first on the lurid aqua bedspread. I can't move. I can barely even breathe.

There's a knock on my door. I groan. It taps again, urgently.

Heaving myself up, I go to the door and pull it open. Tate pushes past me, inside. "What did you tell them?" he says anxiously. "What did they ask?"

I close the door behind him. "I . . ."

"That guy, Dekker, when he brought you back in? He asked what we did all day; what did you say?"

"Nothing! I mean, just what happened." I stare at him, confused. He was there when I got out of questioning, right beside me in the cab ride to the hotel. He didn't ask me anything about my interview then; nobody did. By then, we just wanted to be done with it.

Tate grips my arms. "Tell me, what did you say to him?"

I shrug, trying to remember. "You know, we went to the beach, we took a shower, went to dinner . . ."

Tate frowns. "He didn't push you?"

"Yes." I shudder at the memory. "He kept asking what we were doing."

"But did you tell him? About me going back to the house?" Tate's expression is panicked, and suddenly I realize why: we weren't together all day.

He went back to the house. He was gone for a whole half hour.

"No, I didn't say . . ." I take two steps back. "I forgot. I just said we went to the beach. I didn't remember you went back."

"Oh thank God." The words run together in a rush. Tate

sinks down so he's sitting on the edge of the bed. "I was freaking out the whole time you were in there. I didn't know if you'd told them, if they'd catch me in the lie. Thank you. Thank you!" He takes my hand, kissing it. It's a familiar gesture, something he must have done a hundred times, but this time I want to pull away.

He forgot his shades. I'd just set up camp on the sand: towel in the perfect tanning position, magazine out to browse. *Go ahead*, I told him. *Bring me back a bag of chips.*

"You went back to the house." I repeat it slowly. "But, I don't understand. Why didn't you just tell them? Why did you lie?"

Tate blinks. "Don't you get it? We're each other's alibis."

"Alibis? For what?" I pause, looking down at him. Tate doesn't reply, just stares back at me with a nervous expression. "You mean Elise?" I exclaim, my voice rising. "They think *we* killed her?"

"Shh!" Tate hushes me. "I don't know what they think." He leaps up again, pacing to the door and back. "But that guy, Dekker, he wouldn't let up: Where were we? What did we do? How long were we at the house? He didn't ask me anything about Elise, or who else could have broken in."

"Me either," I say with a sudden chill. "I meant to tell him about that guy, the one who hassled us at the market, remember? But he just kept asking about me, and you, and if we were apart at all."

"That's it," Tate says. "We don't even know when she died. If one of us was alone, they could say we did it, that we killed her."

"But that's crazy." I reach for him, to try to calm him from this paranoia, but Tate shakes me off.

"Is it?" He insists, "Think, Anna: we're stuck in some foreign country, and Elise is dead, and they're asking us about our sex lives instead of out there looking for the killer! The others were off on the dive trip; it's just you and me."

I take a couple of breaths, trying to think through the haze of exhaustion. Was it true? Did Dekker suspect us?

"Then we're fine," I tell him at last. "We said we were together all day, and we'll stick to it. You didn't go back to the house, and we didn't leave each other's side, not for a minute. We'll be okay."

Tate exhales a ragged breath. "You'd do that for me?" He pulls me into a hug.

"Always," I say, muffled by the soft cotton of his sweatshirt. I pull back a little, so I can see his face. "You didn't see her though, did you? When you went back?"

Tate shakes his head. "I promise. I just went in, picked up our stuff, and headed out again."

"But . . ." I pause, "You were gone for kind of a while."

"Like, five minutes."

"It was longer," I say. "Remember? I was waiting for you,

to put lotion on me, and I was already burning by the time you got back."

Tate smiles. "That's 'cause you burn in, like, five seconds flat." He tugs my hair, and bends his head to kiss me. I relax into his arms, savoring the feel of his lips on mine. After everything that's happened, this feels like the safest place in the world.

"We just have to stick together," Tate whispers, stroking my cheek. "You and me, like always."

"Like always," I repeat.

We sleep with our clothes on, curled around each other on top of the sheets. When I wake, it's all over the news: "American teen murdered on spring break." "Possible sexual attack." "Police are pursuing all leads."

They don't have our names yet, but I know it's only a matter of time. I click the TV off. Tate sleeps on.

JUNIOR YEAR

I notice Tate for the first time that spring, a few weeks after I have my breakdown in the girls' bathroom and Elise walks away from her old clique for good.

I'd seen him around in school before then. Even in a school filled with rich, ambitious, smart kids, Tate Dempsey is Hillcrest royalty: star of the lacrosse team, student government, an athlete's body, and golden good looks. We have a couple of classes together, but even with Elise in tow—especially with Elise—we live in different worlds. I would catch a glimpse of him in the hallways sometimes, heading to class with some new, adoring girl beside him, or hanging out on the front lawn after school tossing a football around with his buddies. I would think how he wasn't so much a real teenage guy as the billboard for one. You know, something from a J.Crew catalogue, or the hot guy on a teen TV show who's really in his twenties—square-jawed, strong and sure among the crowds of boys still figuring out their gangly bodies and tufts of new facial hair.

But as the year passes, I realize I was wrong. He isn't loud, or arrogant, like some of those popular guys, but almost quaintly polite: holding open doors if you're behind him in line, presenting his arguments in a low, confident voice in class. He doesn't ever interrupt, or pick on the nerdy kids, or swagger around like he owns the place; instead, he has this air of mild embarrassment about him, as if he knows just how much wealth and privilege have been heaped upon his broad shoulders. Everyone else in school seems to take their status for granted, like they don't realize pure luck is the only reason they're not crammed in a public school across the city, taking the bus home, walking up four flights to a tiny apartment when they get done with their after-school job.

Maybe it's because I wasn't born into this world that I see how random it all is—especially for us kids, who haven't built anything of our own yet, just taken what our parents can provide. My classmates act like they're entitled to their good fortune, but Tate is different, and I admire him for it.

"Don't tell me you've got a thing for Golden Boy," Elise says with a smirk one afternoon, when she catches me watching him from across the library.

"What? No." I quickly turn back. She's sitting cross-legged on the chair beside me, chewing red licorice and doodling in the margins of her world history homework. We have study hall last period on Tuesdays, but Elise is so restless, we barely ever make it through the hour. "It's not like he even knows I exist."

"Which makes you lucky," Elise replies, arching an eyebrow. "He's, like, a total man-whore. He's already dated four different girls this year."

"Really?" I can't help shooting another glance to where Tate is sitting at a table of the popular kids, his sweatshirt sleeves pushed up over tanned forearms, blond hair falling in his eyes. "I don't know, he seems nice."

"Trust me, he's just another asshole jock, but with better hair." Elise yawns, slamming her book shut. "Speaking of assholes, I'm so done with Hitler."

"Stumptown?" I suggest, naming the coffeehouse that's become our regular. "Or we could catch a movie."

"Pie." Elise's eyes brighten. "I've been craving it all day. Dusty's has the best, and all the college boys are going to be out studying for finals," she adds mischievously.

I laugh. "You had me at pie."

We grab our stuff and head for the exit, past Tate's table. He doesn't look up.

As we near the doors, Lindsay and her group saunter

in, armed with razorblade smiles and perfectly glossy bangs. "Aww, look, it's Hillcrest's new favorite dykes," Lindsay sneers as we pass.

Elise doesn't say a word, doesn't even look around, just flips up her middle finger as we pass, linking her other arm through mine. As we push through the doors and outside, I glance over to check her expression, but there's not even a flicker there, just a determined smile. "Peach or pecan?" Elise asks as we head down the steps onto the front lawn.

"You even have to ask?"

"You're right," she replies gravely. "I should have known. Both."

It's startling, how completely they cut her out of their clique, and how fast Elise sheds them, like some unwanted skin. She's grown up with them, after all: sleepovers and birthday parties and after-school hangouts going back years. But in a day—in an instant—she was done. I feel guilty at first, wondering if she regrets her choice, giving up so much and getting only me in return. I didn't yet know that Elise never looked back. Once she made a call, there was no other choice in her mind—she just kept moving forward, never regretting a thing. "Screw 'em," she'd say whenever Lindsay would aim a new barb in her direction— her resentment for me nothing compared to the betrayal of a former friend. "We don't need anyone but each other."

And we don't, not those first few months. The world of girl friendship and intimacy that has always seemed so foreign to me suddenly opens up, just the way I'd glimpsed that very first afternoon. It may sound wrong, but I'm the happiest I've even been that summer, even with my mom's chemo treatments starting up again, and that sickly sweet medicated smell lingering over my parents upstairs bedroom again. Because I have a place to escape now, a place of my own in the world, full stop.

I'm not alone anymore.

Elise and I fall into friendship like it's gravity. We eat lunch together in the shade of the far trees on the east lawn and toil over our homework at coffee shops downtown. We trade clothing and music, passing notebooks filled with lyrics and doodles in the back row of every class we share, and learn the exact texture of each other's bedroom floors from long nights sprawled on our stomachs, watching trashy reality TV. But soon we want more, and weekends become an adventure: fibbing to our parents about sleeping at the other's house, then sneaking out in our best tight denim and chunky boots. It almost doesn't matter where we go, as long as it's somewhere nobody knows us, where we can be anyone we want to be.

Elise buys us fake IDs from some MIT student hacker, and although the door guys look twice, they always let us through. Rock shows, and dive bars, and the college haunts that line Boylston and Beacon—most of the time it isn't even about the alcohol, we just want to see the world waiting for us, after the battle of high school. One night we put on our best vintage dresses and red lipstick and take the elevator up to the restaurant on the top floor of a hotel, high above the city. We sip cocktails from sugar-rimmed glasses and watch the lights over the river, fierce with the knowledge that this will all be ours one day, for real.

The night I meet Tate is near the end of the semester, when summer vacation looms, full of promise and freedom. Elise and I luck into a college party invite from our favorite barista at Stumptown, off-duty with his friends at the table next to ours. Elise shrugs, casual, and says we'll try to make it, but the minute the group leaves, we grip each other's hands, bright-eyed with delight. "Tell your dad you're crashing at my house," Elise orders, and I call him to leave the message, knowing there will only be a hurried text in reply. Ever since I brought Elise home, and he made the connection between her father, Charles Warren, and the state senator of the same name, my father has let me go out with her anytime I want.

So we do: getting ready in a flurry of discarded outfits and lip gloss, then sneaking down the back stairs while her parents are in the den, breathless in the backseat of a cab as we cross the twilight city, heading for adventure.

"If anyone asks, we're freshman at Berklee," Elise orders me as we clamber out of the cab. It's a warm, muggy night and the street is busy with college crowds; music is already spilling out of the upstairs windows of a narrow brownstone. "I'm studying psychology, and you're a business major."

"Boring!" I protest. "I'll be a lit student. No, drama!"

Elise laughs. "Sure, with your stage fright?"

"They don't have to know," I say with a grin as we climb the front steps and push inside the narrow lobby area. "As far as they're concerned, I could be a fabulous actress, auditioning for all kinds of Broadway shows."

"And Hollywood," Elise adds. "You got offered a role in the new Chris Carmel movie, but you turned it down because you wanted to stay in school and perfect your craft."

"I'm very dedicated," I agree, laughing. I can feel a sparkle in my veins, some sense of possibility, and when we walk into the party upstairs, it all makes sense, because there he is.

Tate.

My eyes meet his right away across the crowded room, and I know it's the start of something. I can just feel it.

"Hellooo," Elise murmurs. Tate is with a guy from the lacrosse team, Lamar, but right away he heads over toward us. "I guess you've been wishing on a star."

"Shh!" I hiss to Elise. "Please, don't say anything." But she just widens her eyes in innocence as Tate arrives, casual in a faded gray T-shirt and jeans.

"Hey." He looks at the two of us with a surprised expression, as if he can't quite place us. "What are you guys doing here?"

"Oh, we know a guy," Elise replies, her eyes already roving over the scene. It's hot and crammed with people, music so loud I can feel the bass, and everywhere, there's laughter and noisy chatter, full of the relief of finishing finals. "Well, really, Anna knows him," she adds, her gaze sliding back to us with a meaningful smile. "I swear, the poor guy follows her around like a puppy dog. She's not interested, but we figure, why waste a good party?"

Elise sends me a look that says, *Don't screw this up*, then squeezes me in a sudden hug. "I'm going to go look around. See you two later!"

She disappears into the crowd, leaving me by the side of the room with Tate. I stare awkwardly at the ground, not sure whether to thank or throttle her, but when I force myself to glance up, he's looking at me with something new in his expression, some kind of curiosity.

"You want a drink?" he offers quickly. "There's a bar back in the kitchen, they have all kinds."

"Sure," I agree, just as a new group of guys hurtles through the door. One of the frat guys knocks into me, and I stumble, but Tate takes my arm, steadying me. His hand is hot against my skin, and our eyes meet, just a flash, but I feel it all the way to my stomach.

"Come on," he says, smiling, and I follow him across the room.

I would follow him anywhere.

BEFORE

"Do you love me?"

"You know I do."

"How much?"

"Miles and miles."

"Deeper than the oceans?"

"Yup. More than the wind."

"Higher than Everest?"

"I don't know, that's pretty high. . . . Ow!" (laughter)

"Admit it. You love me more than anyone."

"Maybe."

*   *   *

THE PARTY

Tate leads me to the crowded kitchen, every surface covered with bottles and abandoned red plastic cups. He finds us two unopened beers, and cracks the tops off against the edge of the table. "This okay?" he asks, passing me one. "Because I can find some soda—"

"No," I answer quickly. "This is great."

There's another pause as we both take a sip of our drinks, but I don't feel nervous or awkward. Instead, I'm unnervingly calm. I've never been one to get all romantic about fate and destiny, but there's something so neat about this, I don't have a chance to panic. After all these weeks stealing glances in the hallway, I suddenly have him to myself.

"Cool party, huh?" Tate offers.

"What about you—how much do you love me?"

"Enough."

"Hey!"

"You didn't ask, 'Enough for what?'"

"Fine, then. Enough for what?"

"For anything."

"That's better."

"You think we'll ever wind up like our parents?"

"God, I hope not. Just kill me if I do."

"No, I mean . . . alone like they are . . . My mom shows me her old yearbooks, and there are tons of people in there she doesn't talk to anymore. Old boyfriends, best friends . . . What do you think happened to them?"

"Maybe they drifted apart."

"That's stupid. You don't drift, not if someone matters to you."

"So maybe they didn't matter, not really."

"Anna?"

"Yeah?"

"I'd never do that. Leave you."

"I know. Me either."

"Who do you know here?" I ask, and Tate leans in to hear me. All around us, there's music, and packed bodies—dancing and chatting, voices raised to be heard.

"Some of the guys from last year's team," Tate replies, his breath warm against my cheek. "And Lamar, well, you heard about him and Sophie?"

I nod. They were dating pretty tight all year, inseparable even, until some big blowup over spring break.

"He's been kind of low, so I figured a party would be good."

"Looks like it's working," I nod through to the living room, where Lamar is talking to a couple of college girls in short cut-off skirts and plunging sparkly tops. Tate follows my gaze and breaks into a grin.

"Good for him . . ." The end of his sentence is cut off as the music goes up another level, some dirty club hip-hop track.

"What?" I yell.

Tate looks around, then gestures away in the other direction of the living room, toward the back of the apartment. One of the hallway windows is wide open, leading out onto the flat gravel roof where I can see some people are already hanging out: thin wisps of cigarette smoke drifting up into the night, and the low, sweet scent of something more. Tate bends over to climb through, then holds out his hand to help me after him.

Outside, it's warm, and although the sky is now dark, it's surprisingly bright; the night cut through with the glow from the apartments and traffic on the streets below. We wander closer to the edge of the roof, and find a place to sit, perching on the edge of a brick-built air vent.

"It's weird we haven't really talked before." Tate glances over at me. "I keep seeing you around in school."

"Not so weird." I take a sip of beer. "We don't really run in the same circles."

Tate gives a low laugh. "Yeah, you and Elise pretty much keep to yourselves."

I turn. "That's the way you see it?"

Tate looks puzzled. "What do you mean?"

I shake my head, amused. "Nothing."

All this time, I figured everyone knew I was the outcast, that Elise and I were outsiders because we got blacklisted. But Tate figured we keep to ourselves out of choice, and I guess by now we do.

"What about you?" I ask. "Is it true you're going to be president someday?"

Tate shrugs and looks bashful, and that's when I know that it's for real. He doesn't try and make a joke of it, or deflect the comment away, like people do when they're embarrassed.

He wants it.

"Sorry," I add quickly. "I didn't mean it like that. I think it's great. That you want something so big. I can't even see what I'll be doing a year from now."

Tate checks as if to see if I'm still teasing, then relaxes. "Maybe. Sometimes I wonder if it's worth it, always having to plan ahead."

"What do you mean—school and college and stuff?"

"Everything," Tate replies, and there's a twist in his voice. "I want to go into politics someday for sure, but my parents keep reminding me that I have to be careful, and think how something will look twenty years from here."

"You mean, like, partying underage at a college bash."

"Exactly." Tate gives me a rueful smile. "And they're right, too. But now I have this voice in my head, warning me about everything. To do things right, all the time." He falls silent, looking out at the city. His blue eyes are cloudy in the shadows, blond hair shaded to a dark gold. I can feel the heat of him beside me, just inches between us, and I feel a rush of simple gladness, that I get to see this part of him. The real part.

"So how about you don't," I suggest. "Just for tonight."

He looks at me, a smile playing on the edge of his lips. "Do the right thing?"

"Why not?" I match his smile, playful. "Who's going to know?"

If it had been a Hillcrest party, it never would have happened. He would be the boy who ruled the scene, and I would be the girl on the outside of everything. But here, away from it all, we're just ourselves.

Back inside, we do lime Jell-O shots together, quivering and half-solid in tiny paper cups. The music plays on, loud, and soon we're dancing, lost in the sea of bodies, hot and sweating. He's solid against me, his eyes bright, and then Elise is nearby with some college guy, and Lamar too, wrapped around a pretty coed. We drink and dance until our feet hurt and our throats scratch dry, until it's three a.m. and the cops come and shut the party down, and we flee, laughing, down the stairs and out into the empty streets. We wind up in a red vinyl booth at some twenty-four-hour diner down the street, sharing cheese-covered fries and thick, icy shakes, Elise and I squeezed in the middle of the group like it belongs to us.

Nothing happens with Tate that night, but looking across the crowded diner booth, I see the spark of something in his blue eyes, and I know it's the start. The last few weeks before summer, he stays friendly in school—chatting in the hallways sometimes, or discussing an assignment after class. Elise keeps dragging me out to party and meet guys, worried I'm pining away over him, but I'm not. I've got a certainty about it, like we're fact, even if it hasn't happened yet.

Even if I want to pine, Elise doesn't give me the time. Our summer is a whirl of beach days and road trips, driving through the western Massachusetts country out to explore quaint college towns and hidden-away bookstores and cafés. It's not always just the two of us. Elise's parents insist on introducing her to the kids of an old college friend of theirs, just moved to town from California. Max and his twin sister, Chelsea, turn out to be our age, set to attend Hillcrest in the fall. Max is equal parts surfer and comic-book nerd, Chelsea a laid-back artist-type with a baggie of weed hidden under her paintbrushes. We run into Lamar at a couple more college parties, and soon he and Chelsea are inseparable. Elise's old friend, Melanie, starts hopefully showing up at the coffee shop—regretting her decision to take Lindsay's side now that the queen bitch is off in Europe for the summer—and just like that, Elise and I have our own group, to hang out together in that back booth at the diner after a late night, to drive upstate to her vacation home in New Hampshire, or to just sprawl in one of our big, empty houses, sneaking liquor and smoking weed and watching school loom closer like a jail sentence at the end of summer.

And then Tate is there at a party one night, and just as simple, he's mine, slipping into the place I had waiting for him. Elise on one side, Tate on the other: my hand linked through hers, his arm slung over my shoulder. After so many years drifting, not connected to anything, I'm finally tethered. Safe and loved, in the middle.

We start senior year like kings, like nothing can ever tear us apart.

We're wrong.

AFTER

Our parents arrive on the island by lunchtime the next day, and with them comes every American news team and TV crew within a thousand-mile radius.

They lay siege on the street outside, lining up news vans and portable satellites, snaking electrical wires across the parking lot. The hotel posts security on every entrance, and sets us up in a suite on the fourth floor with full-length windows overlooking the sparkling sands and perversely blue waters of the beach below. I begin to understand the shock of the staff in the police station last night, their dazed tears and murmured apologies. Ugly things shouldn't happen in a place this beautiful.

"Anna."

I turn. Our parents are being shown in by the hotel manager. Elise's mother crosses the room straight to me, her arms outstretched. "Anna, sweetheart." Her face is pale and bleak, and I register somehow that this is the first time I've ever seen her without makeup.

"Judy." My voice breaks, and she collapses against me, sobbing. I hold her tight, feeling the anguished cries wrack through her slim body.

"How could this . . . ?" Her words hiccup against my shoulder. "I don't understand."

"I know." I hang on, arms wrapped around her. "I know."

Of all the parents, I like Elise's mom the best. She and Elise were always locked in constant battle, but right from the start of us hanging out, Judy welcomed me into their lives. She works long hours as a cardiac surgeon at Mass General, and Mr. Warren is always out too, off at political functions and fund-raisers—planning his next move: to mayor, or congressman, even—but whenever she is around, Judy is always sure to ask me about school and college plans. Not in that fake, polite way, like Tate's parents, who always speak to me with a faint icy edge, as if they're just waiting for him to get me out of his system and move on. No, Elise's mom cares—sitting up with us sometimes to watch TV, or eating a late-night snack in the kitchen with us when we get home from parties and she's back from a shift at work. Elise always recoiled from her affection, accusing her of being overbearing and smothering, but Elise doesn't realize how lucky she is to have a mother who even notices.

Had.

I hold Judy until I feel another hand on my shoulder, and raise my head. My father is standing anxiously beside me. "Are you okay?" he asks, moving his hand up to stroke my hair, the way he always did when I was a kid.

I slowly shake my head, waiting until Judy's weeping subsides, and she finally steps away.

"Here." My father offers her his handkerchief. She dabs her face, red-eyed and puffy.

"We should never have let you go. I said it wasn't safe, all of you off on your own." Judy's voice breaks again.

"It's not your fault," I tell her. "You couldn't have known. None of us could."

She nods, wordless, and then drifts across the room to embrace the rest of the group. I move to follow her, but my father pulls me back.

"Let me look at you." He takes my face in both hands, and then hugs me hard against him. "When they called, all I could think was, what if it had been you?"

"It's okay, Dad." I'm crushed against his chest, but he doesn't let go. I feel a sob well up, imagining him back in that house in Boston, all alone. "I'm here. I'm not going anywhere."

He lets me go, taking a step back to recover. "Of course," he says quickly, wiping his eyes with the back of his hand. "You're safe, that's what matters."

Slowly, the rest of our families assemble. Tate's parents, immaculate as ever. Chelsea and Max's dad, with their new stepmom perching awkwardly in the corner. Lamar's mom, short and fierce and not letting go of him, even for a second, and Melanie's dad, scowling at all of us as if we're the ones to blame. We hover on plush sofas and end chairs, as if we don't know what comes next. Then a voice cuts through the low chatter, loud.

"The important thing is that we get on the same page. No one says anything without a lawyer."

We all look over. It's a strange man in a gray suit, setting up a laptop in the next room. He's in his forties, maybe, with an iPhone in one hand, gesturing to a younger man with more computer equipment.

"Sorry—this is Mr. Ellingham, head of our legal team," Tate's father supplies.

"Not one word," Ellingham repeats, moving into the main room. He looks around, pointing at us in turn. "Not to the police, not to reporters. Not until we get this straightened out."

"It's too late for that," Tate says quietly. "They questioned us all night."

"You're minors," his father corrects him. "They can't use any of it."

"I don't understand," Mr. Warren speaks up. He has an arm around Judy, and looks at us in confusion. "Why aren't the police here right now? Why aren't the kids talking to them? If they can help with the investigation, if they can help find who did this—"

"Not without a lawyer," Ellingham cuts him off.

Mr. Dempsey softens. "Look, Charles, I know this is tough. I can't begin to imagine what you and Judy are going through right now. But we have to stick together. Police in a place like this, they'll want to point fingers at the outsiders."

"He's right." Tate speaks up again. "Tell them, Anna. About that Dekker guy."

All eyes turn to me. I hug my arms around myself, but Tate nods again, encouraging, so I talk. "He was asking me all kinds of things," I say softly, "about our partying, and Elise, and what she was doing. It wasn't anything bad," I add quickly, my eyes going to Judy. "Just regular fun stuff."

"But he wouldn't listen when she tried to tell him about this guy hanging around the house," Tate finishes for me. "Or ask about suspects or anything. He's really weird."

"You see?" Tate's father turns back to Mr. Warren. "We've got to protect the kids."

"I've got a public relations team flying in," AK's father

speaks up, formal in a three-piece suit. "They'll take care of the press."

"I've already reached out to a couple of local investigators." Ellingham adds. "Guys who know the island, the people here. We'll find who did this, don't worry."

The adults move into the new conference room to talk about the legal side, about questioning protocols and information appeals, leaving the rest of us to sit, dazed. My dad pulls out his cell and dials.

"Casey? I need you to push my meetings for tomorrow and Wednesday, and see if you can switch Euracorp to a remote conference." He's checking his schedule, flipping through the old-fashioned black leather daybook, and it hits me for the first time that life hasn't stopped. Everything out there is still moving on, like normal. People waking up, and going to meetings, and watching TV—living their lives like a hole hasn't just been punched through the fabric of the world. They don't know Elise is dead, and even if they do, it's no more than a headline on a website, a pretty photo in the top corner of the news report.

They don't care that she's gone.

I feel a wave of dizziness wash over me. I tug my father's arm. "I need some air," I whisper. He nods, not lowering the phone. "No, stick a pin in everything non-urgent. I'll be here several days at least. . . ."

I drift away from the group and slip out onto the balcony, breathing in the warm sea breeze. Down on the beach, brightly colored umbrellas and squares of towels line the shore, people playing in the water. Just another day of their vacation.

"Hey." Tate steps out on the balcony behind me, pulling the door shut behind him. He slides an arm around my waist, giving me a rueful smile. "Who'd have guessed, my parents can stand to be in the same room together after all."

I don't smile. "We have to tell them."

"What?" Tate's body tenses against mine, but I can't drop it, not now.

"You know what." I force myself to look up at him. "About you going back to the house."

"Anna." Tate glances back inside, but nobody is paying attention to us out here. "I told you, we can't."

"But what if it's important?" I argue. "You could have seen something."

"I didn't, I told you. I was there, like, five minutes."

"Maybe you didn't even realize it," I insist. "But if you tell the police, maybe it fits with something else, something someone else reported. You could be a witness without even knowing."

"Stop!" Tate hisses. He grabs me by my arms, his grip digging into my skin. "If we tell them, they'll know we lied. What do you think will happen then?"

"I don't know." I swallow, unnerved by his expression. "But isn't it worth it, if it helps? If it gives them some kind of lead?"

"It won't do anything except make us look guilty." Tate's voice is low and fierce. "Is that what you want? I'm doing this to protect you, too."

I stop. "What do you mean?"

"I wasn't the only one off on my own, remember? I took a nap, and when I woke up, you were gone."

"But . . . I was down by the water," I protest. "I was right there."

"So?" Tate finally releases his grip on me. "Don't you see? Once they know we lied once, they won't believe anything else we say. And meanwhile, the guy who really did this gets away with it."

I exhale slowly. He's right—if Dekker knows we lied on this one thing, he won't trust anything. Reluctantly, I nod.

"That's my girl." He kisses my forehead and hugs me to him.

"I just . . ." My voice cracks. "I can't stop picturing her. The way she was just lying there . . ."

"Don't think about it," Tate tells me. He shifts so he's leaning back against the balcony railing, his hands on my waist. "Think about . . . that time we took my dad's boat out and sailed up to Marblehead."

"Tried to sail." I take another breath and feel my panic

subside. Just his hands on me are enough to anchor me back to Earth again—something solid and real.

He's all I have left now.

"Hey, I got us as far as the Sound. You guys were the ones who wanted to turn right back around," Tate protests, smiling.

"She got so sick." I can't help but grin at the memory: Elise, bundled up in a bright orange life vest, clutching the yacht rail with one hand, using the other to flip us off. "I've never seen so much vomit."

"Yeah, thanks for that." Tate laughs. "I had to pay the deckhand triple to wash it all out."

I pause, feeling sadness swell through me, bittersweet. "That was a good day."

He nods. "The best."

I take his face in both hands and kiss him slowly, trying to pretend we're back there, out on the ocean. Pretend we'll spend the afternoon laughing with Elise in the sun before heading back home together, happy and safe.

Pretend, just for a moment, that nothing has changed.

NOW

Of all the photos, that one is the worst.

The photographer was down on the beach, out of sight, but with high definition and telescopic lenses, it's as clear as if he was just six feet away. My face, bright with laughter, Tate's hands on my waist, his fingers slipped under the hem of my T-shirt. His back is to the camera, hidden, but I look happy and carefree, just another girl sneaking a kiss in the bright Caribbean sunshine—while a bereaved family weeps inside.

And so it began. The reporters, speculating why I was so relaxed. Psychologists, handing out quotes about my social disconnection and worrying lack of empathy. The talking heads on TV, picking over the image as if it were a confession all its own. Sure, some of them tried to keep the hordes at bay, discussing post-traumatic shock and delayed reactions, but those few voices of reason were quickly buried under the chorus of outrage.

Why was I so happy? My friend was dead. I should be sad. Was I happy she was dead? Did I secretly hate her? Did I have something to do with it? Did I do it myself? I did it. I had to. Maybe he did it too. Together. A pact. A game. Something sexual, fucked-up. Drugs and alcohol. Kids today. Where were our parents? Aren't they to blame? Did he pressure me? Did I force him? I was happy. Why was I so happy?

One moment. One picture. One glimpse—that's all it takes to make someone think they know the truth.

FALL

"Let's ditch last period and drive to Providence,"
Elise says in greeting the moment I find her in our usual spot
around the back of the sports shed on a Tuesday afternoon. It's
a glorious blue-skied September day, my favorite time of year. A
day made for mittens and plaid scarves and maple lattes. Not, as
we both agree, a day to spend study hall locked in the library.

I settle beside her, cross-legged on the wall, and wrap
my coat tighter against the crisp breeze. Out here, we're hidden from view from the main buildings—still technically on
school grounds, but far from any wandering teachers. "Can't," I
apologize. "I have French and bio."

"So?" She takes both my hands and smiles at me, her best
You know you want to grin. "That Lex guy from the café said

something about a warehouse rave. Tons of cute RISD guys for you . . ."

I laugh. "Lise! Come on. Miss Guerta's just itching to give me a B. And anyway," I add awkwardly, "I have plans with Tate. We're doing dinner and a movie."

Elise lets me go. "Him? Still?" Her voice has an edge.

"Don't." I dig in my bag for a pack of red licorice, avoiding her gaze. I should be happy: a boyfriend and a best friend, for the first time in my life, but juggling the two of them this past month has been an exercise in exhaustion, both of them wanting all my time, me feeling like a traitor, whomever I pick.

"I'm just saying . . ." Elise shrugs. "I figured you'd be done with him by now. It's been, like, months. You can do so much better."

"I don't want better." I find the pack and offer it to her. She peels off a strip and then dangles it slowly into her mouth. "I want Tate."

"But he's so . . . high school!" Elise exclaims. "With his perfect grades, and his perfect preppy blazer, and all that perfectly mussed hair."

I grin. "He does have great hair."

"It's not a good thing!" Elise's eyes drift past me, and her expression twists again. "And now I know why you wanted to meet here. Because you couldn't be away from him, even for one stupid hour."

I turn. The lacrosse team is jogging out onto the field, Tate and Lamar leading the pack. "I didn't know they had practice," I say quickly.

"Sure you didn't."

"Elise . . ."

She falls silent as we watch them. Tate sprints effortlessly along the far goal line, yelling instructions to the team as he runs passing drills. His blue school sweats hang easy on his lithe frame, his blond hair glinting in the sun. He owns the field, the team, and I can't help thinking he looks like some old-time general, leading his troops into battle.

"Oh Jesus."

I turn. Elise is looking at me. "You're falling for him."

"No!" I protest automatically, but it's just us out here, no one else to gossip. I take a breath. "Maybe. Yes," I finally say, my voice quiet. "You don't know him like I do," I add quickly. "All this Golden Boy stuff, you know it's just for show."

"And what does that tell you?" Elise mutters darkly. She pulls a pack of cigarettes from her bag and slips one out. I watch her light it with a silver lighter and take a long inhale.

"Since when do you smoke?" I ask, distracted.

"Since now. Mom."

"Didn't you dump that banker guy because he tasted like ash?"

"No, I dumped him because he had a two-inch dick and no idea what to do with it."

I laugh as she blows a perfect smoke ring. She looks over, catching my gaze. "Want one?"

I sigh. "I shouldn't."

"That means you want to."

"It means I shouldn't. Mom'll smell it on me." I roll my eyes. "She's getting militant about fragrance. She freaked out last week because I used scented moisturizer, going on about chemicals and toxins and all that stuff."

Elise passes me the cigarette all the same. I take it, sucking in a small pocket of smoke.

"How's she doing?" she asks quietly.

I shrug. "You think they tell me anything?" I exhale, blowing another ring into the crisp air. "You know we're killing ourselves with these things," I say, taking another drag.

"But we look so fucking cool." Elise grins. I laugh.

We share the rest of the cigarette in easy silence, cross-legged on the wall. I know I should leave it, just enjoy the break with her, but I can't help but think about the look on her face when she talked about Tate, the tightness in her voice.

"What did you mean?" I have to ask. "Before, about Tate. Why don't you like him?"

"I like him fine." Elise shrugs. "Just . . . He's the kind of guy who turns out to be a serial killer."

My mouth drops open. "Elise!"

"All that perfection, playing a part." Elise grins. "It's not healthy. His anger's going to build up and up and up until one day . . . boom! Explosion. *American Psycho.* Bodies everywhere. I'm telling you."

I shake my head, smiling. "He's not like that. You'd know, if you spent any time with him."

"I do," Elise protests. "We hang out all the time!"

"In the group," I correct her. "But you hardly talk to him even then."

"Because I'm spending time with you," she shoots back. "It's the only chance I get these days."

There's no lightness in her voice. I pause, my skin prickling with guilt. "I'm sorry. I know I've bailed on a bunch of plans, but—"

"It's fine, I get it, young love, whatever." Elise rolls her eyes exaggeratedly.

"Lise, please . . ." I reach for her. "Don't be like this."

"Like what?"

I pause, suddenly uncomfortable. "This. Can't you be happy for me?"

"I am, doll." She gives me a sideways look, then softens. "I'm thrilled. Go, frolic, be prom queen. But be careful, okay? He's going to break your heart."

I blink. "You don't know that. Maybe I'll be the one who breaks his."

Elise gives me a dubious look. "You don't have it in you."

"Want to bet?"

"You'll lose." She squeezes my hand, watching him on the field. "I'll take care of it. He gives you any grief, he'll have me to deal with."

The fierce note in her voice warms me, deep in my chest. I lean over and kiss her on the cheek. "Love you."

"Miles and miles."

"Always."

SECOND
INTERROGATION

DEKKER: **We ran fingerprints on the knife. Yours were on it, Mr. Dempsey's, too. How do you explain that?**

ANNA: **I . . . I don't know. It was from the kitchen, I mean, I used it before.**

DEKKER: **When?**

ANNA: **The night before, maybe? We made guacamole. I helped Max, chopping stuff.**

DEKKER: **And Mr. Dempsey?**

ANNA: **Yes. Him too.**

DEKKER: **Why are you lying to me?**

ANNA: **I'm not, I promise.**

DEKKER: **And the day of the murder, you didn't leave each other's side.**

ANNA: No, not all afternoon.

DEKKER: And you didn't go back to the house?

ANNA: I told you, no.

DEKKER: How long have you been involved with Mr. Dempsey?

ANNA: Since last summer. Nearly seven months.

DEKKER: And you love him.

ANNA: Yes.

DEKKER: And Miss Warren?

ANNA: What do you mean?

DEKKER: You love her also?

ANNA: I . . . Yes. She's my best friend.

DEKKER: And the three of you, you spent much time together.

ANNA: Sure. I mean, we all did. The whole group.

DEKKER: But you and Mr. Dempsey and Miss Warren in particular.

ANNA: I don't know.

DEKKER: Your friends have said the three of you would often go off on your own.

ANNA: I guess. I mean, we would hang out together, that's just how it was. I don't understand, what's this all about?

DEKKER: I'm just getting an idea of your friendship, that's all.

ANNA: But what does this have to do with her death? You're not asking the right questions! What about that guy hanging around, and Niklas?

DEKKER: I'll be the one to judge what's important. Now, back to your friendship with Miss Warren. Did you fight?

ANNA: No.

DEKKER: Not ever? Surely there were arguments, misunderstandings.

ANNA: No, we never fought. She's like a sister to me. Was.

DEKKER: So you weren't jealous of her?

ANNA: What? No.

DEKKER: Miss Chan said the two of you fought often.

ANNA: Not real fights. We bickered.

DEKKER: So you did argue.

ANNA: You're twisting my words. It wasn't like . . . It was stupid stuff. She borrowed my shirt, I forgot to return her iPod. It wasn't real. We didn't get angry.

DEKKER: And Mr. Dempsey. How would you characterize his relationship with Miss Warren?

ANNA: They didn't have one. I mean, they were friends. We all were.

DEKKER: There was no tension there?

ANNA: What do you mean?

DEKKER: Well, you and she were close, the best of friends. Then you started dating him. Surely that would lead to friction.

ANNA: No, there wasn't any. We all got along great.

DEKKER: So she didn't resent Mr. Dempsey for taking you away from her?

ANNA: No. I don't know where . . . I don't know where you're getting all of this, but it's not true. Elise wasn't jealous; she dated guys too. Tons of guys. She was hooking up with that boy Niklas, right before . . . I told you about it. Have you talked to him yet? Where was he that night?

DEKKER: I'm the one asking questions, Miss Chevalier.

ANNA: But I don't understand, this is all bullshit!

ELLINGHAM: Calm down, please—

ANNA: How can you say that? She's dead, and we're just sitting here, going over the same fucking things again and again and again. What about the guy who did this? Why aren't you going after him?

(pause)

DEKKER: Are you quite finished?

(pause)

DEKKER: Miss Chevalier? Mr. Ellingham, could you

please remind your client that it's in her interest to cooperate fully with questioning?

ELLINGHAM: **Anna . . .**

ANNA: **I'm fine. Whatever. What else do you want to know?**

DEKKER: **The first day, when you arrived on the island . . .**

ANNA: **I told you that already.**

DEKKER: **So tell me again.**

VACATION

"Check out the view!" Max whistles as he drops his bag on the polished tile floor, taking in the beach and deep azure ocean beyond. I catch my breath, following his gaze. The scene through the beach house windows is so perfect, it's like something from a postcard, like there should be *Welcome to Aruba* scribbled in the sky above the gently nodding palm tree.

"Never mind the views: hot tub!" Chelsea whoops. She pulls the balcony door open and steps onto the deck, kicking her flip-flops aside. The breeze slips into the room, cool and welcome after the long flight and ride from the airport; the eight of us crammed into a rickety old van with our luggage strapped to the roof.

I exhale, my carsickness easing now that I'm safe on solid ground. And not just any ground, but gleaming tile, spread with brightly woven mats. The house is modern, set like inter-linked boxes above the sand, with cool white walls and colorful abstract art. The main living space is open: huge windows along the length of the room looking out on the deck and ocean view, with a kitchen area in dark marble and plush couches set up around a vast flat-screen TV.

"This place is amazing." I tell AK, drinking it in as the others fan out to explore. "How long have you had it?"

"A couple of years." AK shrugs, nonchalant, but I can see the excited glint in his smile. "Dad got it as some tax-write-off thing; he hardly ever comes out here."

"Well, you're a genius." I hug him. Elise joins me, kissing his cheek on the other side. She's already stripped down to a bikini top and her cutoffs, shoes kicked aside the moment we stepped in the door.

"Legendary," she agrees. "Now, where do you keep the booze?"

There's a chorus of cheers from Lamar and Max as they sprawl on the couches, but Tate pauses. "Isn't it kind of early?" he asks halfheartedly. Elise rolls her eyes in response.

"What are you, our chaperone? Maybe we should just call you Daddy." She pokes his chest with her index finger. Tate swats her away.

"I'm just saying, we can take it easy. You don't need to be hungover all week."

"*Moi?*" Elise bats her eyelashes in exaggerated innocence, "I can hold my liquor just fine, *Daddy*. You're the one who gets sloppy. Or don't you remember Jordan's party last month?" She gives him a pointed smile.

"Hey," I interrupt. "Less talking, more drinking."

Melanie leaps up. "I'll help," she says brightly. "What does everyone want? Beer or cocktails?"

"Before you get too excited, check the kitchen," AK warns. He's got his cell phone up, recording a slow sweep around the room. "The maid will buy stuff for us if we give her a list, but I'm not sure what there is."

Elise makes a beeline for the kitchen. Melanie follows, opening the huge fridge and checking cabinets and drawers.

Tate collapses on the couch beside me. I put my bare feet in his lap and snuggle closer. "I didn't know you got wasted at Jordan's. Was that why your parents flipped?"

Tate shrugs. "I guess. It was nothing. You were there."

"No, I had that flu thing," I remind him.

He looks away. "I don't remember. Elise is just pushing, that's all."

I drop it. Tate's parents found an empty stash of bottles when they got back from a weekend in New York last month, and even though Tate swore he'd barely touched them, he told me about the massive lecture they dispensed on responsibility, and choice and consequence. Whatever they said, it was enough to make him cut down. Senior year is halfway over, college acceptance on the horizon—he's been wound so tight for weeks, I can understand why he doesn't want to mess anything up, not so close to the finish line.

"Try to relax this week," I say, and kiss his neck, following the line from his jaw to his collarbone. "You've been too stressed."

He gives me a halfhearted smile. "I know. Sorry."

"It's not a crime." I lace my fingers through his. "I just want us to have fun, that's all."

"Fun, I can do." He leans over and kisses me, light and true. I reach up to stroke his hair, and the kiss deepens, lasting—

"Get a room!" A cushion hits us square in the face. Tate pulls back, then hurls the cushion back at Max. He grabs another two and flings them back at us. I duck, my arms up to deflect the barrage, but I'm laughing all the same. There's a buzz of excitement in all of us, I can tell, despite the long trip; the prospect of a whole week away from reality finally sinking in, after all our planning and prep back home.

"Speaking of sleeping arrangements . . ." Chelsea comes back inside, her hair down and already tangled in the breeze. "What is the bedroom situation, anyway?"

"There are five rooms," AK replies, snapping a photo of her on his phone. "So do whatever."

"I call the big one, with the balcony!" Elise calls from the kitchen. "I'm not dragging my shit up those stairs."

Melanie's voice follows, a whine. "But I thought we were going to share."

"Yeah, no," Elise saunters back over to the living area. "I'm going to have fun this week."

"Slut!" Max hollers.

"Fuck yeah!" Elise strikes a pose. I laugh, tossing one of the stray pillows at her.

"We're in the one by the front door." Tate looks to me for confirmation. "I already left my stuff."

"Fine with me." I pull myself to my feet, and grab my case. "I need to go change. I feel like I've got airport all over me."

"Then we need to go shopping," Elise declares. "There's nothing here."

"But the fridge is full." Melanie frowns.

"Yes, with fruit, and salad." Elise wrinkles her lip. "We need limes, mixers, mint for mojitos . . ."

"Chips," Lamar adds.

"Ice cream," Chelsea agrees, resting her hands on his shoulders.

"Beer!" AK adds.

I leave them planning our grocery list, and drag my suitcase back down the hall to the room Tate mentioned, by the front door. I push the door open and smile: there are two bedrooms on this level, and another three upstairs. Those have another deck and even better views, but this one is private, with its own bathroom and nobody next door to hear anything through the walls.

I stash my case by the closet and step into the green-tiled bathroom, already set with fluffy towels and a cabinet full of shower gels and shampoos like some fancy hotel. Not that I'd expect anything less from AK's family. His dad struck it rich in the tech boom and has a thing for shiny toys: AK always has the newest phones and laptops before they hit the market, and a garage of five different sports cars to choose from. Some of the other parents look at them sideways during school events, but if Mr. Kundra notices, he doesn't let on, strolling around with his designer suits and ten-thousand-dollar watches, a chauffeur waiting at the curb.

I pause for a moment, thinking about my dad, and the hushed phone conversations and late hours he's been working recently. Some nights, he's not back from the office until after midnight, looking worn-out and pale, but whenever I ask, he waves away my concern with excuses about tax season and demanding clients. I want to believe him, but even I can't help but pick up the murmurs from everyone's parents, muttering darkly about the economy, and how everyone is cutting back.

But this is my vacation from all of that. I shake off the worry and turn on the multijet shower, stripping off my jeans.

I've got my shirt halfway over my head when I hear Tate in the bedroom. "Hey, do you still have my necklace?" I call. "The one I forgot to take off through security? I think I put it in your bag, the front pocket."

Hands close around my waist, cool, and I squeal, whipping my head around. It's Elise.

"You scared me!"

"Shouldn't leave the door open," she teases, hugging me tight from behind. "Anyone could walk in."

"Most people knock," I point out, but I'm smiling. My eyes meet hers in the mirror, our expressions full of delight. "Pretty sweet setup, don't you think?"

"Fancy," she agrees, kissing my shoulder. "You feeling better?"

"Miles and miles." I agree, and it's true. The stress of Boston and my dad and school is suddenly a world away, dissolving into the bright, clear sunshine that's spilling all around us, warm tiles against our bare feet. "You were right about this place." I hug her back. "And Tate seems better too."

"You didn't say he was down. What's wrong?"

"Nothing, everything." I sigh. "School, family, the usual. But it's fine now. We just needed to get away."

"Told you." Elise lets me go. "You better get moving! We're heading to the market in ten."

"Yes, sir." I mock-salute. She slaps me on the ass and exits before I can protest, leaving me alone with my steamy-edged reflection in the mirror. I take in the sight of my own smile—relaxed and happy—and vow not to give another thought to my dad. For the next seven days, life in Boston doesn't exist. The real world can wait.

We load up at the local market, piling snack foods and beer high on the tiny cart as if we're shopping for a month, not just a week. The checkout girl doesn't even ask for IDs, just swipes through the mountain of alcohol like it's soda.

"It's so weird we're legal here," Melanie glances back behind us as we emerge from the convenience store onto the bustling street. "The whole time she was ringing us up, I kept feeling like we're breaking the law."

"I don't know why it's such a big deal back home." Chelsea sucks on a Popsicle. "When we went to Europe, kids were drinking wine with their meals all the time."

"Ooh," I tease. "Look at you, so continental."

Elise joins me, mimicking, "That time we were in Paris . . . Oh, did I tell you about when we went to Rome?"

Chelsea shoves Elise good-naturedly. "Shut up, you know what I mean."

"Hey, you girls want to give us a hand with this?"

We turn back to find the guys struggling to manage our huge stash of groceries.

"No thanks," Elise calls back sunnily. "I'm sure you big, strong men can handle it for yourselves."

Max replies with an obscene hand gesture.

We leave them and stroll on ahead back toward the beach house. This section of the street is narrow and noisy, packed with garish storefronts advertising local handcrafts, cheap phone cards, and tacky gifts. Some local traders have market stalls set up along the sidewalk, selling beaded jewelry and small carved wooden figurines, and Chelsea and Mel slow to browse the trinkets on display. I fall into step with Elise, peeling strings of red licorice and dangling them into my mouth.

"Wait up!" Mel calls to us.

Elise doesn't slow, just rolls her eyes.

"She's being such a drag." She sighs. "She was moaning at me about the room thing for years back at the house."

"Years?" I laugh.

"Centuries. But like I'm going to cramp my style sharing. She'd probably watch," Elise adds, smirking. "You know she's obsessed with me."

"Come on." I give her a look. "She's not so bad. She's just . . ."

"Whiny? Clingy? Insecure?"

"Wound too tight," I say diplomatically. "We just find her some guy when we're out tonight, then she'll be too distracted to bother us anymore."

"You're too nice." Elise sighs.

"Hey, she's your friend," I point out.

"Fine. *I'm* too nice." Elise catches sight of something on the other side of the street. "Ooh, cute."

She suddenly veers out into the road, and there's a blast of a horn as an old beat-up car swerves to miss her. Elise doesn't slow, just bounds through the traffic to a stall set up on the corner. I wait for the cars to clear, then follow.

"We're just here on vacation." Elise is smiling up at the trader when I arrive. He's tall and muscular, a linen shirt draped open over his black skin, his hair in dreadlocks.

"You like to party? You come to the right place." He flashes a wide grin. "My friend, he owns a bar down by the beach. I can hook you up."

Elise flutters her eyelashes at him. "That would be great." She turns to me. "This is my new friend Juan," she introduces him. "He knows all the best spots."

"Oh. Great." I look dubiously at his stall. It's not so much a stall as a plank of wood set up on two wooden crates, with jewelry and junk laid out on a dirty, frayed piece of blue cloth. Elise picks up a bracelet of metal links and black onyx beading. "What do you think?"

"I think it looks like it washed up on the beach. Come on, we should go meet the others."

Elise stands firm. "I like it."

"Your friend has taste," Juan tells me. "Pretty bracelet for a pretty girl."

"Elise." I tug her arm, my voice low. "These guys are just trying to rip you off."

"Juan wouldn't do that, would you?" Elise flutters some more. She's got her best free-drink face on, the one she uses to charm poor suckers into buying us round after round at the bars along State Street. I drift a few steps away, knowing she won't quit until she gets what she wants.

"How much?" she asks, wide-eyed.

"For you? A gift." Juan beams.

"Really?" Elise checks. "You're not tricking me, are you? Because that would be mean." Her voice is still flirtatious.

"No tricks," Juan slides the bracelet onto her wrist and holds on to her hand. "Maybe we can get a drink. I'll show you that bar, down by the water."

Elise pulls her hand away. "I don't think my boyfriend would like that."

Juan clutches his chest, mimicking heartbreak. "You have a boyfriend?"

"Lots of them." Elise grins.

There's a piercing whistle from down the street. We both look over: Chelsea and the guys are waving to us from outside a beach store—inflatable rafts and pool toys hanging from outside the window. Lamar has a bright duck-shaped inner tube around his waist, over his clothes, and Tate and Max are dueling with neon blow-up swords.

Elise laughs. "Could they get any more phallic?"

"Just wait until they start with the wrestling," I agree. "We done here?"

"Yup." She turns back to Juan. "Thanks for the bracelet." She turns to go, but he catches her arm.

"Wait, wait," he insists. "Where you going? We get drinks, tonight."

"No thanks." Elise pulls free.

"I meet you, at the bar," Juan insists.

Elise's smile drops. "I said no." She turns to me. "Creeper," she says, and rolls her eyes without dropping her voice.

Juan's expression darkens. "So that's how it is, you play me. You think this is all a joke? That Juan is your dupe?"

Elise and I exchange a look and start to walk away, fast.

"Fucking Americans!" His voice echoes after us as we quickly slip into the crowds. "You all whores!"

The minute we're away from the stall, I turn to Elise, pissed. "Why did you have to do that?"

"What?"

"Flirt with him. You can't go around talking to strange guys, it's not safe."

"Relax." Elise looks unconcerned. "Anyway, it was worth it. Look!" She shows off the bracelet.

"Still . . ." I turn around and feel a sudden shiver of panic. Juan is behind us in the crowd, twenty feet away, but closing fast. "Elise," I hiss. "He's following us."

She doesn't turn. "Ignore him. He's just some weirdo, what can he do?"

I'm not so nonchalant. I walk faster, dragging her along with me until we reach the rest of the group, waiting outside the store. "Hey." Tate slings an arm around my shoulder. "Where'd you guys go?"

"Nowhere." I glance back again, but there's no sign of Juan. I exhale a slow breath.

"You okay?" Tate frowns.

"Sure." I force a grin. "It's nothing."

We head back across the street to the beach house, toting groceries and new toys between us. Elise dances on ahead, telling the others the story of how she got her new bracelet.

"You sure you're okay?" Tate checks again as we reach the house. AK unlocks the front door, and the others head inside, their chatter loud and carefree.

"What? Oh yeah, fine." I look behind me one last time, and freeze.

Juan is standing across the street, watching us.

"Anna!" Elise barrels back outside and grabs my hand. "Where did you leave your iPod? We need some tunes for this party!"

"Um, on the dresser, I think."

When I turn back, Juan is gone. Maybe he was never there to begin with. I shiver and follow the rest of them into the house. The door slams shut behind us.

THE TRIAL

"Officer Carlsson, you were a member of Judge Dekker's investigative team on the murder, were you not?"

My lawyer leafs through a couple of the papers on his table, and then strolls closer to the witness stand. Carlsson is young, in his twenties, maybe, with cropped blond hair and an earnest expression. In a police precinct full of suspicious scowls and icy glares, he was a rare friend to me: the one to check if I needed water, or a bathroom break, or to simply speak to me like a decent human being instead of screaming at me for hours, the way Dekker did. Now, on the stand, he sends me a sympathetic smile before he answers.

"Yes. I was assigned to the case the morning after the body was found."

"So you worked alongside the prosecutor, evaluating evidence and assessing leads, from the very start?"

"That's right."

"So you were present during Miss Chevalier's questioning when she told you about this incident with . . . I'm sorry, I don't have a surname for him. The incident with the man known as Juan?"

He clicks his pointer, and Juan's photo goes up on the display screen overhead. It's a mug shot, sullen and dark-eyed, and there's a faint hiss of breath as the courtroom inhales. He looks dangerous.

"I'm sorry," my lawyer adds to the judge, sounding anything but. "It's the only photo we have on record for the man."

Judge von Koppel doesn't look impressed. She waves a hand, as if to say, *Continue*.

"Officer Carlsson?"

Carlsson nods. "Yes. Miss Chevalier told us about meeting Juan at the market, and how he followed them back to the house. She said he was angry when Miss Warren rejected him."

"An angry man, following the victim home . . ." My lawyer pauses for effect. "And you didn't think this warranted any follow-up?"

"Yes, I did." Carlsson looks from us over to where Dekker is sitting behind the prosecution table. "I believed we should have named him a prime suspect in the investigation."

"Because of his threatening behavior?"

"Yes, but there was more," he adds. "There were several break-ins in the area in the weeks leading up to the murder. Juan matched a description of a man seen fleeing one of those robberies."

I look hopefully to the judge again, but she's scribbling notes, her expression unreadable.

"So you believed him to be a criminal, known for robbing the houses along the beach. Houses like Mr. Kundra's." My lawyer pauses again. "Did you try to track him down?"

"Yes. I canvassed his known associates and asked around the neighborhood, but he had disappeared." Carlsson shrugged. "It looked like he'd left the island."

"He fled. So you stopped looking for him?"

"No," Carlsson gave Dekker another glare. "I filed a request for more resources, to liaise with police departments on neighboring islands, and have a team go through surveillance video from the harbor and ports."

"But this request was denied."

"Yes. I was told it would be a waste of time."

"I'm sorry, I don't understand." My lawyer is grandstanding, but I don't mind, not when he's doing it for my benefit. "Here you had a suspect linked to other break-ins—like the one that accompanied Miss Warren's murder—and you were told not to pursue him?"

"Dekker said it was irrelevant." Carlsson looks back to me with regret in his expression. "He'd decided that the break-in was staged, that someone from the group had killed her and just smashed the doors afterward. He ordered me to drop the Juan investigation and focus on Miss Chevalier and Mr. Dempsey. I tried to go over his head," he added, speaking directly at Judge von Koppel. "I thought he was making a mistake. I still do. But they all just shut me down. He was fixated."

Fixated.

My lawyer leaves the word hanging in the courtroom for a moment, and I have to keep myself from smiling. Carlsson was transferred to a precinct on the other side of the island two weeks after they charged me, Dekker and his team did everything to try to keep him away from the trial, but we got him here, and just having him up on the stand feels like a victory—for once, someone not talking about my mood swings, and jealousy, and obvious guilt.

"Let's talk about that crime scene." My lawyer clicks his pointer again, and the image goes up on the screen of Elise's trashed room. He clicks on, to a close-up of the balcony doors and the constellation of shattered glass spread on the floor. "The prosecution has presented experts who testified that the window was broken after the attack, from the inside. Did you agree?"

"It's possible," Carlsson says reluctantly. "There was glass out on the balcony, too, which would fit with it being broken from the inside. But there was glass everywhere," he adds. "People in and out of the room for hours. These photos weren't taken until after the paramedics left. There's no way of knowing how much the scene was contaminated."

"Yet you believe it was a genuine break-in?" My lawyer continues. "But Judge Dekker has told this court nothing was stolen, aside from the victim's necklace."

"That's right," Carlsson answers. "But that doesn't mean the attacker didn't intend to rob the house. He could have been disturbed by Miss Warren, and fled after killing her."

"Like I said, there were others before the murder, and it would fit with the pattern, and this Juan guy."

"So let me ask you, Officer Carlsson, having examined all the evidence—the same evidence that Detective Dekker was party to—what do you think really happened that night?"

Carlsson looks at us. "It's simple. The guy breaks in, finds Elise there, and then attacks her—out of panic, or anger. The ripped clothing indicated it was a sexual attack. She turned him down before, so this guy Juan would have a motive to hurt her like that. It just makes sense—more sense than one of her friends suddenly turning on her, anyway."

"Thank you, that will be all. No further questions."

AFTER

They keep us in a holding pattern for a week, waiting on the island for some kind of news. Every day, one or more of us get called back in for questioning, this time with our parents and lawyers in tow. The news cameras and reporters are still laying siege to the hotel, so there's nowhere else we can go; we just sit around the suite, watching TV, calling up room service and waiting for this all to be done.

AK barely speaks. Melanie cries all the time. Max spends most of the day curled up in his room with the blinds drawn, woozy on anti-anxiety meds.

We all just want to go home.

"What did they ask you this time?" Lamar lifts his head from his laptop as I enter the suite. Dad and Ellingham are off talking legal stuff with the other parents in the makeshift conference room; it's just us kids in here.

I shrug, peeling off my cardigan. "The same. Just, what happened, where were we."

I shoot a look to Tate, over by the TV. He gives me a questioning look, and I nod. We're okay.

"I don't get it." Chelsea is curled in a ball on the sofa beside him. "Why do they keep going over the same stuff? Shouldn't there be security footage, or witnesses?"

I don't reply. Slowly I cross to the kitchen unit in the corner and run the cold faucet over my wrists, closing my eyes against everything but the feeling of the water, icy against my palms. The interrogation room is tiny, and they never set the cold air high enough. After two hours in there with Ellingham and Dekker, my clothes stick, damp and sweaty, to my skin.

"Whoever it was, they planned it." AK's voice comes, and I turn in surprise. He's standing by the windows, staring out at the ocean with the same blank expression he's been wearing since we found Elise. "The front door has cameras. They knew not to come in that way, or they'd have been on the tape."

"So, what, they cased the place?" Lamar asks.

Chelsea scoots closer to him, hugging him close. "That means they would have been watching us. All week. Waiting." She shivers.

"Maybe." AK pauses. "Or maybe they knew all along."

"What are you saying?" Tate speaks up for the first time.

AK turns to face us. "I don't know. All I do know is I spent three hours in that police precinct yesterday, answering questions about you two. How long you've been together. What you do. How Elise fit in with you guys. That's all he wanted to know."

"Because he's crazy," I say quickly.

"Is he?" AK shoots back. "They're the ones who know what they're doing. They looked at the crime scene, and did an autopsy on the body, and all that stuff. Wouldn't they be out looking for the murderer—if they thought he was out there?"

"What's going on?" Melanie's voice comes from the doorway. She's wrapped in a hotel robe, her dark hair hanging limply on either side of her face. She looks back and forth between us. "Did they find something?"

"No, sweetie." Chelsea shakes her head. "It's nothing."

"Nothing you guys want to think about," AK mutters.

"How are you feeling?" I interrupt, asking Melanie. She shrugs, and trudges over to the couch, barely lifting her feet.

"School already started," she says, sitting down across from the others. "When do you think they'll let us go back?"

"Soon, I hope." I give her an encouraging smile. "Even calculus is better than this."

Melanie doesn't meet my eyes. Instead she reaches for the remote, and clicks through to one of the cable news channels.

The familiar sight of our hotel fills the screen, the glossy-haired reporter filming live out from the street below.

"Mel," I say quickly. "Don't. You know they told us not to watch."

"I want to see," she insists, turning the volume up.

". . . and with police yet to make any arrests, pressure is mounting on investigating prosecutor Klaus Dekker." The reporter is blond and wide-eyed, clutching her microphone. She looks like a coed, dressed up in a preppy blouse, as if she was off doing body shots before the studio called her up for duty.

"What's the mood there on the island, Katie?" the man in the studio asks.

"I've been talking to locals, and other tourists, and everyone is still in a state of shock." Katie manages a concerned frown. "Although this is a destination known for its nightlife, photos of the teens' drinking and wild partying have given everyone pause for thought, making some question just what kind of behavior the victim and her friends were engaged in."

"Yes, we've been seeing the photos from the students' social networking profiles. . . ."

"That's right. And the latest photo, of the victim's friends Anna Chevalier and Tate Dempsey, has further fueled speculation." It flashes up on-screen. "Taken just hours after Elise's death, it appears to show them laughing and joking on their hotel balcony, seemingly unconcerned by her brutal death—"

Tate snatches the remote from Melanie and shuts it off. "Enough. You heard our parents, it's all just bullshit, for the ratings."

"You would say that," AK mutters again.

Tate whirls around. "Have you got a problem with me?" he demands.

"Tate." I go to intercept him. "It's been a long day, okay? We're all just tired, and—"

"No, I'm serious." He pushes past me, marching up to AK. "Spit it out. If there's something you want to say, just say it."

AK stares back at him. "Fine." His voice is heavy. "Why didn't you come diving with us?"

Tate stares. "You know why. We were hungover; we just wanted to chill."

"No, you said you were going, you couldn't wait," AK argues. "Then Elise says she's staying home, and you change your mind."

"Tate?" I ask. "What's he talking about?"

"It's nothing." Tate glares. "He's talking out of his ass."

"We both decided to stay," I tell AK, putting myself between them. "It wasn't anything. We just wanted some time to ourselves."

"Is that why you didn't check on her?" AK demands. "You were too busy off on your own? Making out, while she was bleeding to death?"

"We texted!" I protest. "We all did. And if you were so worried, why didn't you check on her, before you left?"

"It was early." AK looks away.

"It was, like, ten in the morning," I correct him. "Remember, she didn't come out for breakfast. And you went and knocked on her door," I add, turning to Mel.

Her face trembles. "You think I don't know that? You think I wouldn't go back if I could, and break the door down, or do something?"

"Hey." Chelsea reaches to comfort her. "Knock it off, all of you. This won't change anything. Nobody's to blame."

"You keep saying that!" AK explodes. "But you don't know it's true. None of us do. We weren't there."

"But we were, is that what you're saying?" Tate steps up, getting in his face. I can see the tension radiating from him, his whole body coiled to strike.

"Will everyone just calm down?" I beg. "We've got to stick together."

"Why?" AK shoots back. "Because you're worried what we might say, if it'll make you look bad?"

"Because it's the truth!"

My voice echoes, plaintive, but it's like a dividing line just got drawn down the middle of the room. Me and Tate on one side, AK on the other. Melanie, Lamar, and Chelsea stranded between us, not saying a word.

"You really think we had something to do with it?" I ask AK, my voice breaking. "That we would hurt her, that we . . ." I catch my breath.

"I don't know," AK finally replies, his voice hollow. "I don't know what the fuck to think anymore."

"Thanks a lot, buddy." Tate's voice is laced with sarcasm.

"He doesn't mean it," I say, but Tate just turns and walks out, the door slamming behind him like a gunshot through the suite.

Silence.

"Go after him," I urge AK. "Apologize. You can smooth this over. We're all messed up, we're not thinking straight—"

"I am." AK looks at me. "I'm probably the only one seeing things clearly."

I shiver. His eyes seem to burn straight through me, harsher than I've ever seen before. AK is the playboy, the joker, the one who suggests we drive out of the city at two a.m. to find some legendary food cart. He doesn't get mad; he never holds a grudge. But right now, he's staring at me like a stranger.

"AK—" I start, but before I can say another thing, the door opens, and my dad comes bursting in, a couple more parents behind him.

"It's okay, sweetie." He crosses the room, pulling me into a hug. "This'll all be straightened out."

"What's going on?" My reply is muffled against his sweater.

He's holding me so tight, I can feel him shake. I feel a sudden chill, blood turning to ice in my veins. "Dad?" I try to push him away. "Dad, what's happening?"

"Mr. Chevalier, please stand aside."

Dad releases me, and I look up to see Dekker, coming through the doorway with two more officers behind him. The look on his face is pure triumph.

"Dad?" My voice has a note of terror in it.

"Just stay calm," he tells me. "We'll be in the car, right behind you."

I back away. "But what's going on?"

Dekker advances. "Anna Chevalier, I have a warrant for your arrest, on suspicion of the murder of Elise Warren."

The ground falls away.

I stumble back, but Dekker grabs me roughly, forcing my hands behind my back. He shoves me up against the wall, and I hear my dad yell out in protest as I feel the cold bite of metal lock into place against my wrists.

"You do not have to say anything . . ."

His voice drifts away. I can see his lips moving, see the burst of panic and confusion in the room, but everything fades to a dull roar as he hustles me toward the door, blood in my ears beating loud to drown out the rest of the world. All I have are glimpses, snapshots of the scene. My dad's expression, panicked and powerless. Chelsea, weeping into Lamar's shoulder.

The maid in the hallway, open-mouthed as they drag me into the elevator. Tourists in the lobby, pointing and wide-eyed, cell phones held high. The news crews outside, already pressed up against the front windows, cameras flashing.

The bright lights snap me back suddenly as Dekker pulls me outside, launching me into the middle of the scrum. Reporters lunge at me from every direction. I'm in the center of a storm, every thought drowned out by their yells. The crowd has swelled to ten times its usual size—all of them jostling their cameras at me, hurling their questions, their faces crude and gleeful.

"Did you kill her?"

"Where's the evidence?"

"Are you pressing charges?"

"Why did you do it?"

I trip, nearly falling, and then Ellingham is beside me, hauling me on toward the police van.

"Don't say a word," Ellingham orders me. "Don't tell them anything until I'm there."

"But what about—"

My reply is drowned out by a fresh roar from the crowd. Tate is being led out of the hotel behind me, handcuffed between two more police officers. His parents and lawyer cluster behind, in a panic.

"Tate!" I call, pulling against my restraints. "Tate, it'll be okay!"

They propel him away from me, toward a waiting van. But before he's bundled inside, he looks up, searching for me in the crowd.

"Tate!" I yell again, helpless.

He meets my eyes for a minute, anger burning in his expression.

Then he turns away.

HALLOWEEN

"Enough photos, you guys!" AK raises a bottle of vodka, yelling over the pounding rock music that fills the kitchen. It's late night on Halloween, and I'm sandwiched between Elise and Tate, posing for the flash of his cell phone camera. AK gestures impatiently, spilling his drink. "Let's get this show on the road!"

"Who votes that AK doesn't drive?" Chelsea laughs as she swipes the bottle from him and takes a gulp. Her tanned skin is dusted with glitter in her tiny Leia bikini, her long hair wound up in fat braided whorls.

"What are you talking about?" AK doffs the cap of his revolutionary war costume. "I am as sober as the grave."

"Bad metaphor, it's the day of the dead," Elise points out, still draped around me, holding the kitchen knife we've smeared with fake blood. "Graveyards are party central—all the spirits going crazy."

"C'mon, you don't believe that stuff." I turn to her. "Ghosts and spirits and all that bullshit?"

"Oh shit!" Elise giggles. "Okay, if this was a horror movie, you'd have just doomed yourself to some serious undead revenge."

"Woo!" I cry, waving my arms around. "You hear that, evil spirits? I mock you and your very existence. Just try to come get me."

"And . . . I vote that Anna doesn't drive either." Chelsea watches, laughing.

Lamar looks up from his phone. "I just checked in with my buddies, they say the party's going hard."

"Then let's roll. Max!" Chelsea yells, without pausing for breath. He wanders in, smoking the end of a fat blunt.

"Dude! Not in the house!" Chelsea snatches it away from him. "Do you want our parents to freak again?" She moves to throw it down the garbage disposal, but not before taking a quick toke herself.

"Whatever." Max grins through the thick zombie scars on his face. He looks down at his football uniform, dirtied and stained. "Hey, can I get some more blood up in here?"

As Elise goes to smear him with more fake-blood makeup, I feel a new pair of arms slip around me; lips kissing, soft against the back of my neck. I shiver, leaning back into Tate's embrace.

"Did I tell you how sexy you look in that costume?" he whispers in my ear.

I laugh. "Only ten million times."

"Well, you do." His lips press against my neck again, but this time he bites down softly, playful. His arms tighten, his breath hot against my skin. "I can't wait to get you out of it."

His words send another shiver of excitement through me—this time edged with unfamiliar uncertainty, but before I can reply, he's pulled me around so I'm facing him, his lips hard and searching on mine. I melt into him, falling back against the kitchen cabinet as we kiss, long and deep. I hear the chatter of the others in the room; music loud; the low, sweet scent of weed, but it all falls away, the way it always does when I'm kissing him.

It still amazes me, how we can create a different place, a whole world, just in the place where our bodies meet. Ours. Even here, in the brightly lit kitchen, it's the same as when we're alone, the two of us, in the dark fort of covers in a bedroom at night. All he has to do is touch me and I feel that quicksilver longing, breathless and expectant—

"Okay people, into the van!" Chelsea yells loudly, cutting

through the drum of my heartbeat. Tate pulls away from me, we're both smiling, bashful but conspiratorial. *"Andiamo!"* she claps, shooing us. *"Vamos!"*

We grab our bags and coats and head out to the front of the house, piling into the Newports' van—crammed together in a tangle of costume hats and fake blood and weaponry. "I told you these costumes would be killer." Elise beams, crushed up against me. Our tiny cheerleader skirts cut off midthigh, and we've streaked blood down our faces, dripping from our fangs.

"You didn't say you were matching," Mel complains from her other side.

Elise and I share a look of exasperation. Mel sees it. "What? You didn't. I would have gotten one too."

"You look great," Elise placates her. "You always look cute in that outfit."

Mel tugs at her catsuit tail, her whiskers quivering. "Still . . ."

Elise turns away from her, back to me. "So"—she drops her voice meaningfully—"you were getting cozy there in the kitchen."

I shoot a nervous look to the front seat, where Tate is scanning through Max's iPod, the music already too loud in the packed van.

"Relax," Elise says, and grins, keeping her voice low. "He can't hear us. Tonight's the night?"

I shrug, blushing.

"Aww, my little girl's going to be a woman," Elise squeezes me close. I fight half-heartedly.

"Don't . . ."

"It's cool," Elise reassures me. "I'll cover with your parents if they call."

"They won't."

My quiet reply is drowned by Chelsea. "Elise, what was that song you played for me? The one from that show . . . ?"

As the group chatters and bickers, I gaze out the window at the dark freeway, hugging my arms around myself. It's clichéd, to plan something like this, to be so nervous, but this is my first time. For all of Elise's and my wild partying, the most I've ever done with a guy is *almost* everything: hot fingers in a dark room, an unfamiliar taste in my mouth. Tate and I have fooled around, sure, but I've been holding back, waiting, never quite certain I should take that step over the edge.

It's not about the physical stuff; I know I want him. I'm consumed with wanting him. That's the problem. I've never felt so reckless in my life before—so out of control. I hide it—from him, Elise, everyone—but sometimes I can't sleep for the desire racing in my system. I lie awake at night, poring over memories of us together: the look of dark intensity in his eyes, a deliberate grind of his hips against mine, the blurring gasps of surprised pleasure. I lie in the haze of desire, imagining everything that would follow if I would only just say yes: mouths and fingers and that final push of friction my body seems to demand, crying out in a language I don't even understand.

The truth is, it's not the act I'm scared of, but giving myself so entirely to someone. As long as there are lines to draw and boundaries to cling to, I can pretend that I'm safe from this wanting that threatens to consume me. I'm separate, still all my own. But after . . .

What then? What comes after, when he has that much of me, to do with as he chooses? When I have him. Will it ever be enough?

"I don't want to pressure you," he told me, his bare chest still rising and falling with quick gasps of air. We were back in his bed last week, the same place we'd been reaching for weeks now: almost naked, almost there, almost too far to stop.

Almost.

His breathing slowed. "I just don't understand why you're not ready." Tate propped himself up on one elbow, leaning over me, a hand gentle on my cheek. "You know I love you."

I nodded.

"And you love me." He grinned, trailing his hand lower, down my throat and across the sensitive skin of my breast. I felt my stomach flip over again—as much from the victory in his expression as the sensation of his fingers, soft against my skin. My love was a prize, a triumph to him.

I nodded again.

"So what are we waiting for?" Tate dipped his head, following the path of his hand with his lips now, kissing a winding trail down my body, while the other hand gently stroked, lower, in a slow rhythm that left me gasping. "I want to know you," he said, lifting his head from my stomach to meet my eyes. There was nothing but sincerity there, hopeful and reassuring. "Completely."

Completely.

The group laughs and chatters as I watch the world blur outside the dark van windows, the word spinning in my head. It's a temptation and a promise, all bound up in one. For there to be nothing left between us—all of him, everything of me.

I want it, and yet I recoil from the idea, all at the same time. But there's only person who I've ever given myself to like that: Elise. And even though it seems odd, even wrong, I wonder suddenly if the reason I'm holding back from sleeping with Tate is because it would mean he'd possess me in a way she never will.

I feel a buzz against my stomach, my phone vibrating with a text message. Tate.

I love you.

I meet his eyes in the rearview mirror. He smiles, the private grin he only ever shows to me—something quieter, and almost sad.

I smile back, shy.

I love you too.

The party is at an old firehouse on the outskirts of Providence, an hour out of Boston on the freeway. It's been transformed into a creepy haunted house: cobwebs draped from every corner; jack-o'-lanterns leering; screams echoing out into the night. The partygoers spill out into the parking lot, a chaotic crowd of zombies, werewolves, superheroes, and the usual slutty story-book-character college girls.

"Disney bingo!" AK whoops, heading toward the firehouse. "I'm going to get me an Ariel!"

We party for hours in the dark firehouse space, the group dispersing and rejoining around me, a steady rhythm like the tide on the shore. I watch as they fall further out of themselves, the way you do when the music is just right and the crowd is dense and forgiving—like an out-of-body experience, nothing but deep bass and movement and hot, sweating skin. But I can't fall, not tonight, with so much on my mind. So I watch them; lost in the middle of the crowd. I see the night in flashes, glittering and dark: AK clutching at a drunk coed Red Riding Hood; Chelsea blissed out in Lamar's arms; Melanie's anxious gaze when she loses sight of us; Tate, oblivious to the stares of admiration from the girls around us; and Elise, Elise with her eyes closed, her head thrown back, her arms drifting high in the air.

She never has a problem letting go, not like me: she'll slip into the rhythm, or a laugh, or a strange boy's arms as easily as breathing, not asking for a moment what happens when the moment fades away and there's nothing left but the pale dawn light and all your old insecurities. I try, but I can't help my mind skipping over the here-and-now and racing on, to what might come next. Consequence and regret and other might-have-beens: plotting out every angle and scenario, knowing all along that the path I take means missing something else.

Soon—too soon, maybe—it's past three. The music scratches into nothing and the party shuts down: neon lights breaking through the dim. Suddenly the creepy skeletons and draped entrails are nothing but cheap props, dangling sadly against cinder block walls and a litter of broken bottles, and our costumes are left smeared and disheveled. The others don't seem to notice the change—they're still laughing, dizzy and drunk, their faces flushed from dancing and illicit hookups. The crowd spills outside, lingering on the curb out front, bumming cigarettes and flirting, calling out after-party plans.

The night is still just getting started.

Elise links her arm through mine as we pick our way back

across the parking lot. "Are you nervous?" she asks. I shrug. "That means yes." Elise grins. "Don't worry, it'll be over real soon. Tate doesn't strike me as a guy with much self-control."

"You'd be surprised," I tell her, and she throws her head back to laugh.

"I guess I keep underestimating him." She swings our hands back and forth, like kids on the playground, but her next words are sobering. "You don't have to, you know."

"I want to. I just . . ." I stop walking, until the group is way ahead and there's nothing but dark and headlights surrounding us. "How do you do it?" I ask.

"It's kind of late to be drawing you a diagram," Elise teases, but I shake my head.

"Not that. I mean . . . You're always *right here*, in the present, and I can't . . . I can't get out of my own mind like that."

Elise tilts her head slightly and looks at me again, serious this time. "It's easy," she tells me. "The way I see it, the future doesn't exist. Nothing does—except now." She looks around, at the party debris and the disintegrating crowd, the couple making out against a car, his pirate hat falling unnoticed to the ground as he gropes higher under her Red Riding Hood skirt. Elise grins affectionately. "You see? It's all we have. It's everything. You can't get tied up in things that might never matter. All that time you waste, you know? You've got to be here." She presses her index finger to my chest, bare through the low dip of the V slashed in my uniform neckline. "Right now."

"But how?" I shrug helplessly. "It's not like I can just turn my brain off."

"Here." Elise steps in closer to me, and takes something from the pocket of her cheerleader skirt. A tiny plastic sachet; two little white pills. She holds her palm out to me.

I hesitate.

"They're my mom's," she adds. "Prescription, nothing crazy, but they'll calm you down. Like a few glasses of wine, but . . . smoother."

"You take them?" I ask, frowning. She's never told me; I've never seen.

Elise shrugs, almost bashful. "Not often. Sometimes. When I don't want to deal with . . . feeling, like this."

"Are you okay?" I ask, suddenly shameful. "I know I've been wrapped up in Tate, and this whole thing—"

"Hey, this is a big deal for you. I'm fine." Elise pulls me into a hug. "Promise."

I stay for a moment in the safety of her arms, catching a breath of her perfume, the light spices of her shampoo. Then she pulls back, pressing the sachet into my hand. "It'll relax you. Trust me," she adds with a knowing look, "you're going to want to be relaxed."

I pause another moment, feeling painfully self-conscious.

My brain has been buzzing all night, caught up in the plan that feels like an inevitability now, whether I could take it back or not. I know what I feel, and what I want—Tate, always Tate— but I'm still frozen on the edge of the drop, waiting. For what, I don't even know. Something to push me over, someone to tell me this is the right decision. Fall. Be his. Let it consume you.

Maybe this is my push.

I take the packet and slip it into my pocket.

They drop us off at Tate's house: the stucco building dark behind the wrought-iron gates. His parents are in DC for some charity fund-raiser, and we have the place to ourselves.

"They texted." Tate grins, unlocking the front door and quickly tapping in the security code. "They won't be back until Monday."

"So no tiptoeing out at four in the morning?" I follow him inside.

He laughs, pulling me in for a quick kiss. "Nope. I can even make you breakfast in bed, if you want."

"You mean, cold cereal in bed," I kiss him back, relaxing into his touch like a drug, but he pulls away, already leading me through the foyer and up the wide staircase toward his room. He stops me in the hall.

"One minute," he says, full of excitement. "Wait here."

He disappears down the hall into his bedroom, leaving me

to loiter nervously on the plush red carpet. My heart is beating like crazy, knowing what's to come. I almost wish we hadn't planned it—that I'd just whispered "now" some other night, when I was already caught up in the breathless grasping of hands and lips and hot skin against mine. This is so deliberate, slow, and sobering.

I take the sachet from my skirt pocket, considering it, but before I can open it, Tate calls to me. "Ready." He beckons me to the bedroom door. I quickly tuck the pills away, take a deep breath, and step inside.

The room has been transformed. Instead of his sports trophies and sailing paraphernalia, the desk and mantle are lit with tiny candles, flickering golden in the dark. He's playing a mix on low, a song I remember from one of our first dates, and there's even a rose lying on the pillow of his freshly made bed.

"What do you think?" He takes my hands, looking almost nervous. "Is it okay? I want this to be perfect for you."

My fear melts away. Not because of the props, the clichéd movie scene he's made here, but because of the earnest look on his face, hopeful and true. This is just so Tate: to try his hardest to make everything perfect. He always wants to be the good guy, and although I don't need this—the candles and the music—I love him for wanting to give them to me all the same.

He'll always do the right thing by me. He'll never let me down.

"It's perfect," I reassure him, feeling my blood start to sing. Desire and love and an unfamiliar sparkle in my veins. I'm done waiting. I want this.

I reach up to kiss his mouth, and give him everything.

WAITING

Lamar comes to visit me the week after I lose the bail hearing. We sit in the visitors' room, with the scratched plexiglass partition between us, speaking through the handsets like a sad, twisted version of kids playing telephone.

"How are you doing?" he asks me, concern clear on his face. I can't think how I must look to him, with my unwashed hair and baggy orange jumpsuit. I won't tell him the truth—about the unbearable wretchedness echoing through every minute of my days—so I don't even try.

"Okay, I guess." I'm glad he's here, but surprised, too. I've been expecting Chelsea, even Mel. But Lamar has always been the solid one: quiet and true in his way.

"Don't tell me they've got you running laps in the yard,

and working sewing footballs or something." He's trying to sound casual, like we're hanging out in a coffee shop or on the front lawn at school, and not in a prison block with two armed guards keeping watch over our every move.

I manage a weak smile for him. "Nope, just sitting around, waiting."

"Same here," he jokes, but his body is folded tensely onto the cheap plastic chair. "My mom's already on me to do something constructive with my time. A project."

"You mean a 'What I Did on Spring Break' essay?" I quip, but my words are hollow. "You should have deferred college for a year. You could write a killer application essay now."

"Right," Lamar agrees. "Killer."

The word sits between us. My stomach drops. "I didn't mean—"

"I know. It's okay." He looks away, his dark eyes darting nervously around the long room. There are two other visitors: a burly tattooed guy, murmuring through the handset, and a cluster of young kids, climbing over their grandmother and pressing their palms to the divider as their mother weeps on my side of the screen. The scene is depressing and bleak, and I wish with everything I am to be anywhere but here.

"Thank you," I say quietly, trying to keep my voice from breaking. "For coming. I know you didn't have to, and you're the only one who's been."

Lamar looks away. "The others wanted to," he says quickly, "but you know what our parents are like. And with the prison . . ."

"I know."

"But they send their best. We're all thinking about you."

I nod. Maybe it's true. I want to believe him, but I've had too much time in here, long, empty days to think about my friends, and all the reasons why they haven't come—haven't even sent letters, or called, even though I made sure my dad told them about the visiting hours and phone privileges.

I'm angry at them for it, hurt, too, but every time I try to muster some kind of sense of betrayal, I can't help but wonder: Would I be any different, if the roles were reversed?

Lamar looks at me again, closer. "You are okay? I mean, you would tell me, if they did . . . If there was trouble, with any of the other girls in there."

"I promise," I tell him. "It's no sleepover, but it's not like a prison movie or anything. The guards keep a pretty close watch on me; I guess I'm high-profile or something." I give him a wry smile. "Mostly the other girls just leave me alone."

"Good." Lamar's dark eyes are wide and expressive. "It'll be okay," he says again, pressing his palm against the glass. "Just hang in there."

I know I should smile and banter, pretend like I'm keeping my spirits up, but the truth is, I've been in a daze ever since the judge made her announcement, the words echoing in my head, so icy and detached.

The defendant is a flight risk, charged with a violent crime of the highest degree. . . .

Dad tried to reassure me, that the lawyer would be launching another appeal, but something in me seemed to switch off, there in the courtroom. I watched in shock as the guard went to release Tate. The handcuffs fell from his wrists, and he turned to embrace his parents, enfolded tight and safe in a circle of celebration while I was hustled out, unseen, through the back door. Away from them all.

The drive back to prison blurred to strips of sand and olive and dusty brown through my red, raw eyes. I didn't even flinch when they strip-searched me, standing numb in a white-tiled room as a middle-aged female guard patted my body down, avoiding my gaze. I don't know what she expected to find—as if I'd managed to duck away from my constant supervision in the crowded courtroom to slip something in my bra. Pills, a razor blade. I can't imagine it, but I've only been locked up here four weeks. Some of the women in my wing have been stuck in here for years.

Years.

The thought of it is too much: like staring straight into the sun, blotting out everything with sheer panic. So I don't. Every time it creeps into my mind, I look away and remind myself of everything my dad and the lawyers said. That this is all a big mistake. That it's a witch hunt, a prosecutor gone crazy. That soon the charges would be dropped, and we could go home. I lie awake in the small, hot cell at night and repeat their words over and over again, wrapping myself in them like a security blanket on the hard, narrow bunk. But still, in the long dark of the night, surrounded by other people's breathing and my own crushing fear, I can't stop the first seeds of doubt from creeping in.

What if they're wrong?

"Just stay positive," Lamar tells me, as if my secret fear is written plain across my face. "This will all be over soon."

I take a breath. "Have you seen him?"

Lamar doesn't need to ask who. He nods. "We went over, after he made bail. They're in a house over on the other side of the island, this big gated place on the beach."

"How is he?" My voice twists, "Did he say anything? Did he ask about me?"

Lamar looks uncomfortable. "We weren't there for long. He didn't really want to talk. He was having panic attacks," he adds, "in prison, so they put him on a bunch of meds. He was pretty out of it."

I exhale slowly. "So he didn't say anything about me."

Lamar shakes his head. "I'm sorry."

He's not the one who should be sorry. Anger flares in me,

as fierce as my fear—and just as deadly. "It's fine." I swallow it back. "I'm sure he'd come if he could. The lawyers are probably keeping him away, and his parents . . ." I force another smile. "Like you said, I'll be out of here soon, and then we'll all go back to Boston, and everything will be okay."

Lamar shifts in his seat. "That's the thing I wanted to tell you." He pauses, his voice heavy and reluctant. "We're . . . going home."

I stare.

"The police said they don't need us anymore," he says, stumbling over the words. "And with school already started, and our parents—"

"No, I get it." I push down the ache blossoming in my chest. "Right, of course. You can't stay, sitting around on the beach all day." I fake another smile. "When do you leave?"

"Tomorrow."

"Oh."

"But I can call, and write, or whatever." He adds, "Until this all gets cleared up."

"Right. Sure."

There's silence as his words sink in, heavy and dark. *Home.* I never felt much for the word before—I didn't get home-sick the summer I spent camp, or feel the same sense of security and place other kids seemed to. For me, home was just a house we lived in, a place my parents picked, and decorated, and filled with the noise of endless renovations and upgrades to the things we didn't need but somehow were necessary now that we were rich. In-room surround sound. Under-floor heating. New skylights, glittering across the back of the house. When they were both there, it was bad enough for me—closed doors, and rooms I wasn't welcome in—but now, it was worse, a silent fortress I could never bring to life, not even with music playing through those brand-new speakers in every room. I spent all my time at Elise's, in the end; even Tate's disapproving parents were better than the emptiness of my own echoing hallways. But now, I ache for that house and all its dark memories with a fervor I didn't know I could possess.

Tomorrow, a plane is taking off, and I won't be on it.

"Do me a favor?" I ask, glancing at the clock on the wall. Time's nearly up. "Keep an eye on him for me. I mean, you guys can talk, and I . . . I just want to know how he's doing."

Something flickers across Lamar's face. He pauses for a moment, then leans closer. "Are you sure?"

I blink. "About what?"

"Tate." Lamar pauses again, and I can see him weighing the words before he speaks. "You were really with him, all day?"

"Yes," I insist. "We said, like, a million times—"

"I know that. But, I know you'd do anything to protect him." Lamar's eyes are watching me, careful.

I don't say anything, and that must be enough, because he exhales sadly. "Anna—"

"Don't." I stop him, glancing around. "We'll be fine. This is all going to be over soon."

"Are you sure?" Lamar drums his fingertips nervously. "Because I've been thinking, about the way he was with Elise. I always wondered . . ."

He stops. I feel a shiver of unease.

"What?"

"It's nothing." He looks away. "Just be careful, that's all. His family is loaded; you know they'll do whatever it takes to get him back home."

"And that's a good thing," I tell him as the buzzer sounds the end of visiting hours. "We have the best lawyers," I add quickly. "They're working round the clock. Everything's going to be okay."

A guard's voice interrupts us, bored. "Everybody out!"

Lamar rises from his seat. "Take care of yourself," he tells me softly, pressing his hand to the glass. I mirror it, matched but not touching, the closest thing to human contact I've had in days.

"I will. I'll be fine, I promise."

My voice wavers, but he's already gone.

THE FIRST NIGHT

"This is Niklas." Elise presents him like a game-show host displaying her prize. "His dad owns, like, half the island."

We're outside the bar in the cool two a.m. breeze, the music muffled and fading as we gather on the dusty street. Niklas is the guy from the VIP booth, the one Elise set her sights on: blond hair artfully mussed over ice-blue eyes, dressed in a preppy oxford shirt and jeans with an expensive watch on his wrist. He lights a cigarette for her with a silver block lighter, nodding a vague greeting to the rest of us.

"Where to next?" Chelsea asks, yawning.

"I'm tired." Mel holds on to her for balance, easing off one heel to massage her foot. "Let's just head home."

"Baby"—Elise's voice is only half-teasing—"the night is young." She smiles flirtatiously up at Niklas. "What do you say, where's a good place for an after-party?"

He shrugs. "Depends. I could show you. . . ."

"I'm sure you could." Elise laughs and leans in closer to him, exhaling her cigarette smoke away in a long plume. She murmurs something in Niklas's ear and he smirks, taking the cigarette from between her figures to suck down a drag of his own, his other hand drifting from her waist to rest on the curve of her ass.

It's fast work, but I'm not surprised. Elise has seduction down to an art. After we started frequenting the bars and clubs with all the college boys, she woke up to her power; we both did. High school is a weird puritanical world of rules and standards, where your reputation matters way more than a sweaty backroom kiss—where every slight and so-called indiscretion gets tallied and tracked. But outside those walls . . . We discovered the rules are different. Better. I could kiss a boy, breathless against the back wall of some club, and then just walk away, not even knowing his name. Or, like Elise, do more. Do whatever we wanted. No rules, no judging stares, or whispers come Monday morning. It's just about us, and the low pull in our gut, the shiver in our bloodstream.

Desire.

Elise meets my eyes with a lazy smile, Niklas tracing idle

circles on her half-naked back. I smile. Mel is scowling suspiciously at him, but I understand—every anonymous boy, every
late-night touch. I would do it too, if I didn't have Tate. And
why not? We want, we take, we have. It's simple.

The guys stumble out of the club behind us, Max already
blurry-eyed and flushed. AK has a lipstick mark on his cheek,
bright pink. I laugh, reaching over to wipe it off.

"What can I say?" AK grins. "I'm irresistible."

"Sure you are," I agree, linking my arm through his. "Or
maybe it was those free drinks you kept offering."

"A guy's got to work with what he's got."

We start wandering back down the street toward the beach
house. I meander slowly between the guys, but Elise and Niklas
hang back.

"I'll see you guys later," Elise calls, Niklas's arm draped
around her shoulder. We stop.

"You're leaving?" Mel's eyes widen. "But Elise—"

"Nik's going to give me a tour of the island." Elise grins
suggestively. "He knows a great Thai spot. See you later!"

I raise my hand to wave good-bye, but Tate speaks up. "I
could get some food." He looks around for agreement. "Guys?"

"Fuck yeah." Lamar nods. Max murmurs something,
slurring.

Elise gives me an exasperated look, but I just shrug. "I'm
kind of hungry too," I say, an apologetic note in my voice.

"Fine," Elise sighs. "Group trip. Yay."

We meander through the town center, still bright and full of activity. The bars spill tourists out onto the street, pop music and cheesy reggae drifting in snatches as we pass. The air is full of celebration, and even though we're all tired, we feel it too: Lamar pulling Chelsea in to dance to a familiar song, Mel and Elise singing along until we reach the takeout spot Niklas mentioned. It's just a run-down shack on the beachfront, but the scent of ginger and hot chilis drifts in the air, and the benches out front are packed with locals.

"So what do you do?" Mel quizzes Niklas as we order a feast of pad Thai and noodles.

"Do?" He gives her an arrogant smile.

"I mean, are you in school?" Mel presses. "Do you have a job?"

"Mel!" Elise protests.

"What? I'm just asking."

Niklas shrugs. "My father has several businesses." His accent is American, but edged with that lilting Dutch tone. "Real estate, import-export. I help out sometimes."

Elise laughs. "Admit it," she says, teasing, "you just sit around on the beach all day and party all night."

Niklas stares at her a moment, his eyes cool. Then his lips crease into a grin. "You got me," he agrees. "And what's so wrong with that?"

"Absolutely nothing, my friend." AK slaps him on the back, sloppy. "Fucking paradise, you've got here."

"And you?" Niklas asks, turning to include me and Elise in the question. "What do you do? Go to school? Do your homework?" His voice is laced with amusement. "Are you good girls?"

"What do you think?" Elise flirts back with a wicked grin.

"I think you like trouble." Niklas reaches out, tracing his index finger down the side of her face, her neck, along her collarbone. Elise doesn't flinch.

"Promises, promises," she coos. The look in her eyes is so intimate, I turn away.

We claim our food in Styrofoam cartons and plastic bags and begin walking back along the beach. I slip off my shoes and sink my toes into the cool sand, listening to the distant rhythm of the waves. My buzz has faded now to a sleepy satisfaction, and I snuggle against Tate, yawning. The ocean is an inky-black shadow to our left, with the lights of the hotels and beach houses string together in a line of glittering neon, snaking out around the bay.

"I don't like him."

Tate's voice startles me from my reverie. I pause for a moment, then look ahead to where Niklas and Elise are a dark shadow, indistinguishable in the dim light. "He seems fine to me. He's into her."

"He's an asshole," Tate replies, curt.

I laugh. "Maybe. But that's her type, right?"

Tate doesn't reply for a minute, but I can feel him, tense beneath his thin shirt. "She can't keep doing this," he says at last.

"What?"

"Picking up strange guys." Tate doesn't let it drop. "It's not safe."

"Come on." I sigh. "She does it all the time."

"Right." He doesn't sound placated. "And it's bad enough back home, when one of us is around, but this is just stupid. She was going to just go off with him? He could be dangerous."

"Sure, he's a real criminal." I laugh. "Come on, Tate. I told you, Elise can take care of herself. And she's not going off on her own," I add. "We're all going back to the house."

Tate kicks the sand. "I guess."

I snuggle closer to him, slipping my hand into his back pocket. My fingers brush against something cool and metallic. "What's this?" I pull it out. "My necklace!"

"Oh yeah, I found it in my bag," Tate replies. "Like you said."

I smile, leaning up to kiss him. "Thanks, baby."

There's the sound of laughter ahead of us. His eyes flick past me, still tense. Niklas.

I sigh. "It's cute you're looking out for her," I tell him. "But Elise does her own thing, you know that."

"I still don't like him." Tate's voice is petulant.

"I know. And if he turns out to be an ass, you guys can kick him out. She'll be right down the hall," I reassure him. "Nothing bad's going to happen there."

NOW

You see it now. It's obvious. You're probably wondering how I could have been so blind.

But I was.

It's not like it was all laid out for me, so clinical and neat. I loved them. I trusted them. It never crossed my mind, not even for a moment. Why would it? We were happy, all of us. We were family. Even now, I go back over every memory, tearing them apart any way I can, trying to see the truth beneath the fabric of all of their lies. Still, I come up with nothing.

There was no reason for it; that's what burns and blazes and aches, filling my days with sick confusion and my nights with restless questions. No fucking reason for them to break everything we had, to just shatter it as if it meant nothing.

As if *I* meant nothing to them.

Maybe it would be different; if I thought for one moment that she really loved him, maybe I could understand. If Tate and I were fighting, bored, unhappy. Something, anything, to explain why they could do this to me. To us.

But Tate? He won't say a word. And Elise took her reasons to the grave. So I don't get my answers. I guess I'll never know.

EVIDENCE:
TEXT MESSAGE RECORDS

ELISE WARREN, PHONE NUMBER 617-555-0173

FROM: ANNA

TIME: 9:17 a.m.

You want eggs?

FROM: ANNA

TIME: 9:22 a.m.

Hey sleepy. Wake tf up!

FROM: MEL

TIME: 9:25 a.m.

You coming? We leave in 10.

FROM: CHELSEA

TIME: 9:30 a.m.

you went hard last night. come dive.

FROM: ANNA

TIME: 9:45 a.m.

god you sleep through anything. we're staying too,
come meet us on the beach.

FROM: MEL

TIME: 9:50 a.m.

r u mad? txt back!

FROM: MEL

TIME: 9:55 a.m.

fine. c u when we get back.

FROM: ANNA

TIME: 11:22 a.m.

down by the café, look 4 the red towel.

FROM: TATE

TIME: 1:10 p.m.

trying to get away. c u at the house.

FROM: CHELSEA

TIME: 1:47 p.m.

FISHES!

FROM: NIKLAS

TIME: 4:12 p.m.

want 2 hook up 2nite?

FROM: ANNA
TIME: 6:32 p.m.
guess ur out. call if u wanna grab dinner

FROM: MEL
TIME: 7:51 p.m.
on r way back. did i do something? talk 2 me.

FROM: AK
TIME: 8:19 p.m.
hey slut, where r u?!

FROM: ANNA
TIME: 8:26 p.m.
This isn't funny. we're worried. where r u?

DAY 52

I know it's important when they come pull me out of breakfast. The routine is carved in stone here, every day the same. Unless you have a court date, visitors wait until the afternoon. No exceptions. So when I'm taken to the interview room and find Ellingham and my dad waiting, pacing in the small, empty space, I feel a shiver of fear.

"What is it?" I go quickly to my dad, forgetting for a moment that I'm not allowed to touch him. He backs away, looking to the guard.

I stop. "Sorry," I murmur, deflating.

"It's okay." Dad gives me a tired smile, but it doesn't reach his eyes.

"You should sit down," Ellingham tells me.

ABIGAIL HAAS

I obey, my fear growing. "What? What is it?"

"There's been a . . . development." Ellingham takes a seat across the small table. "I just got a call from Mr. Dempsey. They're dropping all charges against Tate."

It takes a moment for his words to sink in. My heart leaps. "I knew it!" I spring to my feet. "Did they find Juan? The officer said they were looking for him," I babble, not waiting for a reply. "I knew it would be okay."

I feel a sob in my throat as relief blossoms, sweet in my chest. It's sharp and strong, and I have to hug my arms around my body to keep from embracing him.

"No, that's not it." Ellingham clears his throat, and just like that, my elation wavers, caught on a precipice.

"But, you said . . ." My voice trembles with confusion. "They've dropped the charges. That means I can go home, right?"

I look between them for confirmation, but my dad just glances away.

"They've ended the investigation into Tate," Ellingham says, his voice reluctant. "He's flying home this afternoon. But your murder charge still stands. You'll go to trial as expected in a couple of months."

I sink back down onto the hard plastic chair, reeling.

"I don't understand," I whisper. "What happened?"

My dad finally speaks. "Tate cut a deal with the prosecutor. He admitted you lied about your alibis." The disappointed look in his eyes is enough to break my heart.

"I can explain!" I cry. "He asked me to; he said they'd suspect him if they knew he went back to the house. I never meant to lie."

"But why didn't you tell me the truth from the start?" My dad looks at me, searching. "We could have done something, found a way . . ."

"I don't know," I say helplessly. "He said it would be worse for us, that they'd think we did something wrong."

"They do." Ellingham's voice is matter-of-fact.

I pause, trying to process it. Tate told. After all this time, insisting we had to stick together, he turned around and . . .

"Why did they drop the charges against him?" I ask slowly. "If they knew he was at the house with her, wouldn't that make him a suspect?"

Ellingham clears his throat again. He looks uncomfortable, as if he wishes he could be anywhere but this small, bleak room under the fluorescent strip lighting. Then I remember: he works for Mr. Dempsey. He was never here for me.

"Our investigators uncovered security footage from the convenience store near the house," he explains stiffly. "It shows Elise out that afternoon, around 3 p.m."

I don't get it. I turn to my dad for help.

"The timeline doesn't fit," Dad tells me gently. "She was

still alive, after he went back to the house. His alibi still holds, for the new time of death."

I shake my head. "But why am I still here?" I ask them. "The only reason I was lying was to protect him. And if they're sure he's innocent . . ."

"His alibi holds, but yours doesn't," Ellingham tells me. "Tate says he took a nap when you were on the beach that afternoon. When he woke up, you were gone. That's at least forty minutes unaccounted for, maybe more. Plenty of time to go to the house and back."

"But I was right there." My voice comes out a whisper. I look to my dad again, pleading. "I was down by the water. I walked a little, along the shore. I was right there the whole time."

"Tate says he didn't see you." There's no argument in Ellingham's voice, just plain fact. "That's enough for Dekker to argue that you had the opportunity and means to kill Elise. And with their affair, he can claim you have motive, as well."

NOW

You see? How simple it is, how one little piece of information changes everything. How it all just falls into place.

Betrayal.

THEN

I slowly push my seat away from the table. The legs scrape on the tile floor.

"What are you talking about?" I say slowly.

"Elise and Tate." Ellingham is studying me carefully. "They were having an affair. Hooking up, I believe you would call it."

"No." I shake my head. "You're lying." I look around. "Dekker's watching, he's trying to catch me out. This is some kind of trick."

"I assure you, it's not."

"Tate told the police today," my dad says gently. "When he came clean about the alibis."

"No." My voice is a whisper.

"Apparently they'd been together several months," Ellingham continues, as if he doesn't realize how his words are slicing through me. Or maybe he does and he just doesn't care. "Since January, Tate said."

"No!" My scream cuts through the room. "You're lying! He would never . . ." I catch my breath, ragged. "*She* would never!"

There's a long silence, then Ellingham stands. "I should go," he says, reaching quickly for his briefcase. "Give you time to . . . think things through."

"But you'll call me later?" My dad rises, looking concerned. "We need to talk about her defense strategy, now that Tate is out of the picture."

"Of course." Ellingham's smile is blank and professional. "You have my number."

He sweeps out, the guard closing the door firmly behind him. Dad and I are left alone.

"I didn't know." My voice breaks. "I swear, I didn't know."

"I believe you, sweetie." Dad reaches across and takes my hand. The guard looks away, and that's when I know just how desperate my situation is. That a hand held across the table is the only hope I've got. "We'll be okay, I promise."

"But how?" The full weight of Ellingham's revelations begins to crush me, so hard I can barely breathe. I look around the tiny room, knowing that outside there's nothing but metal bars and security gates and guards, armed and ready to keep me here, locked forever. My panic takes flight, and I feel it all the way to my bones. "It's just me now," I whisper, disbelieving.

"No, sweetie." Dad clutches my hand tighter, but I shake my head. The tears I've been holding back for weeks finally slip through, a grief so deep I could drown.

"He left me." I choke on the words and my own bitter sobs. "They both left me here alone."

I lay my head on the table and weep.

THE TRIAL

"So you didn't know?"

Dekker's question rings out, taunting and full of scorn.

I take a breath, looking for Tate in the courtroom, but he's not here. "No."

"The victim was conducting an affair with your boyfriend for months, right under your nose, and you mean to tell the court you had no clue it was going on?" Dekker turns to the audience, his face a picture of disbelief.

I try to stay calm. There's no jury, my lawyer keeps reminding me, so all of Dekker's wide-eyed performing won't mean a thing in the end. The only person who matters—the one with my fate resting in her delicately manicured hands—is the judge, von Koppel, sitting six feet to my left at the central table at the head of the room.

I direct my answer to her alone, trying to keep my expression neutral and my voice even and resolute. "No. I had no idea—not until he confessed, after he cut a deal with you."

Dekker quickly interrupts me. "Please let the record show, there was no deal, as the defendant implies. Mr. Dempsey volunteered new information that led to his charges being dropped, that is all."

"Sorry," I reply. "My mistake."

It's not. My lawyer told me to bring it up, to bring up anything that might make Dekker look biased, or corrupt, or just plain incompetent. Dekker narrows his eyes at me in a fierce glare, but I try to stay calm. I have to score what points I can, they told me over and over again. It may seem petty, like some silly game, but the rest of my life is on the line. If I can throw him off, even a little, it might make all the difference.

"Also, please note I object to the word 'confessed'," Dekker continues, still glaring. "Mr. Dempsey merely cleared up earlier inconsistencies in his testimony to police."

"Noted." Judge von Koppel sounds bored. I wonder if that's a good thing or not.

"Now, Miss Chevalier," Dekker turns on me again, this time with renewed determination. "Would you say you're a jealous person?"

"No."

"You weren't possessive at all, of your relationships with the victim, or Mr. Dempsey?"

I say it again, calm and collected. "No." My hands are folded in my lap, my legs crossed at the ankles. They coached me for hours about how to sit, how to speak, even how to take a sip of water.

"Not even a little?" Dekker keeps digging. "After all, teenage relationships can be stressful things. A whirlwind of emotions and new feelings."

I keep my gaze fixed on him. "Not really. It was all pretty simple."

"Simple . . ." Dekker goes over to his table and flips through some paperwork. "But what about the incident of the fifteenth of October?"

"I'm sorry—" I pause. "I don't know what that is." I look over to my lawyer, but he just shrugs.

"Then let me refresh your memory." Dekker smiles. "October fifteenth, last year. You were involved in an altercation with a classmate, Lindsay Shaw."

Lindsay, the queen bitch herself. My stomach drops. This can't be good.

"Here's the incident report from the school," Dekker continues, "and Miss Shaw's sworn statement." He passes the pages up to the judge before turning back to me. "Miss Shaw says that you accosted her, during gym class, and accused her of flirting with Mr. Dempsey."

This is what he looks so pleased about? I shake my head. "That's not what happened. It was nothing."

"Nothing? She says you threatened her, physically, and warned her to stay away from him." Dekker continues, "Several witnesses confirm you attacked her, in a violent outburst, armed with a hockey stick."

"It wasn't like that," I protest. "We were playing field hockey; we were on opposing teams. I tackled her, and then she tripped."

"She tripped?" Dekker's voice rises. "Miss Shaw was taken to the emergency room. She required six stitches to a wound on her cheek."

I see the look on my lawyer's face. "It was an accident," I insist, my voice rising. "And I wasn't jealous. She had it out for me, right from the start of school. Ask anyone, she was the one bullying me."

"So she deserved it?"

"That's not what I'm saying." I try to keep a grip, but Dekker keeps badgering me.

"So what really happened? You've said yourself, she was bullying you."

"Yes, but—"

"She flirted with your boyfriend." He doesn't let me finish.

"She taunted you, publicly, until you just couldn't take it anymore. You attacked her—"

"Objection!" My lawyer leaps up. "Relevance? This is a schoolyard argument from almost a year ago—"

"I'm establishing the defendant's state of mind under pressure," Dekker calls back, "and her habit of violent outbursts."

Judge von Koppel pauses. "Overruled. Continue."

Dekker approaches me, but just as I'm bracing myself for more questions about the hockey incident, he gives me a sly smile. "Let's leave your attack on Miss Shaw for a moment, and talk about the victim. We've heard from several witnesses that you had an unusually close relationship."

I pause, regrouping. He's trying to throw me off balance, I can see that—making sure I'm worked up about the Lindsay thing, so I'm still angry and frustrated when I talk about Elise. But I won't fall for that trick. I take a breath, making sure I'm calm again before answering. "We were friends. That's not unusual."

"But you spent all your time together, to the exclusion of Miss Warren's other friends."

"That was her choice." I give a little shrug. "She just preferred hanging out with me."

"And that's what you did together—hang out?" Dekker's got that smug expression again, the one that sends a chill through me. "Tell us about it."

I look to my lawyer again. "I . . . don't understand."

"What did you do together?" Dekker asks. "How did you spend your time?"

"Usual things," I say carefully. "We would go shopping, to cafés, just hang out together, after school . . ."

"You went to bars together," Dekker adds. "Out drinking. And to college parties, with older men."

"Yes," I admit, "but it wasn't just us. We were a group, all year. Chelsea, and Max, and AK—"

"Yes, but you preferred to be alone with Miss Warren, didn't you?" Dekker meets my eyes with that sly look of his.

I stare back, trying to figure out his game. "No. I mean, we were close, but I liked being with everyone."

Dekker goes back to his table to rustle some more papers. "In their statements, both Melanie Chan and Chelsea Newport, and several of your other friends, said that you and the victim would often sleep over at each other's houses."

"Yes," I reply slowly.

"And where did you sleep?" he asks.

I blink. "Excuse me?"

"When you slept over, with Miss Warren?" Dekker manages to keep his expression serious, as if he's asking a deeply important legal matter and not just another of his sleazy suggestive questions. "You didn't stay in the guest suite, did you? You would always sleep in the same room. In the same bed, in fact."

I look across to my lawyer. "Objection!" He leaps up obedi-ently. "This is completely irrelevant."

"Yes, Detective Dekker." Judge von Koppel stares over the top of her gold wire-rimmed glasses, her lips pursed. "I have to agree. This seems highly irregular."

"My apologies." Dekker gives her a smarmy smile. "I'm sim-ply trying to establish motive. If Miss Chevalier was involved in a sexual relationship with the victim, it would surely add to her betrayal and anger on discovering—"

"Yes, yes." The judge waves him on. "I understand. I'll allow you to proceed, but please, be direct."

"Of course." Dekker turns back to me, grinning, as if he's won this round. "So, Miss Chevalier, let me ask: Was yours and Miss Warren's relationship sexual in nature?"

I stare back, stone-faced. "No."

"Not ever?" he presses. "But these photos we've seen . . ." He clicks them up on display again: the shots from Hallow-een, and pictures of me and Elise going back all year. We're draped over each other, hugging, affectionate and close. In one, we have bikinis on, and Elise is kissing my shoulder, her arms wrapped protectively around my bare stomach. In another, we're snuggled on her couch with a blanket, wearing tiny pajama shorts and tank tops, our limbs intertwined. Dekker turns back. "Are you telling us these are purely platonic photos?"

"Yes," I insist. "They don't mean anything. There are photos of all of us like that—me with Chelsea, or Lamar even. Elise and Mel—"

"I'm interested in you and the victim, Miss Chevalier," Dekker interrupts again, but this time, I don't stop.

"You're not letting me finish!" I exclaim. I can see my lawyer's face tense, but I can't let Dekker keep doing this—keep flashing up pictures like they mean something, without showing the rest of them, and what it was really like. "You're asking me all these questions, but you don't care what I say; you just want to show off those photos and pretend like they mean more than they do!"

"Please calm down, Miss Chevalier." Dekker looks smug, and I realize with a pang that this is what he wanted all along: for me to raise my voice, or cry out, or do anything that lets him say I've got a temper.

"Actually, I believe the defendant has a point."

We both turn. It's Judge von Koppel, gazing evenly at Dekker. "If you ask the defendant a question, please allow her to answer fully."

There's another pause. "Of course." Dekker forces a smile, but before I can feel a small sense of victory, he rounds back on me.

"So you were never sexually involved with the victim?"

"I said no."

"You never kissed each other on the lips, perhaps?"

"No."

"The two of you never experimented, with touching, or—"

"Objection!"

"Sustained." Judge von Koppel glares at Dekker. "You're out of line. I won't tolerate this kind of salacious speculation in my courtroom, do you understand?" Her voice rings out, heavy with disapproval, and I see Dekker flush. "That was a question, counselor," she continues. "Do you understand?"

"Yes." He spits the word, resentful. "Now, if I could continue—"

"No." The judge cuts him off, and I feel a wash of gratitude. "I think we've had enough of your questioning for the day. We'll take a short recess, and then I'll see you and Counselor Gates in my rooms to discuss the rules for appropriate lines of questioning. Since you so clearly need a reminder. Court adjourned."

She bangs her gavel, and a ripple of fervent conversation spreads though the courtroom: lawyers and consultants and reporters all murmuring excitedly, but they're a blur to me. I exhale slowly in relief, not moving from the witness seat.

"Are you all right, Miss Chevalier? Anna?"

I look up. It's the judge, leaning toward me, her brow furrowed with concern. "I said, are you feeling all right?"

"I . . . yes." I reply, shocked. It's the first time she's spoken to me like a human being for weeks. All during the trial, she's talked across me, to the lawyers, as if I don't even exist, and the few times she has looked in my direction, it's to press me to answer, or to tell me to be more precise. "I'm okay," I tell her, recovering. "Thank you."

She nods briskly. "We'll continue your testimony in the morning."

The guard approaches to lead me back to the holding room, but even as he snaps the handcuffs back around my wrists, I let myself feel the victory, the smallest triumph in weeks of wretched defeat.

I won this round. Dekker went too far.

Then I look across the courtroom, and my brief joy fades. Elise's mom is staring at me from her usual seat behind Dekker's table. The hatred in her eyes takes my breath away.

I stop, holding her gaze for as long as I can. Pleading. But the guard hustles me on, not stopping, and Elise's mom turns away.

WAITING

The days pass slowly in prison, a repeating parade of early morning wake-up calls, bland meals on plastic trays, and those few precious hours out in the exercise yard, pacing under the endless blue skies. I feel every moment of it at first, trapped and claustrophobic, like the cell walls are closing in on me, about to smother and crush me for good. I find it hard to sleep, or eat, and every time I hear footsteps approaching, I can't stop my heart from leaping, a fierce flutter of hope in my chest. They've come for me. I can go home. It's all over.

But it never is.

In the end, I can't take the heartbreak of disappointment anymore, I decide. Nobody's coming to save me. Although Dad tells me to stay positive, and keep hope alive, I know the truth he can't bring himself to tell me yet: there will be no late breakthrough miracle, no last-minute reprieve. I'm going to stand trial for Elise's murder, and now there's nothing I can do but wait.

In a way, it's easier once I let go of that daydream. I'm not suspended in hopeful limbo, waking up every day rich with the possibility of freedom—and the hollow weight of disappointment when the lights-out buzzer goes off, and the cell doors slam shut again each night. I have the trial to hold on to now: my light on the horizon. When we're in court, when we can shut down whatever evidence Dekker thinks he has—the blood smears, and the knife, and the necklace—then this will all be over. I'll be found innocent. I can go home.

Until then, I just have to stay strong, and wait.

So the days pass. One hundred. One hundred and sixteen. A hundred and forty seven. Mostly, I remember—lying on the narrow bunk in my cell, letting the time drift by as I sink beneath the cool surface of the past. I start at the beginning, the day I met Elise in gym class, and slowly work forward, through school and Tate and the arrival of Chelsea and the others. I play out every conversation, every kiss, like a scene from the movie of somebody else's life. Except I feel it. Hard, and sharp, and slicing with the deep ache of nostalgia, a longing for the time that's gone now and I'll never get back. All the brief moments I took for granted—the afternoons spent slouched, bored, doodling song lyrics in her notebook in the back of history class; the coffee breaks we spent hunched over mocha whip lattes at Luna, and idle free periods window-shopping on Newbury Street. Elise and I, arms linked, limbs intertwined. Dyed streaks in our hair, matching pendants at our necks. Laughter in our souls.

I look for reasons, and answers, for hints and warning signs. I take our final moments on the island apart and spread them flat, like a prospector hunting for the glint of gold in the murky dust of the riverbed. Sometimes, I think I see something: a glance, a worried note in her voice. A hug that lingers too long, the buzz of a text message she doesn't check. But the vision blurs; details mix. Memory and imagination are only a knife edge apart, and I wonder if I'm making it all up: slipping false memories in among the real ones, just to have something to hold on to. Fool's gold.

They argue over trial dates. The days pass, and I wait.

VACATION

I wake in Tate's arms, sunlight falling through the open drapes to where we lie, tangled in the crisp white sheets. It's our third day in Aruba; the window is open, and I can hear the distant crash of the ocean and feel the gentle breeze on my skin.

Bliss.

I yawn, rolling to snuggle against him, cheek against his bare chest. He's a restless sleeper, and the covers are kicked to the floor, his limbs sprawled as if he finally gave up an epic battle and fell into unconsciousness, exhausted. I smile, tracing the line of his jaw down to his collarbone and ribs.

Tate murmurs, still half-asleep, a faint smile on his lips.

I kiss him, my mouth replacing the slow sleep of my fingertips, along the ridge of sinew and bone, down to the taut muscles of his stomach. I feel him laugh against my mouth, awake now. He pulls me back up, kissing me hard as he rolls over and crushes me in his embrace.

I stay there a moment, kissing back slowly, savoring the weight of him. Then the kiss deepens, his hands reaching impatiently for the flesh of my thighs, easing them apart. I feel him harden against me.

"Hold that thought," I say, and tear myself away. He lets out a groan of frustration. "I need the bathroom. I'll be right back," I promise, kissing him again.

"No, it's good. I've got to go for a run." Tate hauls himself out of bed, naked save for a pair of blue boxers. He peels them off, exchanging them for some crazy print board shorts. "Me and Lamar need to stay in shape for the season."

I pause, admiring the view. You would think I'd get used to it, but I don't. His body, the grace he moves with . . .

Mine.

"Okay, I'll see you after." I head across the room, picking my way over discarded clothes and the junk spilling from our suitcases. "I think it's another beach day. AK said something about renting some Jet-Skis . . . ?"

"Awesome." Tate laces up his sneakers, then goes to open the balcony doors. "Laters." He jogs down the steps onto the beach below. I move to the balcony and watch him as he stretches, his arms held high; then he takes off, his feet pounding the sand as he finds his usual rhythm, heading down to where the water laps against the shore. Soon he's a tiny figure in the distance, a dark shadow on the white sand of the bay.

I shower and pull a bikini on, then wander out into the main house. It's early, and the living area is deserted; everyone is still crashed out from the night before. We spent the day on the beach, then wound up drinking at the house until late while Mel and Elise bickered over where to get dinner, until finally the boys revolted and dragged us all out for pizza at a tacky chain restaurant in one of the hotel complexes. They served two-for-one margaritas, lurid in huge glasses as big as serving bowls, and ice cream sundaes smothered in hot fudge sauce and cream. We were all queasy and groaning by the time we made it back, except Elise, of course. She was dancing, alone in the living room, long after the rest of us stumbled off to bed—lit by the eerie blue of the fish tank, swaying and dreamy.

I go to the fridge, and pull out a carton of juice.

"Morning, sweetheart."

I jump, slamming the refrigerator shut. Niklas is just a few feet away, lounging against one of the cabinets. "Jesus." I catch my breath, my heart pounding. "You scared me!"

"Sorry." He looks amused, his eyes trailing me from head to toe. "Guess you weren't expecting company."

I shift, uncomfortable. I'm in just my bikini top and some

cutoff shorts. Beach clothes, fine for hanging out with my friends, or even strolling outside, but here, alone in the kitchen with some strange older guy, I'm painfully aware of the thin fabric and bare flesh on show.

I catch Niklas's gaze again—ice blue and smug—and resist the urge to go pull a sweater on. Somehow I think it would give him too much satisfaction.

"It's early," I say briskly instead, turning back to the juice. "I didn't know you were here."

I reach for a glass from the rack above the sink, but Niklas steps in first, his body pressing against mine as he fetches one down for me. I flinch back.

"Voilà." He offers it with a bland smile, but I can tell he's enjoying my discomfort.

"Thanks," I reply shortly. I pour my drink and then circle around to the breakfast bar—putting a length of polished marble between us. "Where's Elise? I didn't think she was up."

"She's not." Niklas shrugs. I wait, but he doesn't continue. Instead he gulps juice straight from the carton, still watching me with that amused look.

I shiver, despite the balmy temperature. Tate was right. He is creepy.

"Morning, my darlings!" Elise bounds in, dressed in her red bikini and tiny white cutoff shorts. She encircles me in a hug, and cold water drips down onto my skin, her hair still wet from the shower. She kisses my shoulder. "Do you see the ocean? Fuck, I never want to leave."

"Sure, drop out and move here," I say, and laugh, relaxing at her presence. "Become a professional beach bum. Your parents would love that."

"Don't tempt me." Elise hops up to sit on the counter, swinging her legs against the cabinet doors. "I'll send them a postcard. 'Wish you weren't here.'"

She plucks a couple of grapes from the bunch in the fruit bowl and eats, still sitting with her back to Niklas.

I look over at him, realizing for the first time that Elise hasn't spoken to him. Hasn't so much as glanced in his direction.

Niklas must realize it too. His expression darkens for a moment, then the frown is wiped away, replaced with that same bland, smug smile. "I'm out of here. Text you later?"

Elise shrugs. "Sure, whatever."

Niklas salutes at me, and then saunters toward the front door. A moment later, I hear it slam.

I give Elise an expectant look. She grins. "Keep 'em mean. . . ."

"I know, but that was pretty icy."

She shrugs again. "He's kind of full of himself. Going on and on about all his dad's business deals, and how they own, like, half the island. Still, the boy has his uses. . . ." Her lips slip into a mischievous smile, and I can't help but laugh.

"What time did he come over?" I ask, going to rinse my glass. They have a maid come here every afternoon, but I still feel bad leaving anything for her to clean up. "I didn't hear him come in."

"I had him sneak in round back last night," Elise replies, sliding down to the ground. "He had to climb up to my balcony."

"Oh Romeo, Romeo," I quote, holding a hand to my forehead in a fake swoon. She laughs. "You're lucky he didn't fall and crack his head open," I add.

Elise makes a dismissive noise. "It's barely fifteen feet; anyone could climb that. Besides, you've got to make them work for it, otherwise they think you're easy."

"You, the great Elise Warren, easy?" I tease. "Never!"

"That's me." She dances around the kitchen, throwing wannabe gang signs, mock-tough. "Rock hard, baby."

"Like your abs?" I laugh, lightly hitting her stomach.

"Like diamonds, baby!"

There's a groan. AK comes stumbling in, wearing last night's crumpled T-shirt and a pained expression. "Noise. Pain. Dead."

"What's that?" Elise calls, extra loud.

"I don't know!" I yell back. "I couldn't hear!"

AK glares. "I hate you both," he says, falling face-first onto the couch.

"Aww, don't be like that," Elise coos.

"We're sorry," I agree. "Want me to make you some coffee?"

There's a groan.

"I think that's a yes." Elise laughs. She turns back to me, then her eyes widen. "You found my necklace!"

"What?" My hand goes to my throat. "This one's mine."

"No"—Elise reaches around my neck to unfasten it—"I have that chip in the metal, remember? Right here." She shows me the crack through the bronze before fastening it around her own throat. "I thought I lost it back in Boston. Cheap piece of crap." She grins affectionately. "It's going to give us a rash or something one day."

Before I can reply, Lamar interrupts us, strolling into the room with his shades on and a beach towel slung over his shoulder. "What are you guys still doing inside? We've got a schedule, people. Relaxing! Drinking! Lying in the sun!"

Elise laughs, spinning away from me. "Two minutes!" she promises. "I've got to grab my beach stuff, then I'm going to relax so freaking hard."

She dances away, back toward her room, and I'm left there, my fingers digging into the back of the couch, my breath coming slow.

"What's up with you?" Lamar's voice snaps me back. I turn.

"Nothing. Nothing at all."

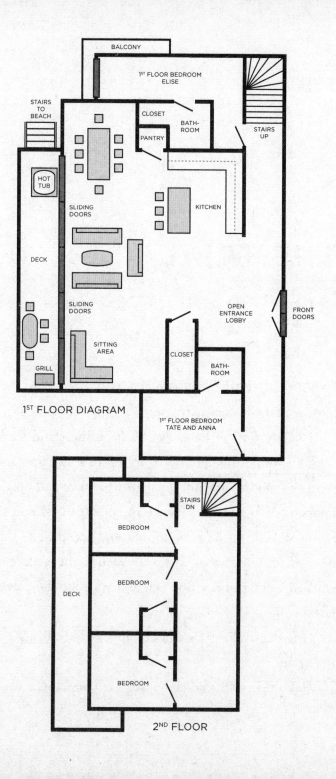

BALCONY

1ST FLOOR BEDROOM
ELISE

STAIRS
TO
BEACH

CLOSET

BATH-
ROOM

PANTRY

STAIRS
UP

HOT
TUB

SLIDING
DOORS

KITCHEN

DECK

SLIDING
DOORS

OPEN
ENTRANCE
LOBBY

FRONT
DOORS

SITTING
AREA

CLOSET

BATH-
ROOM

GRILL

1ST FLOOR DIAGRAM

1ST FLOOR BEDROOM
TATE AND ANNA

STAIRS
DN

BEDROOM

DECK

BEDROOM

BEDROOM

2ND FLOOR

THE TRIAL

"Miss Chevalier, can you tell us what we're looking at up on-screen, please?"

I barely turn to look. I've been on the stand for hours now, answering his questions, trying to stay calm, and not snap or sound sullen, but it's hard when I've had only a few hours of sleep all week. They took me off the sleeping pills, saying it made me look too robotic and detached on the witness stand, but now all I can do each night is stare at the cracked ceiling of my tiny cell and wait for the peace that never comes.

"Miss Chevalier?" Dekker prompts, and I realize I've zoned out again.

"It's a map of the beach house," I tell him, tired.

"That's right," Dekker agrees. "And can you tell us which room you were sleeping in?"

"The one you've marked in black."

"The one by the front door," Dekker continues. He's got an iPad and a pointer, to move around on the screen. "And the victim, Elise, her bedroom was back here, to the rear of the house."

Her room, of course, is marked in red.

"We can see from the diagram, it's barely twenty feet from your bedroom door to the main entrance to the house. So it's a fair assumption," Dekker continues, "that if anyone were to enter or exit in order to get to Elise's room, you would hear them from your bedroom—which, as you've stated on several occasions, you were occupying the afternoon she died, between six and seven p.m."

"No."

Dekker stops. "You weren't in the house at that time?"

"No, I mean, we were. Me and Tate," I clarify, trying not to trip over my words. "But the front door wasn't the only way in."

"But if a stranger broke in to attack Miss Warren, as you claim, then you would have heard him in the process."

"Objection!" My lawyer sighs. "The time of death has not been determined. The attack could have been carried out before the defendant returned to the house, or when she was out at dinner."

"Sustained."

Dekker hides a scowl. "I'll rephrase," he says. "If a stranger broke in while you were in the house, he would have entered by your room, isn't that true?"

"No," I say again, "There were other ways into the house." I turn to the judge. "Can I show, on the screen . . . ?"

"Surely this is something for the defense cross-examination—" Dekker tries to talk over me, but the judge interrupts him.

"You brought up the floor plan, so I'll allow it."

There's a moment's pause, then Dekker reluctantly hands over the iPad and pointer.

"The front door wasn't the main way in," I explain, marking the other exits on the map. "We mostly went in and out via the deck, here, at the back of the house. The whole back wall opened up, like sliding doors, and they were unlocked most of the time. We were coming and going; it was too much hassle for everyone to deal with a key. Elise had a balcony of her own, with doors out over the beach—"

"Her balcony was several stories off the sand," Dekker interrupts me quickly.

"One floor, not very high," I insist. "About fifteen, twenty feet, with easy footholds in the wood beams. Niklas climbed up, just the night before, and Max got in there when we couldn't open Elise's bedroom. Anyone could have climbed up from the beach, and it's set back, so not many people would see."

"Anything else?" Dekker's tone is dangerously polite. "Any secret passages, or hidden exits?"

"Objection!"

"Sustained." Judge von Koppel sighs. "The prosecution should refrain from sarcasm. Anything else to add to the floor plan, Miss Chevalier?"

"Just, our bedroom was across the house from Elise's. We had music on, and . . ." I swallow. "If someone had been in there, we wouldn't have heard. We didn't hear anything." My voice breaks, and my lawyer leaps up.

"We ask to adjourn for the day, Your Honor!" he says quickly. "The defendant is clearly emotional, no doubt suffering due to the prosecution's incessant badgering—"

"Oh, come on!" Dekker interrupts. "This is a blatant attempt for sympathy. She's fine."

They all turn to look at me, the judge peering down with her usual inscrutable gaze.

I stare back at her, pleading. All day, it's been nothing but the knife prints and the blood smears and the precise re-creation of our footprints in that hallway; until now I can hardly remember what I've said, and what Dekker has been drumming away at us.

"I'd prefer to avoid any further delay," she announces, and my heart falls. "Mr. Dekker, you may continue your questioning, but keep it brief."

He turns on me with a grin. "So, back to the floor plan. You claim you never heard anyone enter the house."

"Not through the front door," I correct him. "But like I said, you could climb up the balcony directly to Elise's room. Niklas did it, maybe more than once."

Dekker scowls. "As we've already established, Niklas van Oaten was at home with his father on the afternoon of the murder."

"But if he climbed up, somebody else could have done the same." I can't keep the note of desperation from my voice.

"Somebody?" Dekker repeats, mocking. "Does that seem likely to you, Miss Chevalier? That a random stranger would decide to climb up the side of the house, in full view of the beach, not knowing if anyone is home? And then, when they find Miss Warren there, instead of fleeing, or simply knocking her down, they take the knife from the kitchen, and stab her thirteen times?"

I look down.

"That was a question, Miss Chevalier," Dekker's voice booms out. "Is that a likely scenario? Does it sound at all plausible to you?"

"It's possible," I say through gritted teeth. "Elise could have had the knife in her room. The window was smashed. It was a break-in."

"You claim it was a break-in." Dekker corrects. "Evidence

for which is murky at best. And as for your intruder theory, isn't it far more likely that Miss Warren's attacker knew her?"

"No," I insist.

"Knew, in fact, that she would be alone in the house that afternoon." Dekker ignores my reply. "And that this attacker could come and go in broad daylight, without raising suspicion. That her attacker had keys to the house and knew the alarm codes."

"No!" My voice is shrill. He's making it sound simple, too simple, and I can tell from the expressions in the courtroom that they agree.

"Isn't it more likely that her attacker harbored a jealous rage . . . ?" Dekker is relentless. "And was angry at the victim? Angry enough to stab her thirteen times and leave her there, bleeding to death on the bedroom floor—"

"Objection!" My lawyer finally cries out. "The prosecutor is testifying!"

"Sustained."

"That's fine." Dekker grins at me again, cruel and triumphant. "I have no further questions for the witness at present."

"Would you care to cross?" von Koppel asks my lawyer, but he must be able to tell, I'm beyond helping right now.

"No, Your Honor," he sighs. "Nothing further."

As I step down from the witness seat, I see my dad seated in the front row. He meets my eyes and quickly sends me a wave and a smile, but I catch the look on his face just before he manages to mask it: worried and bleak. The hopeless exhaustion in his gaze is how I feel after my day on the stand, but somehow, seeing it reflected back at me drives the chilling truth home. My legs waver, and a wash of dizziness passes over me as I realize the truth.

We're losing this.

PRETRIAL

"The key is to get on the offensive. Find other suspects, start taking apart the prosecution's case before we even get to trial."

His name is Oliver Gates, and he's an old college buddy of my dad's, recruited to rescue my crumbling legal defense. A short teddy bear of a man in square black-rimmed glasses and a crumpled shirt, he paces in the small interview room, oblivious to the specks of coffee stains on his novelty golf-print tie. I watch, my heart sinking. He's soft-looking and warm, a million miles from Dekker's cut-throat aggression or even Ellingham's snooty professional detachment.

And right now, he's all I've got.

"There's Tate, that's something," Gates continues, checking

his notes. The table is piled with them, loose-leaf and stuffed into cheap cardboard binders.

I frown. "I thought they dropped the investigation into him."

"They did." Gates nods. "But even with his plea, we can cast some doubt, stir it up. And this Juan guy, lurking around. This is good stuff."

My expression must be less than confident, because he pauses, exhaling. "I know I'm behind," he adds, apologetic. "And I'm not from some big fancy firm, like the other guy. But I'm getting up to speed on everything. I'll do my best, I promise."

"It's not you." I feel bad for letting my doubt show. "I'm just tired, of all of this. I thought . . . They told me everything would be okay, that they had a plan, and then . . ." I trail off, feeling tears sting in the back of my throat as I bite back the words I can't bring myself to say.

Then they all left.

Ellingham quit. He's still representing Tate and the Dempseys, of course. He didn't even do it himself: he had his assistant call my dad to explain that it would be a conflict of interest, keeping me as a client. I guess we should have seen it coming, but it still hurt, yet another person walking away. Lamar and the gang are gone, Tate's gone too, and now my dad—back in Boston to try to raise the money for this new legal team, and to pay for all these flights and hotel fees that mount up every time he comes to see me.

"It's okay." Gates sits beside me, puts a hand, gentle on my shoulder. It's the first kind human contact I've had in weeks now, and I have to shrug it off—not because I don't want it, but because I need it too much.

"Did Dad say when he's coming back?" I ask, swallowing back my emotion. For weeks now, I've had nothing but distant phone calls, with Dad's voice so harried and guilty down the line. It only makes me feel worse, to think what this is putting him through.

"He's trying." Gates looks sympathetic. "But there's a lot to do. He's found a firm that has a branch in Amsterdam," he adds in a hopeful voice. "We're talking all the time about how best to proceed, how this is all going to play out. It's a whole different legal system here."

I nod.

"I'm asking around at the police department." The other guy in the room speaks up for the first time. He's younger, in his twenties, I guess, and dressed more casual in jeans and a shirt; dark hair cut conservatively over brown eyes. He's been taking notes this whole time, and I figure him for Gate's assistant, or some junior with his law firm. "Word is, Dekker isn't the most popular guy," he continues. I have to let out a bitter laugh at that. "So maybe we'll find a source to give us the inside track on his investigation, find out why he got so fixated on you—and what he might have overlooked in the meantime."

"Good." Gates nods, making notes. "Any word from the embassy? Some official support could really help us out right now."

The guy shakes his head. "I'm getting shut down at every level. Senator Warren must have gotten involved, or maybe the Dempseys. I shouldn't even be here; this is all unofficial."

I look up, confused. "But aren't you with him?" I nod to Gates.

They exchange a look. "No, this is Lee Evans, a junior consul from the embassy." Gates explains. "I introduced him when we met last week, remember?"

I don't.

"I'm sorry." I shake my head. "I guess things are kind of a blur. . . ."

"No need to apologize." The Lee guy smiles at me.

Gates's phone buzzes. "This is my investigator now; I'll just be outside."

He steps out, leaving me alone with Lee. Now that I'm paying attention, I can see he's cute, preppy, and full of concern. "I can't imagine what you're going through in here," he says softly.

I shrug, still wary.

"Are you sleeping okay?" he checks. "Can I bring you anything? Because we can get you some medication if you're still having problems—"

"No, no more pills." I stop him. "They make me too fuzzy," I fidget with my handcuffs. Even here, in the interview room inside the prison walls, with a guard outside the door, they won't take any chances. I look down at my chafed wrists and the nails I've bitten bloody. "I don't . . . I don't want to sleep anymore."

He nods. There's silence, but it's not like with Ellingham, or any of the police—accusing and cold. This is warmer, understanding.

"You'll get through this," he says. "You're strong."

"How would you know?" I snap before I catch myself. "I'm sorry, I know you're here to help, it's just . . ."

"I'm just another stranger, I get it." Lee looks rueful. "You must be sick of us by now."

"No," I reply after a moment. "It's better you're here than . . . not."

Gates comes back into the room. "Visiting hours are almost over. We should get going."

"Okay." I stand awkwardly, watching them pack all the paperwork away. "Will you be back tomorrow?"

"We have a lot of files to go through. . . ." Gates looks torn, so I keep my voice bright.

"It's okay. It's actually a good thing. Dekker can't question me without you or a lawyer around. I bet he's going crazy out there, having to leave me alone."

"You shouldn't joke," Lee warns me quietly. "From what I've heard, he's a dangerous man."

"You think I don't know that?" I turn to stare at him. "I'm trying, okay?"

"We know," Gates soothes me. "You're doing great. Here." He reaches into his canvas bag. "Your dad sent this to give to you."

I take the envelope. Inside, there's a photo of the two of us from Christmas a couple of years ago. We're in front of the tree wearing the dorky matching holiday sweaters my mom bought for us, smiling into the camera.

I love you. Everything will be okay—trust me.

I say my good-byes to Gates and Lee, watching through the bars as they head down the hallway and out of sight, to freedom.

Everything will be okay. Trust me.

I don't know how many times he's said that to me, not just here in prison but my whole life. When I was scared for the first day of school, or stressed about a big test, when I fell off my bike in sixth grade and split my lip. When my mom got sick. I always believed him. He's my father, he wouldn't lie to me; he's a grown-up, he knows the truth. But now I see his promises for what they really are: hopeful prayers, a mantra he says as much to reassure himself as me.

He can't fix this, not even close.

I drift back through the prison to the rec room. Without Dekker haunting my every day with his relentless questions, there's nothing to fill the time except my own black thoughts. The other women still look at me suspiciously and turn away before they talk, but even if one of them did take pity and try to make conversation, I don't know what I would say. They spend their days watching TV or repeating foreign-language tapes, reading from old school textbooks, mouthing along with the words.

"We return now to our main story of the night, the brutal murder of Elise Warren."

I freeze.

They tell me not to watch any of the coverage, but I can't help taking two steps toward the small TV set up in the corner of the room.

"An innocent spring break, ripped apart by an unspeakable crime. A jealous friend, with a history of violence and wild partying." The anchor is blond and middle-aged, but hiding it under a layer of tanned makeup and a helmet of spray-stiff hair. It's Clara Rose, the biggest name in salacious true crime TV. I used to channel-hop past her show—endless exposés of dead fiancées, kidnapped children, and murderous cheating husbands. Now it's my own photo up on-screen, the mug shot from the police station, the night Dekker formally arrested me.

"As Elise Warren's family and friends still mourn her brutal stabbing, we go behind the scenes to reveal the truth about her accused murderer, Anna Chevalier. What could have driven this straight-A schoolgirl to the edge?" Clara leans in to the camera across her news desk, wide-eyed with fake dismay. "Stay tuned after the break, when we bring you psychologist reports and exclusive interviews with the friends who knew her best."

I feel the eyes of the other women watching me. I know I should walk away, but I can't. My feet stayed glued to their spot, my eyes fixed on the small screen.

I stay.

CLARA ROSE SHOW
TRANSCRIPT

CLARA: **Welcome back. Thanks for tuning in, I'm Clara Rose. Tonight, we go inside the crime that has rocked the island paradise of Aruba, the brutal murder of seventeen-year-old Elise Warren, daughter of former Massachusetts state senator Charles Warren, who recently stepped down from his post— and likely gubernatorial run—to spend time with his family during this horrible tragedy.**

<VIDEO CLIP>

WARREN SPOKESPERSON: **The Warren family appreciates all the support, and they ask for privacy as they deal with this matter.**

<END VIDEO CLIP>

CLARA: **Tonight, we reveal the police investigation into Elise's accused murderer, her former friend Anna Chevalier. Just who is the girl charged with such an unspeakable crime? We'll talk to psychologists and** friends, and discover what could have driven her to the brink. But first we go live to our correspondent in Aruba for on-the-ground updates on the investigation.

MARLEE: Yes, Clara. Hi.

CLARA: What can you tell us about the situation there, Marlee? We're hearing here about new developments, and possible new evidence in the case.

MARLEE: That's right, Clara. Today, inside leaks from the police department have confirmed what we've been hearing in other reports: that there were blood stains in the hallway of the apartment that apparently went unnoticed by Anna and her boyfriend, Tate, for hours on the day of the murder.

CLARA: We're seeing the crime-scene photos now. . . . Yes, on-screen, you can see the bedroom where Elise breathed her final breaths. I have to apologize for the disturbing images, folks, that's an awful lot of blood, but we can see here just how violent the attack was.

MARLEE: Violent, and frenzied—"frenzied" is what I'm hearing from police sources. Elise clearly struggled, fighting her attacker, but was stabbed a total of thirteen times, the autopsy report confirms.

CLARA: Thirteen times! And this blood, yes, we can see on-screen now, photos from the hallway of the beach house where Elise and her friends were staying. There are bloodstains on the tile, visible in several places in the hallway, leading away from the victim's bedroom toward the front door.

MARLEE: That's right, Clara. And it's these bloodstains that police here closed in on as prime evidence in the murder charges against Anna Chevalier. In her interrogations, Anna has supposedly denied seeing the blood, or even that it was there at all.

CLARA: Well, I don't know how anyone can miss those marks; as you can see, the smears are on the tile and up the wall by the door. So it will be the defense's argument that the blood was tracked out later?

MARLEE: Yes, I'm guessing that will be a major defense. These crime-scene photos weren't taken until several hours after the body was discovered, and by that time, of course, you would have had paramedics and police, a whole group of people going in and out of the room. . . .

CLARA: But the detectives there . . . I know that investigation is being led by a Klaus Dekker—

MARLEE: Dekker, that's right. He'll be arguing—and this is something I've heard from several sources within the police department—their case is that the blood was there in the hallway all along, that saying she didn't see it is suspicious, a sign of guilt. And with the fingerprints—

CLARA: The fingerprints on the bloody knife, used to stab Elise. A five-inch blade, from the kitchen—we don't have photos of the murder weapon, but I'm showing you a similar model up on-screen now.

MARLEE: Exactly. We heard just a few weeks ago about this bombshell evidence, with the knife and the fingerprints, and I don't see how you can get around this in court. These are serious questions the defense will have to deal with if Anna is going to have any hope of pleading innocent.

CLARA: And Anna is in custody right now, in the prison, awaiting trial.

MARLEE: That's right. You can see behind me, here, the Aruba Correctional Institute where Anna has been held for the last five months now. It's a small prison; they house the male and female inmates in separate wings.

CLARA: And what other kinds of criminals will she be living with? Aruba isn't known for its crime.

MARLEE: No, most prisoners will be here on smaller charges: drug trafficking, petty theft, that kind of thing. Murder is rare here, and sentiment on the island is that this is very much an outside crime, perpetrated by an outsider.

CLARA: Thanks, Marlee, and we'll be checking back in with Marlee tomorrow for all the latest breaking news in the investigation. Now, after the break, shocking new photos of Anna in prison, and we chat with her friend, Akshay Kundra, who discovered Elise's body that night. We'll be right back.

<COMMERCIAL BREAK>

CLARA: Welcome back. I'm Clara Rose, with a special Elise Warren murder edition of the *Clara Rose Show*. We've seen the shocking crime-scene photos and evidence against Anna, Elise's former friend, now the authorities on Aruba have released photos of the murder suspect in prison. I'm joined by Dr. Martin Holt, a specialist in psychopathic killers, and the author of the true crime book *Beautiful Evil: The Kayla Criss Story*. Now, Martin, let's take a look at these photos just released. I guess there's been speculation about Anna's treatment in prison, and this is the Aruban authorities' attempt to counter those concerns. . . . Well, she looks just fine to me.

MARTIN: Indeed. These are candid photos of Anna about her daily routine in the prison. She looks relaxed, some might even say carefree. She takes a walk in the exercise yard, sits for lunch. In some of these shots, you can even see her smiling, which—

CLARA: I don't know about you, but that seems kind of off to me.

MARTIN: Exactly. In any normal person, you'd see signs of stress, fear, exhaustion. Let's remember, she's lost her best friend to a brutal murder; now she's locked up awaiting trial. If that were you or me, we'd be a wreck, but Anna looks like this is just an ordinary day at the mall.

CLARA: And that's a warning sign to you?

MARTIN: Absolutely. What you have to understand is that psychopaths, and sociopaths, their brains are wired differently. They lack empathy, they lack understanding, they don't care about causing pain and suffering. They are essentially incapable of reacting to situations the way a normal person would.

CLARA: And Anna, here, this isn't a normal reaction to being locked up in prison.

MARTIN: Not at all. And if we look back, to the photo of Anna on the balcony just hours after Elise's body was discovered, again, she looks happy, totally unconcerned.

CLARA: Yes, that photo. I don't know about you, but that gives me the creeps. I think, when we saw that photo, we all thought, "Hang on, something isn't right here." It was the first sign.

MARTIN: Right, and these warning signs, they're always there, but the tragedy is that we don't notice until it's too late.

CLARA: Thanks, Martin; that's Martin Holt there, author of *Beautiful Evil: The Kayla Criss Story,* in stores now. And joining me in the studio after the break, someone who can talk to us about these early warning signs, who was there on the island for the murder, classmate and friend Akshay Kundra. Don't go anywhere.

<COMMERCIAL BREAK>

CLARA: I'm Clara Rose, welcome back. Tonight: the Elise Warren murder, the truth about prime suspect, accused murderer Anna Chevalier. Before the break, we talked to acclaimed psychologist and true crime author Martin Holt about Anna's psychopathic tendencies; now I'm joined here in the studio by a friend and classmate of the suspect, Akshay Kundra. Welcome back, Akshay.

AKSHAY: I'm happy to be here, Clara.

CLARA: We just heard disturbing reports from Dr. Holt about these new photos and Anna's state of mind. Were the warning signs there for you?

AKSHAY: Sure. I mean, looking back, it's a tragedy we didn't see this coming.

CLARA: But why not? If the warning signs were there, then why didn't anyone say anything? Why was this unstable, possibly violent girl allowed to just walk around—I mean, even you yourself considered her a friend.

AKSHAY: We all did. And this is one of those things . . . in hindsight, it's clear, but in the moment . . . You've got to understand, Anna is a really smart girl—she would have known how to keep all of this under wraps. On the surface, she seemed like just an ordinary girl. We trusted her—you know, she was our friend.

CLARA: She was Elise's friend.

AKSHAY: Right. And that's something we're all going

to have to live with, that we never saw—I mean, she was obsessed with Elise, that was clear.

CLARA: **Tell us about this obsession.**

AKSHAY: **They were always together; you couldn't get them apart. She was new to our school, junior year, and she just kind of latched on to Elise. She took her away from all of her other friends, and I think Elise found it suffocating, you know, and eventually she started pulling away, trying to get some distance. That's when we started hanging out, that summer— it was like she needed other people around, to keep Anna at arm's length.**

CLARA: **Because Elise was a good girl, is what I'm hearing. Straight As, drama club, student government, and then Anna comes along . . .**

AKSHAY: **Yeah, she pretty much cut Elise off from all of that. She was a bad influence, we all knew that. They were drinking; I know that Anna took pills sometimes—**

CLARA: **You saw this? Drug use?**

AKSHAY: Yes, a couple of times, but I know it happened more. And Elise went along with it; I guess she felt the pressure, or maybe she was worried about what Anna would do.

CLARA: Did she ever seem scared to you? Scared of what Anna would do if she ended the friendship?

AKSHAY: I . . . I mean, no, not as such, but I don't know what was going on inside. Maybe she didn't feel like she could tell us, or maybe she never thought Anna would do something like this.

CLARA: To all appearances, Anna seemed normal.

AKSHAY: Right.

CLARA: And in the days leading up to the murder, how did the girls seem to you? We've heard a lot about this supposed affair. Tate Dempsey—son of prominent Boston investment banker Richard Dempsey—we've heard he was hooking up with Elise behind the accused's back. Is this what drove Anna to the edge, you think?

AKSHAY: Yeah. I mean, to find out something like that . . .

CLARA: But according to the police investigation, they wonder if Anna knew all along—if, instead of this being a crime of passion—which, in case you don't know, can be used as a defense, you know, temporary insanity—well, they're saying, maybe this wasn't a shock. Maybe Anna knew, for who knows how long, and maybe she planned it. Maybe she came to Aruba with the full intent of getting Elise alone, away from the rest of you, and killing her.

AKSHAY: I . . . I mean, that's awful, to think, if it's true. There was no sign of it; she seemed normal, just having fun, hanging out, you know?

CLARA: So you don't think she knew?

AKSHAY: If she did, then she hid it really well, acting like nothing was wrong.

CLARA: Which could, in fact, be another one of those warning signs. Dr. Holt?

MARTIN: Hi, Clara, yes, from what you're saying, this could be more evidence about her damaged mental state. To plan a murder in this kind of premeditated fashion takes us away from a jealous frenzy and into the territory of a cold-blooded killer. It's a big difference, especially if, down the line, we come to a murder versus a manslaughter charge, or some kind of plea bargain in the trial.

CLARA: "Cold-blooded killer," there you have it people. These are questions I'm sure the police on the island will be following very closely. Was it rage? Was it planned? I don't know about you, but the more I'm seeing of this girl, the more . . . I guess damaged, is the only word for it. Damaged, and dangerous. All right, that's all for tonight. Stay tuned for the news on the hour with Dave and Erin, and coming up tomorrow, more on the Elise Warren murder: the local trader who could have seen everything—a witness disappears. Could he hold the key to the truth? Join us tomorrow here on KLCX, your destination for news and sport.

BACK

The show cuts to commercial again. This time, every woman in the room is staring at me.

I try to remind myself how to breathe.

I knew it was bad out there. Even locked up, I've seen glimpses of newspapers and TV news. It wasn't as if I thought everyone would be lined up, protesting my innocence, but still, Clara's show takes my breath away. I thought it would be more . . . balanced. Isn't that what the news is supposed to do? Present both sides of the story, fairly, not jump to conclusions based on leaked information, and biased statements? We're still months away from the trial; even Ellingham swore they didn't have enough evidence to convict, so where's the support? Some kind of outcry about my arrest? Instead, they showed nothing on my side—no mention of Juan, or Tate's lies and cheating; the balcony issue, or all the problems with the crime scene—nothing, not one hint I might be innocent in all of this.

They assume I'm guilty, and they can't wait to see me burn.

"Killer."

The voice comes from behind me, loud and clear. I turn. One of the other inmates is lounging back on a chair, her legs draped wide. I've seen her before, in the mess hall, or the yard. She's short and bulky, in her early twenties, maybe, with dark tattoos dancing across her collarbone, hair braided in tight cornrows that swing to her shoulders. The girl gives me a sly smile, eyes dark as her stare meets mine, unflinching and direct.

She says it again, with a curl of amusement to her lips. "Killer."

I drop my eyes and start to walk away, heading back toward the far doors, but the girl uncoils herself from her seat and moves to casually block my path. "Where you going, killer?" she asks, folding her arms.

My pulse kicks. I try to sidestep, still looking down. She mirrors, blocking me.

I feel a shiver of fear.

"I don't want any trouble," I tell her softly, holding my palms out, like surrender. I glance quickly around the room, but the guard who usually loiters by the doors is nowhere to be seen. The other inmates start to circle, their body language snapping alert.

My fear shifts to panic.

I've seen this before, the lunchroom fights and exercise yard beatdowns. The women here like to brawl, violent and vicious, and I've watched from a distance how quickly the trouble in here flares, like everyone's a powder keg, waiting for a spark to go up in flames. I've spent every day so careful not to catch someone's eye or accidentally jostle them in the hall. Head down, eyes down, just keep moving, stay out of trouble. But now trouble is here, determination clear on her face in front of me.

"It's okay," I say, backing up. I just have to hold her off until the guard gets back. "Please . . ."

"Please?" the girl repeats, smirking. She turns to the circle. "Killer's got manners. Please and thank you, yes ma'am." She turns back to me. "So, did you ask your girl permission before you slit her throat?"

I look away, knowing it's useless even as I mutter the words "I didn't kill her."

"No? So what are you doing in here?" The girl's sneer slips, becomes something cruel and full of anger. "I seen you, walking round like you're so much better than us. You think we don't know? Huh?" She gets closer. "We're all the same in here, killer."

"I didn't do it." I hear my own voice, stronger, even before I register the words are coming from my mouth.

It's a mistake. There's a pause, so electric I can hear my blood pounding, and then the girl lunges at me. I barely have time to get my hands up in defense before her body is on mine and she's tearing at my hair, clawing at my face.

We tumble to the floor as yells go up from the crowd. I manage to deflect her blows, rolling out from underneath her, gasping for breath, but then she's coming at me again, her face twisted, violence in her eyes like I've never seen before.

For all of Elise's and my adventures in the dark city streets, I haven't come close to violence, a physical threat of any kind. They gave us self-defense classes in gym freshman year: staid, awkward routines where we'd carefully lunge at each other and sidestep in a polite ballet, but this is a world away from the neat choreography: a vicious assault, too quick to think, too fast to do anything but grapple and claw, rolling on the hard tile floor as the other inmates holler and howl, flinching as her blows hit home, blood sharp like metal in my mouth.

The girl drives her elbow into my stomach, making me gulp for air. Her face is lit up, breathless and bright, nose bloody from one of my desperate blocks. She grins through the smear of scarlet, raising her fist again, ready to smash it down into my face, and from some distant place, I realize: she's enjoying this. She likes it. The fight, the pain, the struggle.

Her joy is her power.

I snap.

Ducking to the side, I turn to block her fist, then bring my elbow sweeping up in a glorious arc that cracks against her face. Her head snaps back, her momentum lost, and I pull myself up, rolling so she's trapped underneath me, still dazed. I slam my elbow down against her face, her throat, her chest, again and again. There's screaming, sharp and grotesque, but the roars of the crowd recede like the waves until I can't hear anything but my own drumming heartbeat and the dull thud of bone on tile as her head cracks back, blood spilling on the pale floor like blossoms in the snow. It's almost beautiful, but I don't care. I'm not here anymore, I'm not anywhere—all I am is sheer, pure rage and fists and skin.

I'm still swinging when they pull me off her, strong arms grabbing at me, slamming me to the floor. The screaming won't stop; it echoes through the room long after they carry the other girl out. It's not until they come at me with the syringe that I realize: the screaming voice is my own.

Then there's nothing but black.

WINTER

"Where have you been?"

The voice startles me in the dark. I flip on the living room lights and find Elise waiting on the couch.

"Elise?" I stare at her, startled. She's still in her uniform, neat plaid skirt and blazer. "What are you . . . ?"

"I waited for you," Elise says, her expression bland and unreadable. "Outside school, like we said."

"Oh shit." I feel a flush of shame. "I'm sorry, I forgot. . . . We skipped study hall," I explain awkwardly, "and went back to Tate's."

"I can tell," Elise says quietly. "It's written all over you."

I flush. I'm still breathless from the hours Tate and I spent together, wrapped up in his old quilted comforter and each other. It's no wonder she can see, when I still feel Tate's hands on me, the burning path across my body.

"I called." Elise's voice twists, bitter. "I left you a ton of messages. And then I thought, maybe something happened, with your mom, so I came . . ." She stops. "Your dad let me in."

"My phone died—I never got the messages, I swear." I take a few steps forward, toward the couch. "I am so, so sorry. I completely forgot. It's awful of me, I know. What can I do? You want to order pizza? I was going to just do homework, but we could study together for that test tomorrow, or watch a movie, or . . . anything you like." I'm babbling, I know, but there's something so unnerving about her expression, perfectly detached. "Elise?" I ask again, nervous. "I fucked up, I'm sorry."

The bland look slips, and Elise giggles—but it's not a happy sound, there's something twisted about it. "Do you know what it felt like, just waiting for you? I sat there for an hour, until everyone was gone." She hugs herself, looking painfully young for a moment. "I was worried, thinking about every-thing that could have happened. An accident, or a car crash, or your mom . . ." She shakes her head, her expression hardening. "And all that time, you were off fucking him."

I flinch. "Don't."

"Don't what?" Elise leaps up, and I see her face clearer: the out-of-focus smudge to her gaze. "It's the truth, isn't it? That's all you do these days, hump away like a pair of fucking rabbits."

She laughs, bitter. "And you were always such a good girl. Who would have thought you'd turn out to be such a slut. Well, how was it?" she demands, grabbing my arm. "Go ahead, tell me everything. Is he good? Does he make you come?"

I reel back—from her harsh words and the faint slur in her voice. "You're drunk."

"Bzz! Wrong! Guess again."

"Elise?" My heart skips. I look closer. "What did you take? Oh God, are you okay? Do I need to call someone—"

"Relax." She cuts me off, rolling her eyes. "Don't look at me like that. Just a couple of my mom's pills. Prescription. It's all good."

"A couple?" I demand, still panicked.

"Cross my heart and hope to die." Elise draws an X over her chest, then giggles again. "Irony appreciated, of course."

"It's not funny." I exhale, but the panic doesn't dissolve; it just hardens into something more uncertain, a dark edge that sends a chill down my spine. I watch as Elise wanders over to the bar in the corner and lifts the stopper from the cut-glass bottle of my dad's scotch. "Seriously, Lise, put that down."

"Why?" She dangles the bottle from her fingertips. "Not up for a drink?"

"You're already wasted."

"Not wasted enough."

I go over to take the bottle from her hand, but she pulls

away and lifts it to her lips to gulp. I watch, feeling helpless. This is scaring me, the sudden quicksilver of her moods. She doesn't mess around with drugs. We drink, sure, and even smoke some weed with Chelsea sometimes, but this is something new, and nothing good. "Talk to me," I beg. "What's going on?"

"I told you." She spins in a slow circle, away from me. "I waited."

"Fine, I screwed up, I'm sorry." I hold my hands up, as if in surrender. "What can I do to make it up to you?" I ask, desperation clear in my voice. "Anything you want, I promise."

"Don't you get it?" she yells, her voice loud in the still of the dark house. "Sorry doesn't matter. Not if you love him more!"

There's silence.

"Elise . . . ?" I whisper. She meets my eyes, defiant and wounded.

"It was us," she says. "You and me."

"It still is!"

"But you love him more."

"No," I tell her, but she just looks away.

"You should see your face when the two of you are together." Elise swallows, giving me a sad little smile. "It's like he's your whole world."

"He's my boyfriend."

"So?" she yells. "I'm your best friend!"

"Right," I yell back. "My *friend*! So why can't you just be happy for me?"

"Happy you're throwing me away for some asshole who's going to dump you a month from now?" Elise is wild and furious. "Like I'm fucking disposable? Do you even remember what you said to me? It was us, together, before anything!"

"We still are!"

"No." She shakes her head. "Not since you gave it all to him. I never thought you'd do this to me, that you'd be such a shallow slut!" Elise whirls around and hurls the bottle at me with a cry. I leap back as it shatters against the wall, dark liquid splashing, shards of glass smashing like crystals on the floor around me.

"What are you doing?" I cry, shocked.

"You chose this!" she sobs. "You ruined everything."

Fear chills me, sharp and wild. I don't care about the glass or the mess, or anything but the finality in her tone. Like it's the end. "No," I say, shaking my head against the unthinkable. "Nothing's ruined. I'm with him, and we're still the same as we ever were, I promise."

"I don't believe you!"

"But it's true!" I don't know what to do to make her listen. She's not listening. Panic floods me. I grab her shoulders and shake her, violent with desperation. "It's still you and me; it'll always be you and me!"

"Stop it!" Elise cries, but I don't, I keep holding tight until she shoves me away hard enough to send me flying to the ground among the shattered glass.

I sit up, catching my breath. There's a dull pain in the back of my head, where it cracked against the floor.

"Anna . . ." Elise takes a step toward me, her eyes wide. "Oh God, I didn't mean . . ."

I pull myself up by the couch. For a moment, we're suspended there, across the room from each other. Eyes locked, a canyon of fierce emotion between us. Then there's a noise from the stairs. Elise looks away, quickly grabbing the throw from the back of the couch and tossing it to the floor, so that when my dad appears in the doorway, the mess is blocked from view.

"Is everything okay?" My dad looks between us, confused. "I thought I heard something."

"Fine, Mr. Chevalier." Elise forces a smile. "I was just showing Anna a video on my phone."

"Oh, okay." Dad blinks. He's got that dazed expression on his face, like he's still gone, off in whatever financial documents he was buried in. "Do you want to stay for dinner?"

"No, thank you, I have to go."

"Okay." He turns to me. "Call for takeout whenever you're ready to eat."

"Sure, Dad," I say nervously, but he barely gives us another glance, just drifts back upstairs.

Elise waits until he's gone, then pushes past me, out into the foyer. I trail after her. "Elise. Wait a second, please."

She turns, her face set, then her expression slips. She gasps. "You're bleeding."

I look down. My hand is cut, welling bright red. "It's fine," I say quickly. "I can't feel a thing."

Elise backs away. "I can't . . . I can't be here."

"Wait." I follow her out onto the front steps. "Let me take you home, at least. You shouldn't be out there like this."

I reach for her, but she flinches away. "Elise?" My voice breaks.

"I'll . . . see you tomorrow," she says quickly, her gaze still fixed on my bloody hand. Then she bolts. I listen as her footsteps are swallowed up by the night, remembering the knife-edge to her gaze, something damaged and hard.

Fear shivers through me. I can't lose her, not even a little. Tate has pulled me in and wrapped me up in this new kind of love, but I'm hers, too—I'll always be hers. If I have to choose . . .

"Elise!" I call after her, yelling. "Miles and miles! Do you hear me?" My voice echoes out into the dark. "Miles and fucking miles!"

But there's only silence. I wait on the steps until I'm frozen through, but she doesn't come back. We wrecked it, I realize, and it feels like my heart splits wide open. Something was ripped apart and bared to the world tonight, and we can't ever take it back.

She's gone.

At last I turn and walk slowly back into the warm, bright safety of the house.

Three weeks later, my mother is dead.

My words are a weapon.

They can cut you like glass.

Or they can smooth and soothe over gaps and cracks,

dripping honey.

Sweet and safe.

They can gouge out your heart.

Carve my name into your fair skin.

Write verses in your blood.

Be careful what you say, my friend.

My words are my greatest weapon of all.

THE TRIAL

"And the defendant wrote this poem?"

Silence.

Dekker glares. "Miss Newport, please. You're under oath."

Chelsea looks at me across the courtroom. I haven't seen her since my arrest; her hair is shorter now, the beachy waves an even brown, neat and preppy. She used to be loud and languid, always laughing; now her expression is apologetic and full of regret.

"Yes," she says quietly. "In English class, beginning of senior year."

"And this wasn't the only violent thing she wrote, was it?"

I feel Gates inhale a sharp breath beside me.

Again, Chelsea is silent. She looks down, toying with the

woven bracelets she has still tied around her wrist, the colorful strands that she and I and Elise all bought at a store in Boston together, knotting them tightly to overlap.

Judge von Koppel leans over. "Please answer the question."

Chelsea glances up, reluctant. "No, she wrote other things, for class. We all did."

"Like this." Dekker lifts a plastic-covered sheet between his thumb and forefinger. "Evidence item two-one-seven, a short story written by the defendant, describing the murder of a teenage girl."

"It was an assignment," Chelsea says quickly. "A college girl got shot, in the neighborhood. It was a big deal, everyone was talking about it, so our teacher had us write the stories about it. I did one, Elise did too. Everyone."

"But you could choose, could you not, whether to write from the perspective of the victim or the murderer?" Dekker tilts his head, waiting.

Chelsea exhales. "Yes."

"And Miss Chevalier was the only girl to write from the perspective of the killer."

"Boys did too," Chelsea replies. "Half the class."

"And did the defendant tell you why she chose to take on the killer's role?"

Chelsea bites her lip, looking over at me again. "She said . . ." Her voice trails into a whisper.

"Louder, please."

Another reluctant sigh. "She said she liked putting herself in his shoes. Imagining how it would feel to have that kind of power over someone, to end their life. But it wasn't real," she protests. "It was writing, that was the whole point. Our teacher always told us to get out of our own minds, and imagine being somebody else!"

"But the defendant had a fascination for violent imagery even out of class," Dekker clicks a photo up on the display: the cover of my science lab binder. "She copied the words to several songs, some would even say obsessively writing the same lyrics over and over. Let me quote for you, 'I took a knife and cut out her eye,'" he reads, voice dramatic in the still of the courtroom. "'I'll cut your little heart out because you made me cry.' That's a song by one of the defendant's favorite musicians, Florence and the Machine."

They told me not to register any reaction to his questions, but I can't help shaking my head in disbelief. The photos were bad enough, pulled at random from our online profiles, ripped from any context or meaning, but this? I'd always thought trials were about evidence and witnesses, but those are somebody else's words that I scrawled on my notebook during a boring class, and now he's holding them up as some kind of proof for my "violent urges." Why doesn't he go further, and pull up my DVR records and all the horror movies I used to watch, curled tightly against Tate on the living room couch? Why not go through my bookcase for every crime novel he can find?

Wouldn't we all look guilty, if someone searched hard enough?

"Relax."

I feel a hand on my arm and look over to find Gates leaning over. "You're scowling," he murmurs, too quiet for anyone else to hear. "He's grasping at straws. If he had any hard evidence, he'd be presenting it, but he doesn't. Deep breaths, remember?"

Of course I remember, they've only drilled it into me every day for weeks now. But Gates is watching me intently, so I inhale a short breath and force my face into something I hope resembles a relaxed expression. I can't let the judge see that I'm angry; I can't let her see that I feel anything at all about Dekker's lies.

"Or what about these submissions to the school literary magazine?" Dekker is still reading aloud from the snapshots of my binder covers and English class assignments.

"Objection!" Gates rises. "Does the prosecutor have any more questions for the witness, or is he just treating us to a public poetry reading?"

"Yes, please do stick to questioning," Judge von Koppel agrees with an icy smile. "I believe we've heard enough of the graffiti."

Dekker glares, then turns back to Chelsea. "On the days

before the murder, did you notice any friction between Miss Warren and the defendant?"

"No," Chelsea says. "They were great. Happy."

"Are you sure? No fighting, disagreements?"

"I just said"—she glares back at him—"I don't know why you're even doing this. Anna loved Elise—we all did—she would never do anything to hurt her."

She searches for me again in the courtroom. Our eyes meet, and I give her a tiny nod. It's okay. I know she doesn't want to be here, that Dekker's forcing her up there, to try to slander me. She can't help it any more than I can help the things he's saying about me.

"So you never noticed any jealousy from the defendant?"

"No."

"Never saw her act in any violent or uncontrollable ways?"

"No, nev—" Chelsea suddenly stops. She looks over at me, panicked. Dekker catches the gaze. He brightens.

"You did?"

"I . . ." Chelsea's expression is conflicted.

Gates tugs my sleeve again.

"What's going on?" he whispers.

I shrug. "I don't know."

Dekker clears his throat. "Miss Newport? Did you ever see the defendant have any violent or angry outbursts?"

Chelsea hesitates again, then nods.

"What happened?" Dekker's whole body is alert, his face expectant.

"I . . ." Chelsea swallows, looking nervous. "It was during art class, at school. I went to get something from my locker, and I saw her in the hallway, with Elise."

"With the victim?" Dekker's voice is so gleeful, it turns my stomach.

She nods again. "Anna was . . . She was screaming, and yelling. Elise tried to calm her down, but Anna . . . She grabbed the display—I think it was something for Environment Week—she just grabbed the whole thing and began tearing it apart."

I exhale. Now I know what this is about. I start scribbling a note to Gates as Dekker continues his victorious questions.

"Did you hear what they were saying, why they were fighting?"

"No, I didn't think I should go over," Chelsea looks awkward. "I mean, she was so mad."

"In a violent rage." Dekker draws the words out with satisfaction.

"I . . . Yes."

"And what happened next?"

Chelsea shrugs. "Elise tried to calm her down, but Anna threw her off—"

"The defendant physically assaulted the victim?"

"No." Chelsea stops. "I mean, it wasn't like that. She just, pushed her away and took off."

Dekker beams. "No further questions."

He steps back to his table, and I pass the note to Gates. He glances over it, then nods, rising to approach the witness stand with a confident saunter.

"Miss Newport, when was this altercation you witnessed?"

She pauses, thinking. "Um, before Christmas break."

"Does December tenth sound about right?" Gates suggests.

"Yeah. I mean, I think so."

"Did you know about Anna's mother?" he asks.

"You mean, that she was sick?" Chelsea nods. "She didn't like to talk about it, but, yeah. Elise filled us in, so we wouldn't say the wrong thing."

"Objection, relevance?" Dekker yells.

Gates turns to the judge. "The defendant's mother had breast cancer," he explains, "that recurred in the fall of last year."

She nods. "Continue."

Gates turns back to Chelsea. "So you weren't aware of the state of her mother's disease or how Anna was coping."

"No, not really." Chelsea sends me a look. "She was pretty tough about that stuff. She didn't like to bring us down."

Gates nods. "So you had no way of knowing that on December tenth, the day you witnessed Anna having an emotional breakdown, she'd just been informed that her mother was refusing all further treatment, and was, in fact, preparing to die?"

Chelsea's eyes widen, and I hear the intake of breath in the courtroom. "No. No, I had no idea."

Gates turns back to Judge von Koppel with a frown. "Far from being a violent fight between Miss Chevalier and the victim—as Detective Dekker would have you believe—what Miss Newport witnessed was the perfectly natural reaction of a girl facing the devastating loss of a parent. Any outburst was a result of grief, not violent rage."

The judge nods. "Noted."

I feel her eyes on me, all of the rest of them too. Watching, judging, speculating. Wondering what I felt and how I took the news. The truth is, I can't remember, not clearly—it's smudged with grief and rage and pure, dark disappointment, as if I'm staring at an out-of-focus photograph taken on a gray, rainy afternoon. There are only glimpses left now: the way my mother didn't even have the courage to tell me; my father's gaze sliding to look at the wall behind me when he broke the news.

She'd given up. On herself, on me.

It would have been different if she'd been terminal, even late-stage, but the doctors said there was a 40 percent chance that another round of chemo would work. Forty percent. That was almost half. A half-chance of beating it again, a half-chance at life. With me. And instead, she gave up. Said it was unnatural, that she didn't want the chemicals in her body over and over again. Said that it might work this time, but it would only come back again. Said that this was her time, and that she wanted to go gracefully, with dignity and love.

Except there was nothing graceful about the way she wasted away, a thin skeleton dwarfed by covers and cushions and bathrobes, sitting propped and delicate in bed. Nothing dignified about catheters and bags full of urine, and yellowed skin, and choking pain.

Nothing loving about choosing to leave me.

I sit, silent, as they discuss my dead mother, my grief, my desperation. I dig my fingernails into my palms, and wonder when this will ever end.

AFTER THE FIGHT

They put me back in isolation, saying it's for my own safety, but I know—this is for their sake, not mine. They don't care that I got hurt in here, only that it makes them look bad, makes me more sympathetic to the outside world, maybe. So they take away what little freedom I could pretend I still had, and condemn me to silence, and dark nights, and long days with nothing to do but think. Slowly, my strength drains away, my earlier resolve and determination waning under the brutal onslaught of day after day of loneliness. Those bleak thoughts I've pushed away come creeping back, whispering in the night, slipping their cold arms around my body and their slim fingers around my throat, until the panic is so fierce I double over where I stand, hardly breathing.

I never realized what a privilege it was to get up and leave my cell in the mornings. Now they bring me all my meals, delivered on hard plastic trays, and take me to use the showers late in the morning once everyone else has already had their turn. I still get my few hours in the exercise yard—Gates and my father saw to that—but now I'm escorted out by two guards to a thin strip of land on the far side of the prison, divided from the others by barbed wire and barricades, away from the entertainment of the pickup basketball games and slouching, sullen cliques.

The guy from the American Embassy, Lee, is my only friend. He visits almost every day, bringing me mindless magazines and books to fill the empty hours, a new pillow to try to cheer me, and an old iPod loaded with songs he thinks I'd like, to drown the dark silence and screaming of my bad dreams. He gives me updates on the case, and Gates's new ideas for trial strategy, going over my statements with me for hours and comparing them to the official police transcripts he managed to obtain from his new contact at the precinct. He listens patiently, taking notes, creasing his forehead in a thoughtful frown as he looks for any new angle or possibility to prove my innocence.

Could Tate have left the bedroom while I was in the shower? Did I mention to anyone else about Juan following us back to the house? What about Niklas—did he make any threatening comments, or jokes that could be seen as creepy and aggressive?

"Sometimes it's not about proving you didn't do it," he tells me when I throw the pages down, frustrated after poring over Chelsea's and Max's and AK's interrogation transcripts all week. "Sometimes, you just have to create reasonable doubt. They don't have hard evidence," he reminds me. "They just have circumstantial things, and Dekker's wild theories. *Beyond* a reasonable doubt, that's what they have to prove. But we won't let them."

I lean back in my seat, exhausted. I'm sleeping even worse now, every click and rattle echoing through the isolation wing. "How can you be so sure?"

Lee gives me a quiet smile, his brown eyes soft but resolute. "I just am."

But I can't accept that, not when it feels like everyone in my life has turned out to have some other agenda, a hidden reason for making me say or do what they want. "No, I mean it," I tell him. "Why are you here? You said it yourself, the embassy doesn't want anything to do with me. Aren't you risking a lot, going against them?"

Lee looks down. "I guess I just want to help. You're stuck in here alone, and what they're saying about you . . ."

"Why don't you believe them?" I ask, insistent. "Everyone else does, even people I thought were my friends. You don't even know me, and you're saying you believe me for sure."

Lee pauses. He's weighing something, I can tell, and when he looks up, there's something tired in his expression. "My sister, this happened to her. Not murder," he adds quickly. "Drugs."

I wait, and after another moment, he explains. "She was backpacking down in South America after college," he explains. "It was eight years ago. She wanted to see the beaches, and the jungle, Aztec ruins, you know?" He smiles faintly, and I can see how close they are, that affectionate sibling bond born of shared bedrooms and childhood fighting and all those other tiny moments that add up to something solid and unbreakable. "She was staying in youth hostels, met all kinds of people. They traveled together," he continued. "And I guess someone slipped something in her bag, because they pulled her out of line in customs in Brazil, found close to half a pound of cocaine rolled up in one of her shirts. She never touched drugs," he says, looking up at me, emphatic. "Barely even had a beer. I used to tease her, you know, because she was so straight-edge." He stops, a shadow slipping over his face.

"What happened?" I ask, even though I already know it can't be anything good.

He looks at the floor. "They charged her, locked her up in some hellhole prison. She didn't speak any Portuguese, and my parents . . . It took them weeks before anyone let us in to see her. We got a lawyer, but the trial was a sham, and that much cocaine . . . They found her guilty of trafficking." Lee says quietly. "Ten year sentence."

My heart clutches in my chest.

"She was stuck down there for three years before we managed to get her out on appeal." Lee meets my eyes, pained. "Three years in that place." He shakes his head. "She's back home now—she got married, had a kid. But, it changed her. She'll never get those years back, all because they just washed their hands of her. Like she didn't matter. Nobody fought for her." He stops and looks away, embarrassed. "I guess, I figure if I can help stop that from happening to you . . ."

I swallow, chilled. "Thank you," I say, my voice coming out a broken whisper. "For trying, for believing in me . . ."

Lee manages a smile, reaching again for the files. "Back to work," he says, as if embarrassed by his confession. "I was thinking, we should try to do something about all these biased reports on the news shows. I know your old lawyer didn't want you making any comment, but right now, you're getting slammed, and I don't like how it might look to a judge. Maybe we should do an interview," he suggests, "here in prison. Pick an American network, let you tell your side of the story."

I hear his words but they barely register. Instead, I'm still caught in the horror of his sister's story. A girl like me, a case

like mine—far from home, adrift in a foreign legal system—
and she was found guilty. Abandoned. Left to rot.

Ten years.

Even six months in this place has been unbearable, but year
after year after year stretching into the distant black future ... ?

Now, for the first time, I wonder if this is how my mother
felt. If cancer was her prison; the chemo treatments, torture.

I understand it.

I would rather die.

THE INTERVIEW

"Just lift your head, just a little more . . . okay, perfect."

A bright bulb flashes in my face, blinding me, and the woman holding a gadget near my face takes another reading. "Less on the blues," she yells across the room at the guy fixing the lighting rig. "Let's try it again."

Another light flashes, this time leaving dark circles hovering in the air in front of my eyes. I blink, disoriented. The woman clicks again and then nods briskly. "Okay, we've got it! Don't move." She directs that last part to me, before hurrying away.

I look around. Where would I even go? I'm sitting in the prison cafeteria, except the plastic tables and mealtime madness is gone, replaced with chaos of a different kind. Spot-lights, sound cables, boom mikes and cameras: the room is a flurry of noise and activity, and it's all I can do after so many silent, still days just to watch, drinking it all in. People, regular people, chatting brightly, checking clipboards, scurrying around with papers and coffee cups and reels of cable. I feel like my mind just got an electric shock, jolted awake after so many weeks spent numb and drifting, asleep.

"Let me give you a touch-up." The makeup lady materializes, holding a tray of pots and brushes. She's already spent thirty minutes dabbing at me with foundation and mascara, now she dips a blusher brush into some loose powder and dusts at my face. "I know it seems like a lot," she chats, smiling and friendly. "But these lights get crazy hot; we don't want any shine."

I smile back hesitantly. For all the bustle and activity, most people have stayed away from me: orbiting at a safe distance, as if I'm surrounded by an invisible force field. I guess a prison jumpsuit and handcuffs will do that to you. I'd hoped I'd be getting regular clothes, like the ones I wore for my hearing, but the show insisted on keeping me in my prison gear—and filming in here, with the wire visible on the window, and metal bars instead of walls. They want to show the reality of my everyday life, they told Gates and my dad, but if that was true, we'd be filming the interview in my isolation cell:

crammed into the tiny room with the camera guy balancing over the steel open toilet.

"Are you nervous?" the makeup lady chats, still dusting powder on my face. I nod, embarrassed. "Don't be," she reassures me. "You'll do great. Just keep looking at her, and try to ignore the cameras."

"Don't cover her bruises!" A sharp Southern voice cuts through the noise, and suddenly, there she is, striding toward us on blue patent heels, a paper bib fixed around her neck, and curlers still resting in her blond bobbed hair.

Clara Rose.

On TV, she's larger than life, but in the flesh, she's short: tiny and compact in a bright pink Chanel suit and blue eye shadow. "I told you, nothing on the face," she scolds the makeup lady, snatching the brush away. "She's been rotting in jail for months, not competing in the Junior Miss America pageant."

The makeup woman cringes and quickly begins blotting at my face. Clara looks at me and suddenly breaks into a wide, honey-sweet smile. "Anna, it's so great to finally meet you," she coos. "And thank you so much for agreeing to take part in this. You've been so brave; it's time America got to hear your side of the story."

She holds out her hand, and reluctantly, I shake it. "Thank you for having me," I reply politely.

"I'm sorry we didn't have a chance to sit down earlier," she says, and beams at me with dazzlingly white teeth. "But I'm sure we'll— Kenny, no!" She suddenly barks, looking up at where the lighting guy is fixing the lamps. "What did I tell you about washing me out with the yellow?" She strides off toward him, her stilettos tap-tapping on the dull linoleum floors.

I exhale slowly, watching her walk away. It wasn't my choice: to do the interview, or that it be broadcast as a special extended exclusive edition of the *Clara Rose Show*. After all the things she's said about me, I figured she would be the last person we'd go to, but Lee argued that was the exact reason we need her to do the profile. All of the news channels back home are painting me in a bad light, but Clara's the worst, hammering her cold-blooded killer theories almost every night of the week with so-called experts and Akshay's swaggering guest spots. If we can get her to at least present the possibility that I'm innocent, then maybe people will sit up and start paying attention: petition the American government to get involved, put pressure on the Dutch to throw out the case.

It's a long shot, I know, but they say it could make all the difference. Dekker has been playing the press like a pro— "leaking" photos of me out partying, slipping them information about Elise's body, the beach house, Tate's affair. He holds court on the front steps of the precinct, talking about justice, and morality, and how he won't let outsiders ruin the peaceful tranquility of his home island. I've sat here in prison, silent, for long enough. Now I need to tell my side of the story.

"You ready for this?" Lee comes over with Gates, who looks bewildered at all this activity.

I take a deep breath. "I guess."

"Just remember what we talked about," Gates adds, serious. "Take your time, speak slowly, and ask for breaks if you feel overwhelmed. They're going to edit this together later, so it's fine to stop and then start again, if you get flustered."

"And don't be afraid to show your feelings," Lee interrupts. "She's been trying to paint you as this robot, a sociopath, and we know that's not true. It's okay if you need to cry."

"But don't get angry," Gates is quick to caution. "Don't raise your voice, or ask about her coverage, you need to keep this focused on the facts. What happened to Elise, what Dekker's doing to you now."

I nod again, already worn out.

"You'll do great," Lee reassures me, squeezing my arm in a comforting gesture. "We believe in you."

I smile back, glad that he's here. With Dad still gone in Boston, Lee and Gates are my only link to the outside world, the only people on my side.

"All righty." The older producer guy reappears. "We're good to get started. Mr. Gates, why don't you and your friend come watch from the hallway, where we have the monitors set up?"

Lee looks to me. I nod. "It's okay, I'll be fine."

"Like I said"—he pats me again—"just tell the truth."

They follow the producer out, and soon the mess of cables and stands has been tidied to the back of the room, leaving an unobstructed view from the cameras past the lunch table I'm seated at, back through the bars of the entrance and down the prison hall. Somebody fixes a tiny microphone to my jumpsuit collar and positions the extra boom mike overhead. Then Clara takes a seat beside me, her hair now perfectly styled; her lipstick bright. She's checking note cards, her lips moving as she murmurs under her breath.

"Sound good?" she asks in a regular tone.

"Check!" Comes the reply. I blink, but the lights are dazzling, and as hot as the makeup woman told me they'd be.

"Just ignore the cameras," Clara tells me with that same honey-sweet tone. She smiles, but it doesn't reach her eyes: they watch me, shrewd and darting. "And try not to mumble. Speak clearly, or we'll have to retake the shot."

I feel my nerves kick, a flutter in my stomach.

"Are we ready?" The voice comes again. "Okay, rolling in three, two, one . . ."

Clara's face smoothes. She faces the camera, somber and caring. "Tonight, we take you behind the scenes of the notorious Aruba Correctional Institute to bring you an exclusive interview with Anna Chevalier. Locked up, far from home.

Accused of her best friend's murder. We get a glimpse into this young woman's mind, and ask the questions that need answering, right here on the *Clara Rose Show*."

The questions are simple, at first. We go over the same things I told Dekker in my interrogations. The background for our trip, how we spent those first few days on the island, when we finally realized something was wrong and found the body that night. I pick my words carefully, hesitant at first, always reminding myself that Clara's warm sympathy is an act for the cameras, not any real concern.

"And your time here in prison?" she asks, furrowing her brow. "I can see, you've had some problems."

I touch my face automatically. "I was attacked," I say softly. "It's . . . hard. My dad, he does what he can to come visit, but being alone all this time . . . I just want to go home."

Clara nods. "Now, can you talk about Elise at all? I know there have been lots of rumors, that the two of you were fighting, that you had a destructive friendship . . ."

"It's not true. We—we were best friends," I tell her. "We did everything together, and yes, we had some disagreements, but they were over little things."

"Like what?"

"Just, girl stuff, you know?" I shrug. "She was always borrowing my clothes and then not giving them back, that drove me crazy. And she hated it when I would use her makeup without asking."

"But what about her relationship with Tate Dempsey?" Clara asks, inching forward in her seat. "She was going behind your back with your boyfriend."

"I didn't know," I say firmly.

"But if you had?"

"I didn't."

"But now that you do . . ." Clara changes tack. "How do you feel about it? What would you say to her?"

I blink a moment, thrown. "I . . . I don't know."

"You haven't thought about it?" she presses me. "You've been here, locked in prison for months now. What would you say to Tate, if you had the chance? He hasn't come to see you, has he? Why not?"

"I—"

"Cut!" The voice comes from behind the bank of dazzling lights.

Clara snaps her head around. "What the hell's the problem?"

The producer comes rushing forward. "Nothing about the Dempsey boy, his lawyers made it clear."

"Are you kidding me?" Clara exclaims.

He shrugs helplessly. "You know what we went through with the libel writ. I can't take the risk; they'll have us back in court."

She rolls her eyes, smoothing back her hair. "Fine. Do I need more powder? Debbie?"

The makeup artist trots back over with her brush, but I stay focused on the brief conversation I just overheard. Libel? Back in court? Is this why Tate's barely been mentioned on Clara's show? I always figured it was strange. After all, he's the one person who admitted to lying, and to being back at the house with Elise that afternoon, but he's still barely had a bad word said about him in the press. And this must be why. The Dempsey money has bought him his privacy; Ellingham working round the clock to protect the family's good name.

But not mine.

"Okay," Clara waves the crew away and turns back to me. "Let's pick it up."

The camera man silently counts down, and Clara brightens on cue. "We've seen a lot of, well, I've got to be honest with you, pretty troubling photos over the last few weeks. You girls out partying, drinking. What do you say to claims you led Elise astray, and pulled her into this dangerous behavior?"

I take a deep breath. "It's not true. We . . . liked to go out together, to parties, like most of the other kids in school—"

"But this wasn't just your regular sleepover, good, clean fun," Clara interrupts. "There was drinking, college boys . . ."

"We went out," I admit. "And maybe we went down some bad roads, but that was Elise. She . . . loved to have a good time.

She was the outgoing one, you know? She was always looking for an adventure."

"So she was the one initiating the drinking, the drug-taking . . ."

"No, that's not what I mean." I stumble over my words, "I just . . . It wasn't one-sided, like people are saying. She did bad stuff too, it wasn't all my idea."

"So what would you tell her parents, if you had the chance?" Clara leans in again. "What would you say to these fine folks, who've lost their daughter in the most tragic, violent way?"

I blink. "I . . . I don't know."

"Why don't you try?" Clara urges gently.

I slowly turn, and look at the camera, at the empty gaping lens, with its distant reflection of myself. I open my mouth, hesitant. "I . . . I'm sorry, that's she's gone. There's not a single day that goes by that I don't . . . that I don't think about her." I can feel myself choking up, the glare of the lights hot on my face, Clara's expression so fixed and hungry. But all I can think about is Elise dancing around the kitchen in the beach house that day, bright and free and alive.

"I'm sorry," I sob, tears coming fast now. "I'm sorry I wasn't looking out for her, that I couldn't stop this. I miss her too," I add, pleading. "She . . . She was like a sister to me, and now, now I'll never get her back!"

My eyes blur with tears. I wait for the producer to call to

cut, for them to stop rolling, but nothing comes. They keep filming, watching me weep, counting the long seconds as my body shakes with grief.

This is what they wanted, I realize, too late. They don't care about my story, or presenting the other side. They just want to see me crying, and begging, and broken. They want a show.

BEFORE

"Crushed by an elephant or trampled by bulls?"

"Umm, trampled. You'd go quicker. Every hair in your body plucked out one by one or all at once?"

"Shit. Uh . . . all at once. I'd get doped up on painkillers and get it over and done with. You?"

"God no, can you imagine, a bikini wax all over your body?"

"You're such a pussy, you can't deal with any pain. Remember you cried that time Elena did your eyebrows?"

"Did not! I have a very sensitive forehead! Oww!"

"Pass me that."

"Drowning or gunshot?"

"Depends . . . Where's the bullet hit?"

"Stomach. It's slow and painful and you bleed to death."

"Drowning, then. It only takes a few minutes, right?"

"Yeah, but you're suffocating. And then your eyeballs explode."

"Bullshit."

"It's true. I saw it on some Discovery Channel show. The pressure builds up and squeezes all your insides out."

"You're so dumb. That's only if you're really deep—diving or something. Or in space."

"Would you still bleed to death in space?"

"What? You're crazy."

"Shut up, I'm serious. There's no gravity, right? So why would the blood come out?"

"See?"

"Why are we even talking about this? It's morbid."

"You're telling me you haven't thought about it? Come on, how would you do it?"

"Pills, I guess. There's a bunch left from when . . . Mom . . . I wouldn't even feel it happen."

"Coward. You've got to feel it, all the way to the end. It shouldn't be a get-out-of-jail-free card, you know? You should have to earn it."

"So how?"

"A knife, I guess. Slice my wrists, bleed out all over the new cream carpets. Give my mom something to complain about."

"Elise!"

"What? It's the point. One final fuck-you."

"But you wouldn't."

"No. I'm just messing with you. Besides, who'd hold your hand for Elena at the salon if I'm gone?"

DAY 196

Elise's mother, Judy, comes to visit me in prison the week before the trial begins.

I've already taken my sleeping pill, so I drag, disoriented, as the guard leads me down the hallway, past the interview rooms, and up into a part of the prison I've never been before. "Where are we going?" I ask, confused, but he doesn't reply, doesn't say a word at all as we climb a flight of stairs. There are no bars here, I notice, looking around: the walls are painted a soft peach, the flooring, polished and new. If I didn't know any better, I would think it a school or office building: someplace productive, where things were made and minds molded, not the opposite, a place that takes time away from us, day by day.

He knocks, once, on a door at the end of the hallway. It

opens, and I'm ushered inside the room, an office. After so long with the basic plastic furniture and metal fixtures bolted to the floor, it's a shock to see the decor here: a plush rug, bookcases, framed pictures on the wall. Warden Eckhart sits behind a wide wooden desk; he gestures for me to step farther into the room. My heart leaps with expectation, just as I hear a gasp behind me. I turn. Judy is sitting on a narrow sofa, her hands folded in her lap. She rises, staring at me with horror. "Anna . . ." The word trails away.

"Judy?" My voice tilts upward, a flight of hope. "What's going on? Did they drop the charges?" I look around, but there's no sign of Gates or my dad. Wouldn't they have called them in, if I was being released? "Where's my dad?" I demand. "Did something happen? Is he okay?"

"Oh yes, he's fine." Judy blinks, her face falling. "I'm sorry, I didn't think—"

"This is just a quick visit," the warden interjects. He looks between us. "I'll give you some privacy."

He exits with the guard, leaving us alone. I don't move. They didn't put me in handcuffs, I realize, absently rubbing my wrists. This is as free as I've been in weeks.

"Oh, Anna, sweetheart . . ." Judy sinks back down onto the sofa. "Look at you."

I don't know what to say, so I walk slowly to the other chair and sit. It's the first time she's spoken to me since my arrest. She's never visited me, or written, or even looked in my direction during the bail hearing or our pretrial motions. I've seen her in the courtroom, her head bent, holding on to Charles's hand as if to save her from drowning. I know how she feels, but I haven't had that luxury—someone to cling on to, to stay above the surface.

"I don't understand," I say softly, my fingertips tracing the fabric of the cushions, rich and brocade. "Why . . . ? Why are you here?"

Judy looks down. "I guess . . . I had to see you, before it all begins."

It. The reality of the situation hovers between us in the small room, full of unspoken words like "death," "murder," "killing," "accused." I can't say them out loud any more than she can right now, so I don't say a word; I just study her, feeling strangely detached, as if there's more space between us than just these few short feet. A canyon, an ocean. Her face is worn and tired, even beneath the slick of makeup, and she's wearing one of her usual pantsuits in crisp navy, but it hangs around her thin frame, draped and oversized. I have to fight the urge to go sit beside her on the sofa, to hug her casually the way I've done so many times before.

She left me too.

"I'm not supposed to be here." Judy finally speaks, giving me a nervous smile. "Charles, he told me not to come. The lawyers, too."

I don't reply. There was a time when she was more of a mother to me than my own, somebody to ask how my day in school was, how things were going with Tate. I wound up crashing at Elise's most Friday nights through last spring and summer—it made sense, when we were out until dawn, but the truth was, Saturday mornings at her house were my favorite place in the world. Judy would make cinnamon French toast, and confiscate Elise's cell phone, and we would all wind up sitting around the table out in their glass-covered conservatory, drinking English tea and sharing the new fashion magazines that arrived with the newspapers. Elise always rushed her food down and then demanded to be released, like it was a terrible burden to be trapped in such tranquil domesticity, but those brief mornings held a sweetness for me that I can still taste, even trapped in my tiny cell, with Saturdays bringing nothing more than an extra apple on my breakfast tray, grapefruit juice instead of orange.

I wait for Judy to explain why she's come, but she just sits there, looking anywhere but directly at me. Then she seems to remember something, and rummages in her expensive leather bag. "Are you hungry?"

"It's late," I reply, still confused. "They bring dinner at six."

"I brought you . . ." She holds out a bar of chocolate to me, covered in a familiar blue wrapper. "It's that Swiss make; I remembered it was your favorite."

I pause a beat, then slowly reach out to take it. "Thank you," I say politely.

"I remember, when I came back from that conference in Zurich"—Judy gives me a weak smile—"and brought all that candy. You girls nearly made yourselves sick, eating it in one night."

I nod. I don't know what to do with the chocolate, but I doubt they'll let me take it back to my cell, so I slowly unwrap it, sliding my finger beneath the crisp paper wrapping and then scoring my fingernail down the crease of the foil. The bar breaks with a snap. The candy is smooth on my tongue, creamy and sweeter than the American brands that Lee used to bring me.

I offer her a square. She takes it.

"They had a memorial, at the school," Judy says hesitantly. "There was one after the break, but this was for the unveiling. They built a lovely fountain in the side courtyard. They said that was where you all liked to sit, at lunch. In the shade there." Judy stares at the piece of chocolate, still in her hand. "Charles wants me to start a scholarship in her name. Fund someone's tuition. Or maybe a charity foundation. To honor her."

"Elise would have loved that," I murmur, sarcastic. Then I stop, horrified. "I . . . I'm sorry, I didn't mean—"

"No, you're right." Judy meets my eyes and then, to my amazement, she begins to laugh: a tiny twitch at her lips that spreads until she's gasping, a hollow sound ringing out in the small room. "It's all wrong. I kept thinking, all through the ceremony, that Elise would hate it." Judy shakes her head. "You know they had the choir sing that song, that awful one about being in the arms of angels . . ."

"Sarah McLachlan?" I ask.

She nods, trying to control herself. "They were all so sad, and all I could imagine was Elise making that face of hers, you know the one, where she'd just roll your eyes at you."

"As if you were beyond saving," I finish, "and she deserved a medal just putting up with you."

"That's the one." Judy smiles at me, shaking her head. "I swear, I got that look every day of her life." She takes a tissue from her bag and dabs at her eyes, the laughter fading away. "Nobody knew her like us." She says it quietly, but I feel the words strike through me. "Everyone comes around saying what an angel she was, how perfect, how precious. But they don't know. Nobody does, except you."

Her eyes meet mine again, aching and lost. This is why she's here, I understand it now. This is her only way to feel close to Elise: the memory of her, as she really was. Not the girl on the front page, or the glowing paragraph in her obituary. But the daughter who screamed in a rage because Judy had looked at her phone again; the friend who curled, sandwiched between us on the couch those late nights when Judy got back from the hospital and found us, still awake, watching bad reality TV and eating Doritos. We were poisoning ourselves, she'd warn us, plucking the remote and bag of chips from our hands, but inevitably she'd wind up tucked under the blanket too, interrupting to ask who this one was, and why was she mad at the other guy?

I'm her only link to Elise now. We're coconspirators in the crime of loving her daughter.

"She hated me." Judy's voice cracks. "We fought, right before she came away. Did she tell you that?"

I shake my head.

"She was threatening to defer college," Judy says, and clutches her tissue tightly. "Go out to California, or Europe, or volunteer in some godforsaken tribal village. Not that she would have done it," Judy adds. "You know she couldn't bear to be without her creature comforts. But still, I let her get to me, every time. She always knew just the hurtful things to say. . . ." She trails off for a moment, then shakes her head. "We were screaming, all night. And then I went to work in the morning. I didn't even say good-bye." Judy swallows back her tears, but her hand shakes. "The last time I saw her, and I didn't even wait to say good-bye."

She looks at me, plaintive, wanting something. Absolution.

I exhale, suddenly clear. I can give her that much, at least. "It doesn't matter," I tell her gently. "She loved you. I know she didn't like to show it, but none of the fights, none of that matters. You know that; you have to know."

Judy's eyes meet mine, hopeful this time. "I just hate to think of her . . . If she thought I didn't care . . ."

"No, I promise. She loved you, both of you. She didn't even mention your fight," I reassure her. "She didn't give it another thought. She was having fun. You know how she is." I pause. "Was," I correct softly.

Judy nods, and some of the tension in her body seems to ease. She takes a long breath, her expression smoothing out, peaceful now. "Thank you," she says softly, and rises to her feet.

I blink. "But . . . You're going?"

"I should get back." Judy pulls on her jacket.

"You're not going to help?" My voice twists. "But, if you talked to the judge, if you explained to him that you know me, and I would never . . . You could do something!"

"It's out of my hands now." Judy looks away, and I see for the first time, the flicker of doubt in her expression; the shadow drifting in the back of her eyes.

Doubt.

It strikes me like a dull blow, blood ringing in my ears as if from far away. My stomach drops, my body turns ice-cold. If Judy can doubt me—if she can think I'm capable of murder, after all the time we've spent together—then what hope do I have in court tomorrow, with Dekker snapping at my heels, and the judge sitting so icy and remote?

I push the fear down, desperate. "You didn't ask me," I say.

She glances up, caught. "You didn't ask me if I killed her."

I thought it was because she believed me, unquestioning. She wouldn't be here otherwise, would she? Alone, bringing candy and memories?

She has to believe me.

Judy shrinks back, looking anywhere but me. "Anna, let's not . . ."

"No. Ask me," I demand. "Do it."

Judy pauses, as if gathering her strength. She takes a breath, and then looks at me straight-on, with fearful eyes. "Did you . . . kill her?"

"No!" My voice breaks. I reach for her, pleading. "No, I promise you. I never . . . You know I loved her. It's all a lie."

"Then everything will be okay." Judy cups my cheek for a moment, then steps back. "Just tell the truth and be yourself. It'll all work out."

My mouth drops open, helpless, as she knocks against the door. The guard steps inside. This time, he has the cuffs waiting.

"Judy, please." My voice breaks. She smells of vanilla, and family, and lazy weekends wrapped in fluffy bathrobes and somebody else's slippers. She smells like home.

"Look after yourself, sweetheart," Judy says, not meeting my eyes, and then she's gone.

NOW

She was wrong, they all were. Telling the truth doesn't make a difference, nor does being true to yourself. If it did, I wouldn't be here now, awaiting the verdict that's going to decide the next twenty years of my life.

The next twenty birthdays and Christmases, the next twenty first days of summer, and last nights of fall. One thousand and forty Mondays. Seven thousand three hundred days of waking up here, penned in under an endless blue sky.

Except I won't. I can't.

Looking back now, I see how naive we all were. I stepped into that courtroom believing I'd have a fair shot—a chance to state my case and be heard, the way you're supposed to. But the real truth is, it's all a performance. The trial is no different from the *Clara Rose Show*, in its way, only instead of a film studio with lights and cameras, we have the courtroom as our stage. The lawyers and witnesses are all actors; the judge is our audience, and whoever can sell their version of the script—make you believe it, whether it's fiction or fact—they're the one who wins. It's that simple. Evidence is just a prop; you can ignore it and look the other way, and even the script doesn't matter when some supporting actor can improvise their scenes and steal the whole show.

Maybe if I'd known that, I could have played my part better, maybe even stopped it from getting this far at all. I guess it's too late for that now.

Dekker knew it, though; he knew it from the start. What else was he doing, by leaking police reports and crime-scene photos weeks before even the trial date was set? He was setting the stage for his story, like a movie trailer cut with the juiciest scenes so people would go in already expecting the big showdown, anticipating the final twist. Watching him in court was like watching a conductor, like the time Elise's parents dragged us out to the symphony. There was a tiny man up above the orchestra pit, waving and swirling that baton, painting whole landscapes in the air with every breath, making the music lift and fall, steering us effortlessly through the song.

Dekker wasn't half as elegant as that tuxedoed man, but his power was just as strong. He carefully steered the performance, bringing in each new section of the chorus with a well-timed flourish: a scandalous photo, words of a fight, testimony of my anger and partying . . . He led our audience deftly through the script along his chosen path so that they would end the show with only one obvious conclusion in their minds: my guilt.

The curtain's down now, but I won't forget so easily: the performance never ends.

CLARA ROSE SHOW
TRANSCRIPT

CLARA: . . . and a few times, even outright lying, or at least contradicting a lot of the testimony and statements we've already heard about the case.

<VIDEO CLIP>

ANNA: We went out. And maybe we went down some bad roads, but that was Elise. She . . . loved to have a good time. She was the outgoing one, you know? She was always looking for an adventure.

<END VIDEO CLIP>

CLARA: Well, Martin, we've had time now to go over the footage—exclusive footage, by the way, exclusive to the *Clara Rose Show*—so what's your take on this? Is Anna telling the truth here, or is this just the latest in a long series of lies from the accused killer?

MARTIN: Looking at the clips we've seen, I've got to say, the thing that strikes me is the complete lack of personal responsibility. Time and again, she blames everybody else for the situation she's in: her friends wanted to go on vacation; her boyfriend told her to lie about their alibis; the prosecutor has some kind of personal vendetta—

CLARA: Even blaming the victim herself.

MARTIN: Exactly. And seeing this, you've really got to ask yourself, is she just trying to pass the buck, or does this go much deeper, to an almost pathological detachment from reality?

CLARA: Now, I've got body-language expert Heidi Attenberg on the line, author of several books on the subject. What does this footage tell you, Heidi?

HEIDI: Thanks for having me, Clara. First of all, if you look at her posture during these answers, it's very composed, controlled. Her hands are folded, she doesn't twitch or move around at all; this tells us she's a very self-possessed person, someone who likes control.

CLARA: Too controlled, perhaps? I mean, this is a girl who's been locked up in prison for months now. I have to admit, I was expecting her to be . . . more raw, a lot more emotional . . . Even before the cameras started rolling, she sat quietly, barely speaking, like she was analyzing the scene.

HEIDI: Right, and then when she does have a more emotional moment—here, where she's talking to the parents and she starts crying, it's almost too emotional, coming after all that calm.

CLARA: You're saying she's faking it?

HEIDI: It's certainly possible. When people cry, for real, it's an almost involuntary action; they just can't help it. In the footage, if you keep your eye on Anna's hands—

CLARA: We're highlighting it on-screen here—

HEIDI: They stay folded, again, very composed. We'd expect to see her touch her face, wipe her eyes, maybe.

CLARA: That's fascinating. Now, can we backtrack a moment and show you some footage from before the interview? This is background roll of Anna talking to her legal team, she's got her lawyer there, and I want to show you this: Anna, getting very friendly with a young man we've identified as Lee Evans, age twenty-three; he's a junior consul at the American embassy in the Netherlands. We contacted the embassy for comment, and all they'll tell us is that Evans is not in Aruba in any official capacity. So, Heidi, what do we think? Is this a friend? A secret boyfriend? What does their body language say to you?

HEIDI: Whoever he is, they have a close relationship. You can see the physical affection when he touches her, the way she smiles at him.

CLARA: I would say he looks smitten with her.

HEIDI: Definitely not just a platonic relationship.

CLARA: Well, then, I've got to ask: What does this tell us about Anna Chevalier? I don't know about you, but if I'm in prison, awaiting a murder trial, boys are going to be the last thing on my mind. But here she is, apparently flirting with a young man, in plain view of everyone.

MARTIN: And if I can add, we know there was confusion about her and her boyfriend, Tate Dempsey, and their alibis, which were later recanted. Anna's always claimed he was the one who told her to lie, but looking at this tape, now I've got to wonder, you know—this is a girl with considerable feminine power. She's got this new guy under her spell, even from behind prison bars. Getting a loyal boyfriend to lie for her would be easy.

CLARA: And we'll get back to that later. But quickly, Martin, before the break, let's talk about her bruises. A lot of people were shocked to see them.

MARTIN: Right, and I know this fight, this prison fight, has gotten her a lot of sympathy from some quarters—

CLARA: Even though the prison authorities have assured me she's being kept in isolation now, away from other inmates.

MARTIN: I think seeing her like this, up close for the first time, has really driven home the reality of the situation. I mean, whether she's falsely accused or not, this is a young girl, a teenage girl locked up in a foreign prison with women—all kinds of criminals, most of them older than her.

CLARA: Now, Anna says she was the one who was attacked, but the other girl in the incident, a Johanna Pearson, she says Anna is the one who started it. That Anna flew at her in a rage—well, that sounds familiar, doesn't it? We've actually got some photos released to us, showing Johanna's injuries after the fight. Well, clearly, it looks like Anna got off lightly here.

MARTIN: Wow. I mean, that's some serious damage. The wounds to her face, a broken nose—

CLARA: And the hospital records say Anna broke two of this other girl's ribs.

MARTIN: I've got to say, this is . . . This changes a lot for me. If Anna can do this with her bare hands, then I bet I'm not the only one wondering, what would she be capable of with a knife in her hand?

CLARA: We'll be right back, after this message.

WAITING

I lie out in the prison yard every afternoon leading up to the trial. It's the only perk of isolation, I guess, that I'm alone in my tiny, fenced-off strip of land, far away from the rest of the inmates. I don't have to watch my back for fights, or gossip, I can just sprawl flat on my back in the yellowed grass, watching the sky.

If I tilt my head just right, I don't see the barbed-wire fencing or the top of the guards' tower, just the expanse of blue sky overhead. Every ten minutes or so, a plane takes off, banking in a wide semicircle across the island before heading out—to America, or Europe, or some other place that's anywhere but here. You'd think the ache would lessen watching them go. I must have seen hundreds of planes leave by now, day after day;

but every time, I feel it fresh, the same sharp longing in my chest, to be on one of those flights, squeezed up against some noisy seatmate in the tiny row, spilling peanuts and watching bad movies on an eight-inch screen.

Going home.

A wolf-whistle cuts through my reverie, sharp. I sit up, turning to find somebody leaning up against the barbed-wire fence. I squint, confused, until the figure shifts out of the sun, and I make out his familiar blond hair and ice-blue eyes.

Niklas.

I freeze.

"How did you get in?" I finally scramble to my feet, slowly approaching him. He's on the guard's side of the wire, lounging and smug in loose surfer shorts and one of his preppy pastel polo shirts, the collar popped. I study him suspiciously, staying back from the wire. "You're not allowed. Visiting hours finished this morning."

"I pulled some strings." Niklas's eyes trail up and down my body, with its baggy prison jumpsuit now dusty from the dirt.

"Why?" I fold my arms across my chest, remembering sharply how unnerved I felt around him, like he was imagining me naked. Of all the guys in the bar that first night, Elise had to pick the creepiest of them all.

"I saw you on TV." He smirks, casual with his hands in his pockets. "Nice show. I liked the part where you cried, very touching." His tone is amused, almost mocking.

I shiver. "What do you want?"

"Can't I pay a visit, show some moral support?" Niklas asks. "It must be tough for you here, all alone. Your friends all went back home, didn't they? Guess they didn't want to stick around for a killer."

"I didn't do it," I say quietly, before I can stop myself.

Niklas tilts his head at me. "Maybe not." He smirks again. "But that won't make a difference, will it?"

I take a step back as he chuckles to himself. "Found yourself a prison bitch yet? Some action in the showers?" He waggles his eyebrows suggestively. "I always wondered, you and Elise . . . I suggested you come join us, but she said that wasn't her style. That she didn't like sharing you."

I glare at him. "Stop it."

"Funny, isn't it?" Niklas looks around. "You were the ones saying I'd never make anything of my life, never *be* anyone, and here you are." The smile slips, and his eyes turn hard as glass. "You girls thought you were so much better than me, didn't you? Laughing at me, making me look a fool. Well, look where you are now." He gestures around at the bars and wire. "And Elise . . ."

"What?" I demand. "What about her?"

Niklas stares back at me, hard and unflinching. "Maybe the bitch got what she deserved."

VACATION

I down a shot of tequila, then another, the burn shooting down my throat like fire.

"Look at you go!" Elise whistles. "My girl's going wild!"

I ignore her and grab another shot, this one lurid blue and peppermint-sweet in my mouth. We're back in the bar from the first night on the island: the music still loud, the floors still sticky, the crowd still packed half-naked and sweaty in the shack of a room. I can't believe it was only three days ago we partied here, happy and blissfully naive.

I drain the glass, wincing at the taste.

"What's the deal?" Elise slips her arm around my waist and pulls me in close. "Not that I'm not a fan of this new party-girl you, but I thought you said you were taking it easy this week."

"Things change." I duck out of her embrace and cross the bar, to where Lamar's waiting against the wall, watching Chelsea and Mel dance and spin around the room.

"C'mon," I take his hand, pulling him toward the dance floor. "Tate won't dance. I'm all alone."

"The girls are out there."

"Yes, but I need a big, strong guy to protect me," I tease. "It's no fun without you."

"Just one song." Lamar laughs and lets me lead him into the crowd. It's a fast song, with a grinding dance bass. I feel the alcohol seep through me: the giddy lift, the sweet veil slipping over my mood. This is what I need, an escape from the doubts creeping into my mind and all the questions as heavy as the flaking pendant against Elise's neck.

I let the music take over, swaying close to Lamar. My arms are loose around his neck, my body against his. He's more built than Tate—muscles from the football field, taut under my fingertips as I run them across his shoulders. He backs away slightly.

"Are you okay?"

"Why wouldn't I be?" I spin out, and then back to his body again, close enough to feel the heat beneath his loose T-shirt. He's still frowning, but his body moves against mine with the beat of the music, slowly relaxing.

He's always liked me. It's nothing he's ever said or done,

but I can tell all the same. Like the way he'll look at me some-times, when I'm tucked in Tate's embrace, or when we're all dressed up for a night out—heels and skirts and hair falling down low—and I'll feel his eyes on me, edged with some-thing more than friendship. I never thought of doing any-thing about it, of course; it was just nice to know. Validation, I guess. And there's Chelsea, and Tate, always Tate, filling my mind until there's no room for anything else. But now, through the gentle haze of tequila and dark, pulsating lights, I wonder what it would be like if I'd picked Lamar instead. Easy, and sweet. Fun. Not this all-consuming hunger I have for Tate, the dagger-shards of insecurity slicing through me. He would be a satellite, not my gravity, the pull so strong it scares me sometimes.

I move closer, sliding my hands down his back. He sways for a moment, leaning in, and there's a longer moment when we're in sync, closer than we should be, then Lamar detaches himself from me awkwardly. "I should get back, to Chels . . ."

There's a hand on my shoulder, and Lamar's eyes go past me. "Hey, man," he says quickly. "We were just going to find you. She's all yours." He swiftly hands me off to Tate, then slips away through the crowd.

I slide against Tate, still moving, not pausing for a sec-ond. He places his hands loosely on my waist and gives me a crooked grin. "Should I be worried?" he teases.

"Maybe." I smile back, still feeling off balance. "Maybe I'm having a torrid affair with Lamar behind your back. You ever think about that?"

Tate laughs, pulling me closer. "No way," he says, stroking my hair possessively. "He wouldn't dare. You're my girl."

I fall into his arms, until he's half holding me up and we're barely moving on the dance floor, just standing there together. His.

It's weird and maybe wrong, but ever since Halloween— my costume pooling on the floor, an unfamiliar lust in his eyes—I've felt that way too, like I belong to him. Branded, by his kisses, his touch, all those nights grasping precious time and each other under the soft down covers in his room after dark. I'm as much his as Elise's now, but the one thought that never slipped in, never even drifted across my mind, was that they could belong to each other.

Without me.

"I need to sit down," I say, suddenly dizzy. I push him away, breaking for the edge of the dance floor. I grab on to the back of a booth, my head spinning. *This is crazy*, I tell myself, struggling to breathe. *I don't know anything; I shouldn't even be thinking . . .*

"What's up, baby doll?" Elise collapses beside me. I blink.

"I . . ." I stare at her, the smudge of black glitter liner on her lids, the gentle pink swell of her lips. "I don't . . ."

Her forehead creases into a frown. "Hey, you don't look so good. Come on." She takes my hand.

I don't move.

"Anna? Come on, you just need some fresh air, then you'll feel better." Elise smiles, reassuring me. "It was the fifth shot, wasn't it? What am I always telling you? You've got to pace yourself."

I nod, and follow her out toward the exit. She grabs a bottle of water from the bar as we pass, and then the night air is cool against my face. I pause, disoriented, as the blast of music and voices recedes behind the closed doors, replaced with the hum from other bars on the main street—traffic and passers-by, and the distant crashing of the ocean.

"Easy there," Elise murmurs, steering me carefully across the concrete walkway and onto the sand. "Give me some warning if you're going to barf, okay?"

She bends, undoing the straps of my wedge sandals in turn and gently lifting my feet out of them as I lean on her for balance. She straightens. "Rule one: suede and vomit don't mix." She grins at me, and I blink back, still dazed. In the dark out here, her eyes are almost violet, large and luminous.

Elise rolls them good-naturedly. "Man, you really went hard tonight." She kicks off her own shoes and then scoops both pairs in one hand, taking my arm in the other. "You good to walk?"

I nod again, and we slowly strike out across the sand, heading toward the dark stretch of ocean.

"Nik texted me again," Elise chatters, swinging our sandals back and forth. "I swear, it's like the tenth time tonight. Wanting to know where we'll be, what time I'll get there . . . It's kind of tacky, I mean, he seemed kind of cool to begin with, that whole 'lord and master of all he surveys' thing, but I don't know, he kind of gives me the creeps now." She pauses. "You know he did this weird role-play thing, when we were hooking up? He got off on the whole domination thing, you know, holding me down, trying to make me beg. I mean, I like getting thrown around as much as the next girl, but this was different. I don't know. . . ."

We come to a stop just on the shoreline, where the soft, cool sand turns damp from the slow sweep of the waves. Elise crumples to the ground, her legs folded beneath her. I sit, hugging my knees to my chest. "Feeling better?" she asks, concerned. "Here." She unscrews the cap and passes the water bottle to me. I take a sip. It's warm but clear in the back of my throat.

"So . . ." Elise pauses. She sifts sand through her fingertips. "You going to tell me what's wrong?"

"What?" I flinch. "Nothing's wrong."

Elise fixes me with an even gaze. "C'mon, Anna. You can't pull this with me. Something's been up with you all day. You barely said a word on the beach, and then you took that nap all afternoon—"

"I had a headache!" I protest weakly.

"And now you're drinking like you want to pass out," Elise finishes. "I know you, remember? Better than anyone. This isn't you."

I don't speak for a minute, watching the dark shadows of the waves. The words are there, jumbled up in my mind, but I can't bring myself to say them out loud. To accuse her, based on what—a bad feeling in the base of my spine, a mixed-up necklace, a shiver? It's crazy. They wouldn't do this to me. *She* wouldn't do this.

"I guess I'm just stressed," I say at last, looking down. I trace circles in the sand, pushing the grains into spiraling shapes. "College, and school ending. What happens after, you know?"

"That's ages away."

"It's not." I shake my head. "Graduation's in a couple of months, then we all go off in different directions. This could be the last time we're all together like this."

Elise reaches out and squeezes my hand. "It's okay. Some things aren't meant to last."

My eyes must have widened in horror because she laughs and says, "Not us. We're set, remember? You and me, doddering around an old estate somewhere in our nineties. *Grey Gardens*-ing it up."

"Turbans and paste jewelry," I agree quietly.

She grins. "With fifteen cats. And a hot pool boy."

I laugh. It feels like a release somehow. Relief. And I realize the worst part of my stupid suspicions wasn't even Tate, and his terrible betrayal, but the idea of losing Elise. Of her being gone from my life, cut away and buried for good.

Elise squeezes my hand again. "It'll be okay, I promise," she tells me. "It's you and me. I don't know about the others—maybe Mel, and Lamar, and AK and everyone come back every holiday, and we hang out and visit one another, and nothing changes. Or maybe we drift apart and don't speak until our ten-year reunion. Shit happens, you know? You can't control it. But us? We're forever."

I lace my fingers through hers in response. "I know it's stupid," I say, feeling as foolish for the things I haven't said as the things I did. "It's high school. We always couldn't wait for it to be done. But now, everything so close . . . I like how it is, right now. I don't want anything to change."

"But it does," Elise says softly. "Everything changes. But it can be better. Think about it, if we both get in to USC . . . you and me, California. We can hang out on the beach like this all the time, and not die of hypothermia."

I smile, leaning to rest my head on her shoulder. I never told her I've spent these last weeks split, wavering between schools on the East and West Coasts, between proximity to her or to Tate. Now I'm glad I didn't make a big deal of it, because it doesn't feel like a choice anymore. Of course I'm going with her. Of course.

"Do you love me?" I ask, repeating our familiar refrain.

"You know I do."

"How much?"

"Miles and miles."

We sit on the beach until the world slowly stops spinning on its axis, then head back across the sand to the bar. I'm almost not surprised to find Melanie waiting outside the back exit, pacing back and forth and clutching her phone.

She sees us approach, and rushes up to meet us. "Where were you guys?" she demands. "I've been texting and calling. Why didn't you tell me you were going somewhere?" she adds, a whining note to her voice. "I thought something happened."

"Jesus, we were gone ten minutes," Elise says, and sighs. "Do you want me to wear a tracking chip?"

Mel blinks. "I was worried, that's all."

"So don't be." Elise pushes past her to head back inside the bar. The blast of music swallows her up, and I make to follow but Mel moves to block my path.

"Why do you have to keep doing this?" She glares at me fiercely.

I step back. "What?"

"Dragging her off somewhere, always coming between us." Mel's eyes are wide and almost tearful in the dim light, and her words pour out in a furious torrent. "I know you hate me, but she's my friend too, and you won't let her spend any time with me at all."

"Let her?" I repeat slowly, caught there in the doorway. I don't have space for Mel's desperate insecurities, not after days of her sighing and whining and moaning, tagging along in the background for everything. "For fuck's sake, since when does Elise do anything she doesn't want to do?" I demand. "If she's not hanging out with you anymore, that's her choice. It's got nothing to do with me."

Mel's mouth drops open. "She would never . . . ," she manages, as she starts to cry. "We were friends first! Until you stole her from me. Everything was great until you came along—"

"What are we, stuck in grade school?" I cut her off, my anger blazing now—at her or myself, I'm not sure. I just know that Mel is pouring all her fear and insecurity out onto the dark asphalt in front of me, when I've fought so hard to keep mine hidden. *This could be me*, I realize in a terrible flash. *This could be my future.* Without Elise: abandoned and alone. "Grow up. It's not finders keepers, okay?" I tell her, my voice ringing out, harsh. "Maybe if you were less of a whiny, needy brat, she'd still want you around."

Mel recoils, as if I'd hit her. "You're such a bitch!" she cries.

"Hey, those are Elise's words, not mine. You think she's your bestie?" I add. "You should hear what she says when you're not around. 'Mel's such a baby,'" I mimic. "'She's, like, obsessed with me.'"

"Stop it!" Mel yells, her mascara running in two pathetic streams down her cheeks. But I can't, not with the anger flooding hot in my veins.

"She makes fun of you, how clingy you are," I continue, relentless. "She doesn't get why you don't just take the hint and leave us alone for good."

"You're lying." Mel sobs.

"I'm not. She didn't even want you coming on vacation," I tell her. "I was the one who said to invite you. I figured we could put up with you for another few months, until graduation, but God, look at you—you don't know when to give it a break!"

Mel gives another sob, then whirls around and flees. I watch her hurry down the street, unsteady in high heels, and feel a sobering wash of shame. I shouldn't have done that, I know it right away. I shouldn't have been so cruel, but she just kept pushing me—acting like this was all my fault. And her naked desperation . . .

I shiver, turning back to enter the bar. It's dark and loud inside, and I fight my way through the crowd, looking for the familiar faces of our group. Elise is up by the bar, a flash of red and blond, and I duck past a group of drunken frat-boy guys, yelling along with the music.

Her back is turned when I reach her. "I told you, it was just a one-time thing," she's saying. She shifts, and I see the guy beside her: Niklas.

"Everything good?" I ask, positioning myself between them.

"Just peachy," Elise says, and nods, but I see the relief in her smile.

"The lovely Anna," Niklas drawls. He grabs my hand, kissing it before I can pull away.

"Let me buy you ladies a drink."

"I'm good, thanks," I reply, but Elise beams.

"A margarita for me."

As Niklas turns to order from the dreadlocked bartender, I lean in closer to Elise. "I thought he creeped you out," I murmur.

She laughs back. "Doesn't mean I can't take his drinks. What did Mel want, anyway? Don't tell me she was calling in a Missing Persons because we were gone five minutes."

I sigh. "She freaked out, it was a whole thing. I'll tell you later." I glance around. "You seen Tate anywhere?"

"Yeah, I think he was fucking some tourist up against the bathroom wall."

"Elise!"

"What?" She grins. "I'm just messing with you. I'm sure he's sitting quietly in a corner, gazing at photos of you."

I shove her lightly. "Don't say shit like that, okay?"

"Why? Worried Prince Charming's going to run around on you?" Elise's tone is light, but I swear I see something flicker in her expression. Or maybe that's just the five shots still spinning in my system, and the crash of the electronic dance beats. I shake my doubts away.

"No, of course not. I trust him," I reply forcefully, but I can't help adding, "He knows it would break my heart."

Elise doesn't flinch, just pulls me into a hug. "And then I would have to break his skull." She laughs.

I rest my cheek against her hair for a moment, calmed. Behind her back, Niklas is claiming a margarita from the bartender, a vast frothy concoction with fruit and a tiny umbrella balanced on the lip of the glass. I smile to myself for a moment—for all her bad-girl posturing, Elise will always choose the fruity, girly drink over a straight whiskey shooter—and then I catch a glimpse of something, out of the corner of my tired eyes. Niklas's hand, passing over the drink. A flash of reflection, as if from glass, or a vial. And then it's gone, back in his pocket again, and he's turning to hand Elise the drink with a bland smile.

"Ready to get this party started for real?" he asks.

Elise takes the glass and raises it to her lips.

THE TRIAL

"So you saw the victim at the bar, the night before she was killed, isn't that right, Mr. van Oaten? Before the group left, around two a.m.?"

"Yes."

"What was the nature of your interaction?"

"I don't understand."

"What did you do?" Gates clarifies, pacing in front of the witness stand. "You fought, did you not?"

"No." Niklas slouches back, his arms folded. He looks utterly at ease, as if he's relaxing in front of the TV, not in the middle of a tense and crowded courtroom.

"No?" Gates repeats. "But we have statements from several

people at the club; they all say you fought with Miss Warren. In fact, she threw a drink at you."

Niklas smirks. "It was nothing. A lovers' quarrel."

He looks for me across the courtroom, and meets my eyes with that same smug, chilling smile I saw through the barbed wire of the prison fence.

I shiver.

The trial is winding down now. Dekker's prosecution case dragged on, but now that it's the defense's turn, the list of people appearing on my behalf is painfully short. Gates has done what he could: attacking the flaws in Dekker's case any way he can. He sent a parade of forensics experts up on the stand, arguing everything from how the time of death was wide open to how the crime scene was contaminated and the blood spatter suggests someone taller and larger dealt the fatal wounds.

But our strongest hope has always been Niklas. With Juan still vanished into thin air, Nik was the only suspect we can put up there on the stand, to show how he makes more sense as the killer: how he had motive, and opportunity, and practice climbing up to Elise's balcony. All through the trial, I've been holding on to this brief shard of hope—that once they see him, sneering and slouching, cavalier in the face of Elise's brutal death—the judge would have no option but to think twice about my guilt.

I sit forward in my seat, willing Niklas's mask to slip, for some incriminating words to slip out.

"So, the night before the victim's murder, you fought—wait, I'm sorry, you *quarreled* with her." Gates layers on the sarcasm. "Why?"

Niklas shrugs, nonchalant. "She was jealous, of my . . . attention. You know how girls are." He flashes a conspiratorial look at the judge. She glares back, unmoved.

"She wasn't angry because you attempted to spike her drink with liquid Ecstasy?" Gates demands. Niklas snaps his head back around.

"What? No." His face darkens. "Who said that?"

"Again, we have statements from several witnesses at the club—"

"Objection!" Dekker rises. "The witnesses say Miss Chevalier accused Mr. van Oaten of spiking the drink. We have no evidence that any drugs were actually—"

"Withdrawn." Gates sighs.

I knew this would happen, but I still dig my nails into my palm with frustration. They warned me that without chemical tests, and drink samples, it was my word against his that Niklas even spiked the drink at all.

As if reading my mind, Niklas gives me another look, this one dark and full of loathing.

"So, Mr. van Oaten," Gates continues, "You didn't attempt to drug the victim that night?"

"No." Niklas keeps his gaze fixed on me, furious.

"Have you ever taken liquid Ecstasy?" Gates presses.

"No."

"Never? Interesting. But did you know that it's a drug most commonly used by date rapists—"

"Objection!" Dekker flies to his feet.

The judge nods. "Sustained."

Gates walks back to our table and leafs through some papers, regrouping. "He's lying," I whisper frantically, but Gates just shakes his head at me and gestures to me to keep quiet.

"The victim rejected your advances that night, isn't that true?" Gates returns to the stand. "She insulted you, publicly, made a laughingstock of you, in fact?"

Niklas shrugs again. "It was nothing."

"You weren't hurt, or angry at all?" Gates asks. "A pretty girl, making fun of you, in front of your friends . . ."

"I didn't care what she thought." Niklas is relaxed again, his mask back in place.

"Why not?"

"Would you care what a dog thought? A roach?" Niklas smirks. "She was just some American slut."

There's an audible intake of breath in the courtroom, and even the judge's mouth drops open a little. I can picture Judy and Charles behind me, listening to this, but as much as my heart breaks for them, I feel hope rise again in my chest. This is what we need.

"You didn't value her opinion," Gates muses. "What about her consent?"

"Objection!" Dekker leaps up again before Niklas can reply. "There is no evidence that Mr. van Oaten made any attempt to rape the victim. In fact, we've heard testimony that their encounters were entirely consensual."

Gates steps up too. "Miss Chevalier has testified that the victim was increasingly uncomfortable with Mr. van Oaten's sexual fetishes—"

"Yes, well she would say that," Dekker interrupts with a snort. "I urge Your Honor, please stop the defense's smearing Mr. van Oaten's good name. These are not allegations to be taken lightly."

"Yes, yes." Judge von Koppel stops him, then pauses for a long moment. I wait, clutching the table in front of me, silently urging her to let Gates keep going. All the things Elise said about Niklas being weird in bed—dominating, wanting to make her beg—it would fit with the murder. We just have to push him far enough.

After thinking, Judge von Koppel sighs. "I'm afraid I have to agree with the prosecution on this. It's hearsay. We have nothing except the defendant's testimony regarding Miss Warren's feelings. Please move on."

My heart falls. *Stop!* I want to cry out. *He needs to answer this. You have to see!* But Gates just checks his notes again, figuring out another move.

"Where were you, the afternoon of the murder?" Gates asks, but I already know it's over. We'll get nothing from him, not when he's lying like this.

"At home," Niklas drawls. "With my father."

"The whole afternoon?"

"Yes."

"What were you doing?"

Niklas shrugs. "I don't remember."

"But you remember that you were home? The whole afternoon?"

"Sure."

"Is there anything that can verify your story?" Gates presses. "Security records, perhaps. You live on a large estate—I assume there are security cameras and alarms posted."

Niklas lifts his body forward toward the mike as if it's a great effort. "The system was down."

"Down?" Gates repeats. "For how long?"

Niklas shrugs. "I don't know."

"So you have no way of proving—"

"Objection!" Dekker rolls his eyes this time. "The witness has accounted for his whereabouts the afternoon in question. We have statements from him and his father."

The judge surveys Gates over her glasses. "I agree, we should move on. Do you have anything else to ask?"

Gates pauses for a moment, but there's no delaying the inevitable. "No. No further questions."

The judge bangs her gavel, calling a short recess. Disappointment crashes through me. After everything, I thought Niklas was the key—that once he was up there on the stand, it would all come out. The drugs, the balcony, the fight. Surely they would have to see how crazy he is. How dangerous.

I was naive to believe it would make a difference at all.

The crowded courtroom disperses briefly in a wave of chatter and conversation. Gates takes a seat beside me at the table, staring blankly at his notes. "That's it?" I exclaim, fighting to keep my voice low. "Their security cameras conveniently go down the afternoon she's murdered, and he's still not a suspect? He could have done it!" My voice breaks with frustration.

"His father gave him an alibi." Gates shrugs, helpless.

"He could be lying to protect him!"

"Even if that's true, there's nothing we can do. Niklas's father is a respected man; he has interests in shipping, and hotels, and—"

"Owns half the island," I finish, sitting down with a thump. "I know."

I look around, watching Niklas saunter from the witness stand. He flutters me a wave as he passes, and then heads on back to meet his father: a large blond man in a designer suit, flanked by other lawyers. They smile and nod, clearly pleased with Niklas's testimony.

His lies.

"This is how it works, isn't it?" I murmur softly, seeing it all play out so clearly now. For weeks, I've had my faith in justice chipped steadily away with every one of Dekker's half-truths and sneering implications, but now, the last fragile pieces crumble into nothing. This is a sham, all of it.

"Niklas, and Tate—they've got money, they can buy their way out of anything." I realize. "Say what they like, just to protect themselves. And here I am . . ." I trail off, thinking of my one lawyer compared to their dozens; Dad's company, sinking under the weight of my fees and expenses; the extra mortgage on the house, and all the fresh worry lines on my dad's face. "It's no contest, is it?"

Gates doesn't reply, he just takes off his spectacles and polishes them on his tie, exhaling slowly.

That's when I know—it's over.

I swallow back a sudden rush of tears. It's not his fault. He's done what he can, but sometimes, David doesn't beat Goliath—not when they've got an army at their disposal.

A noise comes from the back of the courtroom. We turn.

It's Lee, pushing through the crowd, flustered but determined. His shirt is rumpled, and he looks as if he hasn't slept in a week. He hasn't been in court the last few days, but I figured it was just too much for him—the memories of his sister's trial.

"I've got it!" he announces, arriving at our table.

"Got what?" I ask, confused, but Lee doesn't answer me— he's passing a slim memory drive case to Gates, carefully, like a treasure.

"It's all there, just like Carlsson said." Lee catches his breath, running one hand through his hair. "Just play the files. The first one's the official cut, then the full clip."

Gates grasps the memory drive, and slaps Lee on the back. "You did it." He smiles, as if he can't believe it.

Lee gives nod. "Time to nail the bastard."

"Someone tell me what's going on?" I ask again. My heart is already beating faster—their energy infectious even though I still have no idea what's caused this change. "Is there new evidence? What's happened?"

Lee turns, giving me a happy grin, just as the judge returns to the room and people begin taking their seats again. "Something good," he promises as von Koppel bangs her gavel for quiet. "It's the break we've been looking for."

I don't want to get my hopes up, but I stay forward in my seat, on edge, waiting for their reveal. After Niklas's testimony turned out to be a joke, we need something now—anything to turn this trial around.

The judge looks up from her notes, over to Gates. "Any further witnesses?" she asks.

"Yes, Your Honor. For my last witness, I'd like to call Klaus Dekker back to the stand."

Dekker looks surprised, but he makes an expression as if to say, *Sure, why not?* He saunters up to the witness chair and settles in, looking amused.

Gates loads up the memory stick, bringing up the video on the screen overhead. "You've been in charge of the investigation from the beginning, is that true?"

"Yes," Dekker replies bluntly.

"And all evidence, all materials relating to the case, they run through you?"

"Everything." Dekker nods. "We have a chain of command, and I'm at the top."

"So you decided what leads to pursue, and, in fact, what evidence to present here in court today?"

"I have presented all evidence relevant to the case, yes." Dekker frowns, like he's trying to figure out what Gates is leading toward.

He's not the only one. I wait, breathing softly, praying that this big break is something real and substantial, and won't just fade away like Niklas or Juan or all the other arguments we've made these last weeks.

"Can you tell me what this is?" Gates asks. He hits the

controller, and a familiar video begins to play, up on the screen.

I exhale, disappointed. We've already seen this: the security footage from the grocery store down the street from the house. There's a date and time stamp in the corner showing the afternoon of the murder, and Elise is clear in view, idly browsing the snack aisle.

Lee leans forward from the seat behind me and puts his hand on my shoulder. "Just wait," he whispers with another grin.

Gates hits pause on the video, still waiting for an answer.

Dekker answers cautiously. "It's the tape from the store, the last time the victim was seen alive."

"You already showed us this footage, I know." Gates smiles. All his previous weary defeat has disappeared, now he's the shark, circling for the kill. "In fact, you used it to establish the time of death, and prove that Tate Dempsey couldn't have been the one who killed her."

"Yes, that's right." Dekker is looking worried now. His eyes dart to the back of the courtroom, like he's seeking someone out. "The time of death gives him an alibi, but not her."

"And by her, you mean the defendant."

"Yes, of course," Dekker snaps. He's riled, I realize, watching carefully. He knows what this is about—what's coming. Lee's grip on my shoulder tightens in matching anticipation.

ABIGAIL HAAS

"Where did you get this tape?"

"From a source," Dekker replies. "An outside investigator hired by the Dempsey family."

"But this isn't the full tape, is it?"

There's a beat. Silence. Dekker opens his mouth, but nothing comes out.

The judge leans over. "Detective?"

"I . . . I'm not sure what you mean." Dekker's sweating, his forehead shiny and red. He looks guilty, although of what crime, we don't know yet. The courtroom is totally still, all of us waiting for the next words.

"Then let me show you." Gates beams. "This is the video you submitted as evidence." He starts the video again and the frames run through on the screen, grainy and black-and-white. Elise enters the store, browses the aisles. She grabs a bag of chips and a soda, pays, and leaves. The video cuts.

"But that wasn't the only footage given to you, was it?" Gates says loudly. Dekker is silent. "There was footage from a second camera, outside the store."

This is news to me—and everyone else. Fevered whispers fill the courtroom.

Gates hits play and another video starts, this one angled from the doorway, with a view out into the busy street. We see Elise stroll toward the store and enter, but there's another figure in the frame, several steps behind.

326

Juan.

I inhale in a rush. Even in the grainy recording, it's him: dreadlocks and a loose linen shirt. He follows Elise down the street, then drops back as she enters the store. He stops, waiting on the other side of the road.

Gates pauses on him lurking there, watching the grocery store. "Is this the man known to you as Juan?" he asks.

"Yes," Dekker replies quietly.

"The man named as a suspect by the defense, whom the defendant says argued with the victim and followed them back on their first day."

Dekker is silent, but then offers a grudging "Yes."

"And in this footage, does he appear to be following the victim, again? Stalking her?"

Dekker doesn't say a word.

"Let's take a look for ourselves." Gates hits play again.

The video continues: Juan loiters opposite the grocery store. Elise emerges, just a blond head in the frame. As she exits to the right of the camera shot, Juan crosses the street, moving closer toward us—and Elise. Gates freezes the video just before he disappears from the frame: the large figure heading determinedly after Elise.

There's a long silence.

I can't believe it—that the video existed, all this time. Dekker saw this and tried to bury it. I knew he hated me, but

I didn't realize he would tamper with evidence just to see me go down.

Lee's hand slips from my shoulder, but I reach to grab it, holding tight. We share a breathless, hopeful smile as Gates circles for the kill.

"When did you decide to edit this video?" Gates demands.

"I . . . It wasn't a decision, as such," Dekker fumbles. "There were many leads—"

"But this offers clear proof that Juan was the last person to see the victim alive."

"We don't know—"

Gates talks over him. "So not only did you ignore a crucial suspect but you deliberately withheld evidence that would help clear my client!"

"I—"

"Why did you ignore this evidence?" Gates demands. "Why pursue this unjustified and deeply flawed prosecution against my client when you knew full well there were better suspects more likely to have committed this crime?"

"We tried to locate Juan," Dekker argues weakly. "But we couldn't find him."

"And you needed a suspect," Gates mocks him. "Someone to put on trial, to prove to the world you weren't a bungling, incompetent detective. So you picked my client—a young woman with no criminal record, no motive, no history of violence—"

"She does, she could have—"

"You picked her to be the scapegoat for this farce of a trial!" Gates finishes with a roar.

Silence. Dekker is slumped in his seat, sweaty and broken. He knows he fucked up, and now we all know it too.

"No further questions," Gates finishes. "The defense rests."

THE TRIAL

After Dekker is humiliated on the stand, my dad presses Gates to file for a mistrial. "We can argue incompetence, withheld evidence," he argues, but Gates stands firm.

"A mistrial isn't the end," he explains. "Another prosecutor could launch another case, and then we'd wind up back here, a year, two years from now. They might not even let her go home before a new trial."

"Seeing this through is the only way," Lee agrees. "An 'innocent' verdict finishes this for good."

But what if I'm not found innocent after all? I want to ask, but they're all so upbeat and optimistic, I can't bring myself to be the lone voice of warning. "The video changes everything," they say over again, with a breathless enthusiasm that tells me

I'LL NEVER TELL

just how dire my situation was before. Now we have proof of Juan's stalking and Dekker's vendetta against me. The judge will have to question everything, and see Dekker for the corrupt man he really is.

I try to stay calm, but their hope is infectious, like sunlight warming me in my dark cell, and I sleep straight through the night for the first time in months. When I'm taken to meet Dad in the conference room of the courthouse the next morning, he greets me with a box of fresh-baked pastries and a clutch of brown manila envelopes.

"What are those?" I ask, sinking my teeth into a soft pillow of flaky donut.

"College letters," he replies with a smile. "They came for you months ago, but I didn't want to get your hopes up, before . . ."

My hand freezes, outstretched. "But won't it jinx things?" I whisper. It feels way too soon to be thinking about the future, not with the trial still in progress and everything still ready to fall apart.

"Gates is going to finish up the defense today," Dad says. "He thinks we should end on the video, and not throw anything else to distract the judge. So, with closing arguments and some final motions, we'll be wrapped by tomorrow." He gives me another hopeful smile. "The judge could have a verdict before the weekend."

I sit down with a thump. "So soon?" I feel a shiver.

"I called and spoke to the admissions people. They all deferred your place until next year, if you want it. But you've got options. Your college fund is safe," he adds awkwardly. "The money, from your mother. I never touched it. . . ." He pushes the envelopes toward me again, and despite every instinct screaming that this is a bad idea, that I'm tempting fate somehow if I look, I reach for them.

University of Chicago. Bryn Mawr. Georgetown. Smith. USC.

I open each envelope in turn, the paper already slit and waiting for me to slide out the cover sheets.

Congratulations!

Acceptances, a fat stack of them. I line them up in turn on the table, still feeling strangely uneasy. When I pictured getting my college letters, this was never how I imagined it. I was going to be waiting for the mailman at home, grabbing the pack from his outstretched hand and racing into the house to excitedly tear them open, already speed-dialing Elise.

"I'm sorry I opened them," Dad apologizes, watching my face. I can feel the happy expectation radiating from him. "I didn't want you to see, if there were any rejections."

"I got in," I say softly, staring at the admissions booklets, the glossy pictures of undergraduates strolling across leafy campuses. It's a world I haven't let myself imagine, or even think about, the great prospect of *after*.

Dad beams. "I know you want to try the West Coast," he adds, but I shake my head.

"We were going together," I say, stroking the cover of the USC packet. "It wouldn't be right, walking around there, without her." I take a breath. "Besides, I want to stay close to home—to you. An East Coast school."

Dad smiles widens. "That . . . that would be great, sweetheart. I'd love to see you."

I nod, still staring at the papers when the guard comes to summon us to the courtroom. My future, right there on the table: one path, the possibilities, but only if I make it out of this hell first.

I'm close. So close.

THE TRIAL

I walk into court the next morning knowing it's one of the very last times. There's nothing but legal motions and closing arguments now, before the trial ends and it's all down to Judge von Koppel and her cool, blond deliberations.

I expected to feel relief, but instead, I almost don't want it to end. This trial has been the only constant thing in my life for months now. First, it was the light on the horizon, keeping me going through the endless nights in prison. Now, there's a comfort to the daily routine: dressing up in normal clothes; fixing my hair as best I can in a borrowed mirror; drinking in the view from the darkened windows of the prison van as we drive across the island to the courtroom.

It's not just me—we've all fallen into a regular pattern

here. Dad fetches coffee on his way in for us all; Elise's parents sit in the same spot in the back left of the courtroom every day, staring straight ahead through every witness and piece of evidence. Even Dekker has his small habits and rituals, like the way he'll straighten the papers on his table into perfect angles before the judge calls us all to order, and unbutton his jacket before standing to interrogate a witness. I know it sounds crazy, that something as dramatic as a murder trial could become normal and everyday, but it is to me now. And soon, everything will be different.

"Ready?" Lee gives me an encouraging grin as the judge settles in at the front of the room and we take our seats. "Nearly over now."

He's not the only one smiling. The mood in the courtroom is visibly lighter—they know we're at the end too, and I guess the reporters and families are all relieved to be able to go home soon. Tate and Lamar and everyone have had to stay on the island throughout the trial, in case they were needed to testify. Only AK comes to court every day, probably making notes for his televised trial roundup on the *Clara Rose Show* each night. But the others stay away, and although being stuck in Aruba isn't the worst fate, I know they must be ready to leave the minute the judge says that they can.

I'm the only one here who's scared for this to be over.

"Counselors?" The judge bangs her gavel for silence.

Gates rises, but the other table sits empty—Dekker nowhere to be seen.

Von Koppel frowns. "Have we seen the prosecution judge?"

There's silence. I look around, confused. Dekker is always punctual and precise—in all the weeks of the trial, he's never once been late.

"Let's try to find him." The judge doesn't look impressed. She beckons Gates and a couple of people closer, and they begin to murmur in hushed tones.

I sit back, on edge now. "Where do you think he is?" I ask Lee. I drum a pencil against the table, my nerves suddenly jittering.

"Who knows? Maybe he had a crisis of faith and is off contemplating his sins," he jokes, but I shake my head.

"Don't."

"Sorry." He clears his throat. "Have you thought about what you'll do?" Lee leans in close. His brown hair is longer than when I first met him, months ago, and brushes against his collar. "When you get out of here, I mean. What's the first thing on your list?"

I feel that flash of panic again, like he's tempting fate, but I know he's only trying to keep my spirits up. I pause to think about it. "A bath," I say at last. "I'm going spend a whole day in the tub—lock the door, use a whole bottle of bubble bath, just lie there for hours."

Lee grins. "Sounds good."

"What about you?"

He shrugs. "I don't know, go back and see my folks, I think."

"You won't go back to the embassy?"

Lee gives me a look. "I don't think so. Technically they're calling this leave, but, I don't think I'll be welcome back in the diplomatic corps again, at least not for a while."

"I'm sorry," I say softly. He's never said anything, but I know being a part of my team has caused all kinds of problems with his job, and after Clara Rose started speculating about our relationship, it only got worse.

He shakes his head. "It's not your fault. I was thinking about going to law school, anyway, do this for real."

"You mean rescuing damsels in distress from foreign jails?" I joke. "You should, you'd be great. But first," I add, "can I recommend a haircut?"

He laughs. "You should talk."

"Don't remind me." I groan, touching the split, sun-damaged ends of my hair. It seems silly, to care about my appearance when the rest of my life is on the line, but I quickly found out in prison that vanity can almost be a form of hope. You try to keep hold of the person you used to be, with all the same shallow, flimsy worries, because letting them go would be a form of surrender. "I'll put that on my list," I tell him. "First, a bath, then eight hours in a salon."

"I think you look great," Lee says, almost shy. Our eyes meet for a minute, and then there are footsteps, loud, as Dekker sweeps in. He's clutching an armful of papers, his assistant scurrying behind.

"And here he is," the judge says icily. "I believe we have some pre-closing motions to argue. Shall we go to my chambers?"

"A moment, Your Honor." Dekker deposits the papers and pauses to take a breath. He turns and shoots me a look so full of triumph that it freezes the blood in my veins. "I would like to call a witness to the stand."

"What's going on?" I whisper, anxious, but Gates is already approaching the front of the room with Dekker quickly following behind. They argue there for a moment with the judge, their voices too low to reach me. "What's he doing?" I ask Lee again, but he just shrugs helplessly. "I don't know."

"But he can't, can he?" I ask. "The prosecution finished; it's against the rules."

"Sometimes, the judge will let them," Lee watches the front of the room. "If it's important enough."

Dekker's new witness must be, because after another few minutes of hushed argument, Gates returns, downcast. "She's allowing it," he says. We all look to one another, not sure what this means. "Is there anything I need to know?" Gates leans in close, his expression like stone. "If there is, you need to tell me right now."

"I . . . No!" I shake my head helplessly. "You know everything."

Dekker clears his throat. "I'd like to call Melanie Chan back to the stand."

Mel?

My head snaps around to watch her enter the courtroom. She's dressed in a neat blouse and pleated skirt, hair smoothed back under a wide blue headband. Mel takes a seat in the witness chair, and raises her hand to swear the oath.

"Anna?" Gates urges again, under his breath. "What does she know?"

"Nothing," I insist again, but Gates doesn't look convinced. I wrack my brain, but nothing comes to mind—nothing that would have Dekker swaggering around so confidently, like the trial is as good as won. "She was off diving with the others, she wasn't even there that day!"

Gates nods grimly, scribbling a note. "Let's see what this is about, then," he says, turning back to the front.

There's silence, and then Dekker begins.

"You already testified here before, Miss Chan."

"Yes."

"But you contacted my office yesterday to retract that testimony."

"I . . . Yes." Mel meets my eyes briefly, then looks away.

"So what you told this court several weeks ago wasn't true?"

"No, it was, I just . . . I didn't tell you everything."

Gates leaps to his feet. "Objection! The witness has admitted perjuring herself. Anything else she has to say now cannot be seen as reliable."

"I'm inclined to agree." Von Koppel flickers an eyebrow to Dekker.

"I understand. However, given the gravity of the situation, and the fact that the witness voluntarily recanted her statements knowing full well the consequences she'd face. I believe her testimony should be heard."

I hold my breath until the judge nods. "Carry on, for now."

My heart sinks. I look desperately at Mel, but her gaze is fixed straight down on her hands, clasped in her lap.

"Miss Chan." Dekker approaches gently, his tone soft and encouraging. "What did you tell me, when you contacted me?"

Mel looks up. "Anna knew. About the affair, that Elise and Tate were hooking up."

I freeze.

"She says she didn't, but she's lying," Mel continues, her voice ringing out. "She knew, and she hated Elise for it. She was so jealous, she couldn't take it."

I grab Gates's arm. "It's not true," I whisper. "She's making it all up!"

Gates shakes me off, staring intently at Mel.

"How do you know this?" Dekker prompts her.

"I heard them fighting about it, before she died."

"But you were on the dive trip, on the other side of the island."

Mel shakes her head. "This was the day before. In the afternoon. Everyone else was on the beach, but I came back to the house, and I heard them fighting. Anna was screaming and yelling. It was so loud. I stayed for a minute, but I didn't know what to do, so I left."

I shake my head, heart pounding. It's lies, all of it. There was no fight—none. We were back at the house, mixing drinks and hanging out, laughing over some dumb Internet video. That was the night we went out to the bar again—when Elise and I went to go sit on the sand, and I wound up yelling at Mel.

I stop. Is this what it's about—the things I said to her, about her tagging along? Could she really be so petty, to lie up on the witness stand just to pay me back?

Dekker wheels around. "You heard the defendant fighting with the victim?"

"Yes." Mel's lips are pressed together in a thin line, determined. "She was saying, 'How could you do this to me? I'll never forgive you. I'll kill you.' All kinds of things."

"'I'll kill you.'" Dekker stops. "You heard her say that? Threaten the victim?"

"Yes," Mel says firmly. "That's what she said."

I can't take this. It's hard to breathe, like something's pressing down on my chest. I clutch for Gates again, but he's staring stonily ahead.

The judge interrupts, leaning down toward Mel. "Do you understand the charges for lying under oath, Miss Chan?"

She nods again. "I'm sorry. I know I shouldn't have, but I didn't want to make her look bad." Mel's lip trembles, but there's something defiant in her expression. "I'm sorry, Anna." She looks out at me, tearful. "I didn't want to think that you could do it. But I have to tell the truth."

"She's lying!" I can't stop myself. I yell out, rising to my feet. "Can't you see it? She's lying!" I feel hands grabbing me—Gates, or Lee, I don't know—but I struggle against them. "Why are you doing this to me?" I scream at Mel as they drag me from the room. "Why won't you tell them the truth?!"

THE FUNERAL

My mom dies on a Wednesday, the week before Christmas.

Any other year, there would be parties and holiday dinners, cards and twinkling lights, and holly wreaths hanging from the mantel. We would bake sugar cookies from a box mix and decorate the tree, playing carols and old Frank Sinatra songs. But instead, I sit at her bedside, watching her die.

It's not like the movies. She doesn't pull me close and whisper inspirational words—about how I'm brave and strong, and she'll always be with me—before gently closing her eyes and drifting away. No, my mother dies slowly. Angry. She falls away, then claws her way back with a gasp and a groan, clinging to the edge of the world with brittle, cracked nails and wheezing breaths. She spits and babbles, furious that this isn't the peaceful slide into oblivion she was promised. It was her decision all along, but still, her body fights death—betraying her all over again as she begs for an end, and it keeps holding on.

It takes the whole day for my mother to die. I sit there, clutching her cold hand, watching every minute of it.

"Anna?" The voice comes in the dark, hesitant. I look up numbly to find Elise, silhouetted in the light from the hallway. "Anna, baby, it's time to get ready."

I don't reply. I'm on the floor at the foot of my bed, my legs folded beneath me; a half-empty bottle of vodka at my side. I don't remember how I got here, or how long I've been huddled under my comforter. It's days since Mom finally sucked in her last desperate breath and ceased to exist; they've slipped past in a dark blur of sympathy and hushed voices, and strangers traipsing in and out of the house; my dad's blank stare, and the welcoming cocoon of my bedroom and the black burn of alcohol in my veins.

"I'll pick you out something to wear." Elise pries the bottle from my limp hand, then crosses the room to open my drapes. I flinch from the light that floods in from outside: gray clouds and snowy winter skies. "Did you eat something?" She crouches beside me. "Anna? Can you remember when you last had something to eat?"

I stare at her blankly.

"Okay, I'll go fix you something." Elise strokes my hair softly. "People have been bringing casseroles, there's all kinds of stuff. You get in the shower." She takes me by the shoulders and pulls me slowly to my feet.

I sag against her, my head on her shoulder. I'm empty, too numb to even try. She holds me up. "Come on, Anna. You have to."

I shake my head. "I can't."

"I know, but it's just today; you just have to get through today."

I stay there, clinging on to her like she's the only thing keeping me from going under. And maybe she is. Our fight is nothing now—it was swept aside the minute I found out about Mom's plan to end treatment. I called Elise right away, hyperventilating through my tears, and she was on my doorstep within the hour. We drove all night, just circling the city, the neon lights blurring through my tears as I huddled there in the passenger's seat beside her and tried to understand. But I can't—not then, and not now, either.

Finally, Elise pulls away. She cradles my face. "I know you don't want to do this, but I'm here, okay? I'll be right by you, the whole time. I'm not going anywhere."

I manage a nod.

"Let's get this over with, then."

I let her steer me to the bathroom and into the shower. I barely notice as Elise undresses me, I just stand, dumb, under the hot jets of water, while she bends me like a doll to rub shampoo into my scalp and carefully rinse the suds away. Back in the bedroom, she feeds me lasagna from a Tupperware dish, then dresses me—fresh underwear, thick tights, a plain black dress she or my dad must have bought, because she lifts it, fresh, from tissue paper in a crisp paper bag by the door. She brushes my hair out and braids it, damp against my neck, then paints my face with concealer and blush.

It's soothing, in a way; her soft hands against my skin. She puts me back together, like broken pieces, and slowly, the haze of drunken grief slips from me. I wake up.

"There," she murmurs, stepping back to examine her work.

I stare at my reflection: pale skin, almost as pale as my mom's. "I look like someone died."

Elise's eyes widen, then a faint smile tugs at the edge of her lips. "You're right," she agrees. "Anyone would think we're going to a funeral."

I feel a laugh rise in me, bitter and bleak. I reach for the red lipstick on the edge of my bureau, then slowly paint my mouth until it's a vivid scarlet slash across the pale plains of my face. I tilt my head, assessing. "Better."

Elise takes it from me and quickly does her own. Matching. She blots her lips together, meeting my gaze in the mirror. "I'm right here," she says again quietly, taking my hand. "I won't let go."

She doesn't. Not through the service, sitting on the hard pews of the cold, echoing church. Not through the receiving line, as Mom's friends and survivors' group supporters envelop me in a never-ending parade of hugs and cooing sympathy. And not as we sit in the back of the car, driving slowly through the cemetery to a fresh grave near the top of the hill.

The wind is icy, and it whips around us as I get out of the car. I see the others assemble at the graveside: Chelsea, Max, AK, Lamar, and Mel, all wearing matching dark coats and expressions of sympathy. There's one face missing.

"Did you talk to Tate?" I ask, unsteady in the black pumps she picked out.

"He's still in Aspen." Something stiffens in Elise's expression. "He says they'll be back on Sunday."

"It's not his fault," I defend him weakly. "It's the holidays; it's hard to switch flights."

She doesn't reply, just tucks my scarf tighter around my neck; smoothing back a strand of hair flying free around my face. "Nearly over," she whispers, guiding me into position in the front row beside the grave.

The next part of the service begins: interring her bones

back to the earth; ashes to ashes, dust to dust. I let the priest's words drift over me, thinking instead of Tate. The truth is, I'm glad he's not here to see me like this. Such a wreck. I feel raw, and bruised, as if the worst, darkest parts of myself have been spilled out onto the frozen ground beside my mother's grave, on display to the world. Tate knows me laughing and at ease, centered and calm, not this ragged mess of a girl. And it may be shallow, but I want to keep it that way: to be bright and good for him, not an endless black hole of grief.

"'Do not stand at my grave and weep. I am not there. I do not sleep.'"

I look up. It's my dad's turn, reading, with a single red rose clutched in his hand. They're lowering the body now, a slow grind down into the ground. The words wash through me, and I let out a sharp, twisted laugh.

"Of course she's there," I mutter, suddenly so angry. "Where the fuck else would she be?"

Elise's grip tightens on me.

"'I am the sunlight on ripened grain. I am the gentle autumn rain.'"

Suddenly I can't breathe. After sitting, numb, through so many saccharine poems and Hallmark-card consolations, I can't take it anymore. They're pretending like this is all some big tragedy, an accident. As if she didn't choose to leave me. But it's a joke. *Cruelly taken from her family*, they say, but the truth is, she killed herself. She chose this. She could have fought it, stayed with me longer, but she didn't love me enough.

She never has.

The pain comes welling up, and with it, a rage that burns so fierce, I feel like I'm about to pass out. "Elise," I gasp, my chest burning, but she holds me up. She holds me through it all, until Dad finishes his poem and tosses the rose down onto the coffin, and the glossy lacquered wood is swallowed up by the dark earth forever.

We drive back to my house, silent in the backseat of a town car. Dad has invited more people over, to "celebrate her life," he says, but I've played my part. I'm done. I hurry straight up to my bedroom, and find the bottle of prescription pills tucked in my drawer. I sneaked them from my mom's room, before the doctor cleared it out. I shake out one, then another, small and white in the palm of my hand, sweet against my tongue.

There's a noise. I look up sharply, but it's just Elise. She's got a bottle of whiskey with her. "You started without me," she says, kicking her shoes aside. She holds out her hand, so I pass the pill bottle. She reads the label.

"Xanax, good choice." She slips one into her mouth, and sighs. "When I die, I want a real party. None of that poetry, weepy bullshit." She leaps onto my bed, scooting back against the pillows. I flip the main lights off and follow, so we're lying there together in the glow of my bedside lamp.

I sink deeper into the pillows, exhaling. "Don't talk like that."

"About what, death?" She props herself up on one elbow, looking down at my face. "Too soon?"

"Very."

"Very soon. That doesn't make any sense."

"You think any of this does?" I feel the chemicals start working their magic, the smooth hiss and fizzle as they slip through my bloodstream. Elise reaches down and gently strokes my face, trailing her finger along my cheek, my nose, the line of my jaw. I smile, relieved that it's over now, that she's here just like she said.

"Tell me I'll be okay," I say, slipping further into the numbness. "Tell me it won't always feel this way."

"It won't." Elise curls in closer to me, her head resting on the pillows just inches from my face. I stare into her eyes, the promise there. "You'll be just fine."

I know she's right, but somehow, that makes it sadder. I've been losing Mom for years now, ever since that first diagnosis, and I realize that part of this pain is more from the mother she'll never be to me than the mom she really was.

Something in me finally breaks. I start to cry, quiet tears slipping out of my body like release. "I can't do this," I whisper, clutching Elise. "I can't, I can't. She left me. She could have stayed and fought this, and she just gave up instead. Maybe if I'd been better . . . ?"

"No." Elise stops me with a kiss, sweet and tender on my lips. She cradles my face, unblinking. "It's not on you, it's on her. It's all on her."

I inhale, shaky. "You won't leave me," I say, a quiet note of desperation in my voice.

"Never." Elise wipes the tears from my cheeks and kisses me again. "I'm yours, and you're mine. Always."

"Always." I fall into her, feeling the gentle pull of oblivion. It's dark, and warm, and safe here in her arms. I kiss her back, and wait for the pain to be over.

RECESS

They take me back to the conference room after Mel's testimony, and threaten to put me back in handcuffs and shackles unless I calm down.

"She'll be fine," I hear Gates reassuring the guard, but I can't focus; I can't stop shaking. I tear away from them, pacing back and forth in the small space. I was so close to the end, so close, and now it's all ruined.

Lee edges closer, holding out a bottle of water, but I push it away.

"She's lying," I tell them again, my voice scratched and sobbing. "She couldn't stand it that Elise picked me. She always hated how close we were, that we didn't need her tagging along." I look up, to Gates and my dad, but they're frozen, their eyes cast away from me. "I bet she's been waiting for this all along." My voice rises with desperation. "To pay me back, for all those mean things I said. It's not true. You have to believe me," I yell. "None of it is true!"

I can't believe she's doing this to me. It's not some high school bitch-fight, a war over BFFs and party invites. This is life-and-death, my whole future on the line, and it's just her word against mine.

"The maid," I suddenly remember, stopping dead. I turn to them, gripping the back of a chair. "She was there, in the house, with me and Elise. She can testify, say there wasn't any fight!"

Gates exchanges a look with my dad.

"What?" I demand. "It's true, she came every day. What's her name—Marta, Martha? Where is she? We have to get her on the stand. She can back me up!"

"Marta and her family moved off the island," Gates says slowly.

"So?" I cry. "The judge can make them come, can't she? Force her to testify."

Gates and my dad share another look, then Gates lets out a sigh. "They moved to America, to work for the Dempseys."

I stop. "I don't understand."

"It was a payoff," he says slowly. "Back before Tate cut his deal. Remember, he was a suspect too. She probably saw him with

Elise, something they wanted to keep hidden." Gates explains. "They gave her a job, probably got her a visa, a house, too."

"But . . . that doesn't mean she can't testify," I say, desperate. "She was there. She can tell them all, Melanie's lying."

Gates shakes his head. "Even if the judge compels her to come back, it won't be credible. Dekker will say part of the payoff was lying about this."

"But *we* didn't pay her off!" I cry. "That was Tate!"

"It won't make a difference."

I grab the chair and hurl it to the back of the room. It clatters against the wall with a screech of metal. "But it's not true!" I gasp, the pressure pinning down on my chest again. "None of it is true!"

I sink to the floor, tears coming now, uncontrollably. How could Mel do it—sit up there and lie like that? She had to know what it would mean for me, that I'll spend the rest of my life in prison now, because of something she made up to spite me. I gasp for air, shaking. From a long way off, I hear a knock at the door. Gates goes to answer it, but my dad doesn't move, he just stands there, stranded on the other side of the room.

I don't know how long I'm huddled there, weeping, but eventually my sobs fade away, leaving nothing but a thundering headache and the dry soreness of my throat. Lee crouches down beside me and offers the water again. This time, I take it.

The door opens. Gates returns.

"We should ask to recess until tomorrow," Lee says, but Gates shakes his head. He rights the chair from where I hurled it, then sits down at the table.

"Anna?"

I look up from the floor.

"I just talked to Dekker," he says slowly. "He's willing to cut a deal."

I freeze.

"What kind of deal?" my dad asks urgently.

"Manslaughter," Gates says with a slow exhale. "He wants a ten-year sentence, but you'd be up for parole before then. Eight years."

There's silence.

I look around the room. Gates looks relieved. My dad is still staring at the floor. Lee is thoughtful. "Why would he do that?" I ask finally. "With what Mel said, why would he offer me something?"

"Plenty of reasons." Gates can't stop smiling now, like this is a good thing, like he's relieved. "Mel lied the first time on the stand; maybe he doesn't want to risk the judge ignoring her. Then there's the video, with Juan. He's trying for first-degree murder here—he has to prove you meant to kill her, that you planned it."

"But I didn't!"

"This is a good deal," he says. "Better than I thought we'd get."

I try to think, to pull back from the edge of despair and see this clearly. Manslaughter. A plea. "I'd have to say I did it," I say, realizing. "I'd have to say I'm guilty."

"Manslaughter is unintentional death," Gates quickly replies. "He's saying you didn't mean to kill her. You fought; you lost control. A crime of passion, in the moment."

"But I didn't." I look at them, plaintive. "I didn't kill her."

"I know it's a lot to think about." Gates's tone is gentle. "But this is a limited-time offer. He wants it wrapped up before the judge calls us back for closing arguments."

"I have to decide now?"

"I'm sorry." Gates looks apologetic. "I know it's fast, but this is a good thing."

"How can you say that?" I cry. "It's prison! I'd be guilty. I'd go back there for years!"

My words echo. Gates looks away.

"You think I should take it." My heart twists.

He sighs. "I do. A lot of evidence is circumstantial, but it doesn't look good. The affair, Mel's testimony—"

"She's lying!" I cry again.

"Either way, do you want to risk it with the judge?" Gates leans across the table, solemn. "If she convicts you of murder, that's a twenty-year sentence, minimum. Twenty years. At least, this way, you'd be out sooner. You'd have a life, after."

After.

I choke back another sob. "Daddy?" I ask, my voice wavering. "I don't know. . . . I can't think straight. What should I do? Tell me."

My father swallows and finally meets my eyes. "Gates is right, sweetie," he says quietly. "You should take the deal."

The words are soft, but they crash through me like thunder. I stare at him, dumbfounded, and then I see it: the faint flicker in his eyes. He tries to look away and hide it, but it's too late. I see.

He thinks I'm guilty.

My heart breaks wide-open.

"Eight years isn't so long." He hurries to my side, trying to cover the betrayal. "You'd be twenty-five. That's still young, you could have a life, do whatever you want."

"But I didn't do it." My voice is thin and tired. I can't move, not a single limb. He sits beside me on the floor. "I didn't . . ."

"I'm sorry, sweetie" is all he can say, over and over. He hugs me close, and for a moment I'm a kid again, crawling into his lap. Before the long work nights and the hospital rooms, and everything began to change. Before I wound up here, staring into the bleak abyss of years in prison, my whole youth, locked away in that terrible place. "I'm so, so sorry."

EIGHT YEARS

I was going to go to college, some sun-drenched campus far away.

I was going to take film, and women's studies, classes in literature and ancient philosophy.

I was going to study abroad in Prague, and walk those golden bridges. Sip coffee in tiny cafés and flirt with cute waiters.

I was going to learn to surf, and learn to speak Italian, and how to change a flat tire.

I was going to try bangs, and dark eyeliner, wear scarlet lipstick and tartan capes.

I was going to fall in love again.

I was going to road-trip across the country, stay in cheap motels and collect postcards from every state.

I was going to see the world.

I was going to move into my own apartment and furnish it with cheap thrift-store finds, sip tea in the afternoon from mismatched vintage china, in a space that was all my own.

I was going to be alone in a strange city where nobody knew my name.

I was going to finish reading *Great Expectations*.

I was going to have another macaroni night with my dad in our kitchen back at home.

I was going to see a midnight screening of *The Rocky Horror Picture Show* with a rowdy costumed crowd.

I was going to get two kittens and name them Eleanor and Marianne.

I was going to volunteer at the cancer hospice.

I was going to fight for something I believed in.

I was going to grow herbs in terra-cotta pots outside my kitchen window.

I was going to write something one day, that people would read. Maybe even love.

I was going to kiss a lot of boys.

I was going to stay up all night talking, and know that it was just the beginning.

I was going to get married, in a strapless white dress with my mother's veil.

I was going to graduate high school in my cap and gown.

I was going to dance through a hundred more rock shows, drenched in sweat and songs.

I was going to spend a summer backpacking through Europe.

I was going to sing along to the radio every day.

I was going to get my boots fixed before fall.

I was going to buy that red belt I saw in the store.

I was going to watch all the shows I left on my DVR.

I was going to see it snow at Christmastime in New York.

I was going to get an A on my history midterm.

I was going to get a new car for graduation.

I was going to make him proud.

I was going to start all over again.

I was going to be brave, and good, and bold.

I was going to love him forever.

I was going to hold her hand till the very end.

NOW

I tell them no.

Eight years is too long. Even just one year more of this would destroy me, but more than that, I can't plead guilty. I won't sign the deal and say I killed her, when I've spent so long fighting to clear my name. I'll take my chances on the judge instead, and all of Dekker's failings.

I know I'd rather kill myself than go back to that prison again. I have to try for freedom, or nothing at all.

CLOSING ARGUMENTS

PROSECUTION:

"Elise Warren was the light of her parents' life. A kind, fun-loving girl who loved to spend time with her friends, volunteer, join school clubs and activities. A straight-A student, she could have had any future that she chose. But Elise will never get to live those dreams, because her life was cut brutally short by a frenzied attack. On the afternoon of March twentieth, Elise was attacked in her bedroom as she prepared to go meet her friends. This wasn't an accident, or a quick death, no; you've heard from expert forensic witnesses how Elise was stabbed thirteen times in the chest and stomach with a kitchen knife and then left to die in a pool of her own blood. She would have died gasping for air, feeling her own life and that bright future slip away as she slowly bled to death.

"Now, the defense has tried to pin the blame for this murder on anyone but the woman here on trial today. They've told you that this was a break-in gone wrong, that somebody scaled the back wall to the house in broad daylight and, when faced with Elise, instead of turning and running, or simply knocking her down, they instead picked up the knife and killed her. But a murder case isn't about theories; it's based on evidence. And the evidence in this case points to one woman, and one woman alone: the defendant, Anna Chevalier.

"Experts have testified that the deadly wounds inflicted on the victim were the result of a passionate frenzy, from somebody who likely knew the victim. The defendant's fingerprints were found on the murder weapon. Her physical DNA and hairs were near the body. And as you've heard over the past weeks, the defendant had both motive for the killing and a pattern of violent behavior, which makes Elise Warren's death seem like a tragic inevitability.

"You've heard how the victim was having a secret affair with Miss Chevalier's boyfriend, and that the defendant was sent into a jealous rage when she discovered the truth, fighting with the victim and threatening to kill her. Now, threats are one thing, but we've found that the defendant has a long record of violent physical outbursts. Time and time again, she's lashed out at the people around her, inflicting serious physical damage. What's more, the defendant has no alibi for a portion of the afternoon of the murder, and even lied to police about her whereabouts that day. These lies undermine everything the defendant has said to you during this trial. How can we believe a single word she's said? She denies knowing about the affair, when her friend has testified to overhearing the defendant fight with the victim about it. She denies coercing her boyfriend into giving her an alibi for the afternoon, and she has even tried to pin the blame on the victim for their partying and reckless behavior, when other friends have all testified that the victim was a model student and citizen before she became friends with Miss Chevalier.

"As we've seen, since the murder and throughout the trial, the defendant displays a troubling lack of responsibility. In the days after the murder, she was seen laughing and joking with her boyfriend, and in fact, just hours after discovering the body, Miss Chevalier seemed more concerned with buying a soda than the fact that her best friend was dead. These are the marks of a remorseless killer, who struck the victim in a premeditated attack fueled by sexual jealousy and rage. This is a woman who deserves to pay—for the life she's taken, and the lies she's told.

"A young woman is dead. Nothing can bring her back, but justice must be done. So, I ask you to deliver justice, to Elise

Warren's parents and friends, and to the memory of Elise herself. Find the defendant guilty, and award her the maximum sentence permitted for her crimes."

DEFENSE:

"Justice. The prosecution likes to talk a lot about it, as if prosecuting an innocent teenage girl for a crime she didn't commit could ever be justified. The fact is, Klaus Dekker has botched and mishandled this case from the very start. Responding to 911 calls from the scene of the crime, police found broken glass in the room, indicating a break-in. The victim's friends testified that Elise had been harassed by two men in the days leading up to the murder—Niklas van Oaten, and the market trader known only as Juan, who had a record of theft and break-ins. Yet instead of pursuing these suspects, Dekker instead concocted an outlandish theory about the crime, deciding that the defendant—a young girl with no criminal record, with no real violence to her name—had somehow plotted to kill her best friend, a girl she counted closer than any sister.

"You've seen the extent to which Dekker has gone to prove this so-called theory: tampering with video evidence to conceal Juan's stalking of the victim, and putting witnesses on the stand to contradict their own testimony. He wants you to assess the evidence in this case. The fact is, the evidence against my client is purely circumstantial. Due to police failure to preserve the body, the exact time of death of the victim is still unknown. No blood from the victim was found on the defendant's clothes or person. Several other fingerprints were found on the knife, including that of her boyfriend, Tate Dempsey, and others who were staying in the house. The room was easily accessed from the beach, and several other people knew of the way inside.

"As to the defendant's behavior after the murder . . . It's clear that Anna Chevalier was in shock. You've seen expert psychologists testify about the effects of post-traumatic stress disorder, and how the delayed reaction to grief can affect different people. Seeing her dear friend lying in a pool of blood was a deeply traumatic experience for the defendant, a trauma worsened only by the aggressive interrogations she suffered at the hands of the prosecution. In her testimony here, Anna has shown she is a caring, empathetic young woman who has remained admirably strong in the face of her imprisonment. The prosecution has tried to paint her as a cold-blooded killer, somehow sexually fixated on the victim. He has shown you photos, and isolated incidents to try to build his case, yet this is nothing more than baseless slander. Any one of us could be made to look a monster, with selective readings of our history, but for every photograph he shows you out of context, I can show you another side to the defendant: a caring, thoughtful, intelligent young woman who has bravely faced tragic loss before in her life, with the death of her mother. That is the real

Anna Chevalier, not the wild party girl the prosecution would have you believe.

"The law calls for you to convict my client only beyond a reasonable doubt. Time and again, we have shown that this doubt exists: in the lack of evidence supporting the prosecution's case and Miss Chevalier's supposed motive for the crime. To convict her now would be a tragedy no less than Elise Warren's murder, for just as that young woman lost her life, so too would Miss Chevalier if sent back to prison to serve decades for a crime she didn't commit. Justice demands her acquittal. The *evidence* demands her acquittal. I place her life in your hands, and urge you to do the right thing. Thank you."

WAITING

The judge doesn't come back with a verdict that day, nor the next one. I get up every morning and leave prison like it could be the last time, then spend the day in the conference room at the courthouse, pacing, nervously waiting for news. Gates and Lee swear it's a good thing, that it means she's taking her time to pick apart every little detail of the case, but I won't let myself get swept up in false hopes.

"She could have made her mind up on day one," I tell them. "And just be back in her office, catching up on her DVR and gossip magazines."

Lee gives me a look. "I know this is hard, waiting," he says. "But it's the best you could hope for, it taking so long.

We always knew Dekker's case was weak, and now she gets to see that for herself."

I sigh. "I know, I just . . . What if—"

"Don't." He stops me. "You've just got to have faith."

I look at him, his brown eyes so calm and trusting. He's the one person who has stuck with me through it all—despite the lies people told about me, all the terrible things they have said. "How can you still believe in me, after everything? Even they don't . . ." I drop my voice. Gates and Dad are on their cell phones, deep in two different conversations about legal process and our chances of getting the verdict overturned. For all the delay, I know they still expect the judgment to come back guilty. Maybe they even think I deserve it.

Lee leans closer. "I know you," he says softly. "I know you're a good person. And even if this comes back wrong, it's not the end. We can appeal," he reminds me. "Get Dekker's evidence thrown out. Whatever it takes, I'll be here."

I want to believe him. He's been here before, after all, but I'm not his sister—I can't stay hopeful through years in prison. I'm not that strong.

The hours tick past, with no news. Then, just before four p.m., a knock comes on the door. We all leap up. A guard beckons Gates out; he exits, giving me a nod as he passes.

"Oh God," I breathe. My skin prickles hot with nerves; my stomach turns over. "This is it."

Lee grabs my hand and squeezes, but when Gates comes back in a moment later, he quickly shakes his head. "It's not that," he says. "There's someone who wants to see you." He pauses, uncomfortable. "Tate Dempsey wants to talk with you."

Tate.

I blink. Months of silence, all my letters left unanswered, and *now* he wants to see me?

"You don't have to," Lee tells me, but I slowly shake my head.

"I . . . Yes," I say, suddenly calm. "Let him in."

Gates nods to someone in the hallway. My dad gets up, clearing his throat. "We'll, uh, give you some privacy."

They exit, but Lee is the last to leave. "Are you sure?" he asks. "I can stay, if you want—"

He stops talking as Tate steps into the room.

I glance up, almost afraid to look at him after all this time. But there he is, looking just the same as ever: neatly dressed in a preppy oxford button-down and dark pants, his hair golden and tousled. He stands by the doorway, awkwardly slouching with his hands in his pockets. Finally, I let my gaze settle on his face.

God, how I loved that face.

"It's fine," I tell Lee softly. "Really."

He nods. "I'll be right outside," he says, stepping around Tate and closing the door behind him.

Silence.

I watch Tate scuff the ground with his spotless sneakers, looking anywhere but directly at me. Finally, I sigh.

"What do you want?"

He walks closer, then stops. "Can I . . . ?"

"Sit?" It's almost funny, that he would think it matters. "Sure. Whatever you want."

He lowers himself carefully onto one of the folding metal chairs, and takes a breath. Then another. "How are you doing?" he asks.

My mouth drops open. *Is he serious?*

"Just great," I reply, sarcastic. "Except for this whole pesky murder conviction hanging over my head."

Tate seems to crumple in front of me. "God, Anna, I'm so sorry." He reaches for my hand across the table, but I flinch back. "It wasn't my idea, to cut the deal, I swear to you. But my parents said I had to. Dekker was coming after me; they said I would go on trial for sure." Tate stares at me, imploring, with those blue eyes I know by heart. "I didn't have a choice."

"You always had a choice!" I burst out. "I'm here because of you. I lied for you. You're the one who sold me out—you betrayed me!"

Tate hangs his head.

I fight to stay calm. There's nothing he can say, I realize. Nothing at all. He was weak, and selfish, and he let me down in every way he could. But what else was he going to do? He always wanted to be so good: the perfect son, the best boyfriend. Elise was right, in the end: all that perfection had to fall apart sometime.

I swallow, gathering my strength. "When did it start?" I ask softly. "You and Elise. Tell me. Please."

Tate reluctantly lifts his head. "Anna . . ."

"You owe me this much, at least."

He looks away again. "Jordan's party," he says finally. "It was . . . maybe a month before the trip?"

I nod. I remember.

"My parents were on at me, about summer internships, and volunteering, and . . . I just wanted to forget it all. You were home, sick, and . . . I wound up out in the gazebo with Elise and a bottle of tequila."

Even after all this time, hearing it still stings. I fight the image of them together, sprawled, laughing. The looks that turned into more.

"But, why?" I ask. "I don't understand. You said you loved me."

"I did." Tate looks helpless. "It just . . . happened."

"And kept happening."

He looks shameful, at least. "You know Elise, what she was like. She made you feel . . . like everything was dangerous. A risk. Like, you were the center of everything, you know?"

I do.

He stops, tugging at the skin around a hangnail. "She said she wanted to know—what it felt like for you. Being with me."

A noise comes from the door, interrupting us. Gates is there. "It's time," he says. "She has a verdict."

Oh God.

I get to my feet, unsteady.

"Anna . . ." Tate looks up at me. "I'm sorry, you have to know. I never meant for any of this—"

"I have to go," I cut him off. I follow Gates and my dad back down the hall to the courtroom, the guard flanking me every step of the way.

"It's okay, sweetie," my dad says, but his voice is weak and uncertain. I falter in the doorway, suddenly realizing everything that's waiting for me.

My freedom, or the end of my life completely.

A hand goes to my back, steering me gently across the threshold. I walk, numb, to the table, and sit one final time. Dekker is already in his seat, looking smug and confident.

"Daddy?" I whisper, panicked, but he doesn't hear me. He's staring straight ahead, his foot tapping in an uneven rhythm.

The judge enters and takes her seat. She looks out at us

from over those thin gold spectacles. "Would the defendant please stand?"

I don't know how, but somehow, I manage to rise to my feet. My whole body is shaking, blood pounding in my ears. I try to find some clue on her face, but her expression is unnervingly blank. Wouldn't she smile at me? Wouldn't she give me some kind of sign if the verdict was good?

"I have reviewed all the evidence presented to me, and in the matter of the prosecution versus Anna Chevalier, I have reached a verdict."

The courtroom is completely silent as the judge's voice rings out. "On the charge of murder in the first degree . . ."

I don't move. I don't even breathe. My heartbeat takes over as I watch her lips form the words. I can't hear a thing, but I see it now, written on all their faces. My dad lets out a sob. Lee's body crumples. Gates hangs his head, slack-jawed.

My legs give way. I fall into blackness, and it's over.

THE NIGHT

Her body is on the floor, half-naked in pink bikini bottoms with her tank top ripped away in ribbons and stab wounds cutting scarlet across her chest.

Tate gets to her first. He hugs her torso against him, the trails of blond hair matted with blood, her face pressing against his blue shirt.

"Elise!" Melanie whimpers over and over again by the wreckage of the door, her voice shrill and gasping. Chelsea falls to her knees in the blood, taking Elise's lifeless hand. AK and Lamar stand beside me, not breathing.

"She was like this." Max's voice is breaking, tears streaming down his face. He's crumpled in a heap by the open balcony doors, broken glass scattered on the floor. "The door was smashed and open, and she was just, lying there. I didn't touch her."

There's blood everywhere. Dark and thick, pooling around the body, smeared across the terra-cotta tiles. Her body is sticky with it, and for a terrible moment, we're all frozen. Staring.

She must have struggled. Clawed for rescue, gasping and half-dead.

And now she's gone.

"God, someone cover her up," my voice breaks, but nobody moves, so I quickly pull off my jacket and lay it gently over her body. It's too small. Her legs splay out from underneath, pale against the blood. Her arms hang limply from Tate's clutched embrace.

Melanie sobs louder.

"We should go," Lamar says suddenly, backing away. "This is a crime scene, right? We shouldn't be in here, messing things up."

Chelsea whirls on him. "This isn't *CSI*! This is Elise, this is . . ." Her whole body shudders, and Lamar rushes to hold her up.

I swallow, looking around at the devastation. "Come on, he's right. We can't be here."

AK pulls Max from his corner, and Melanie stumbles on ahead. Tate doesn't move.

"Tay?" I put a hand on his shoulder. "Tay, she's gone. There's nothing you can do."

His body shakes, and then he places her carefully back on the floor, tenderly brushing hair from her eyes. They stare up at me, blue and lifeless. A wave of nausea rolls through me, and I have to look away.

I pull Tate to his feet, and we slowly head out front, to where the others are waiting on the paved driveway in the glare of security lights.

"Who would do this?" Melanie finally demands, her voice raw. "Who would do this to her?"

I close my eyes and sink back against Tate's chest, feeling his arms press tightly around me. But the sight of her body stays, vivid in my mind: so red, and torn, and empty.

"They'll find him," Lamar says quietly, Chelsea sobbing into his neck. "We'll make him pay."

We wait in a silence punctuated by sobs. Headlights pass on the main street nearby; we can hear faint music from the hotel down the beach. Behind us, the ocean is an inky shadow beyond the bright lights of the bars. And Elise is gone now, forever.

THREE MONTHS LATER

"Now, Anna, I know that we all want to hear: What did you feel, when you heard that verdict being read?"

I pause, flashing back for a moment to that day in the courtroom and the few seconds that changed everything. "Relief," I finally answer with a small smile. "Just, relief. I was overwhelmed, I could hardly speak. After all that time, expecting the worst, to finally be found innocent . . . And it wasn't just about me," I add quickly. "I was relieved for Elise, too. The worst part of all of it was knowing that if I was found guilty, the person who really killed her would be getting away with it. At least now, maybe they can find him."

Clara smiles at me, warm and supportive. She's walking beside me in the graveyard, spring blossoms bright on the trees. The interview setting was their idea, of course: to cap my homecoming tell-all with a heartfelt visit to Elise's grave. I didn't want to do it—I didn't want to ever lay eyes on Clara Rose again—but the money they were offering was too big to pass up. From the moment the verdict came back innocent, we've had networks and newspapers all clamoring for my exclusive interview. Every time I said no, it only made them chase harder, so in the end it was easier just to pick one and be done with it. And after all the money I cost him, it's the least I can do for my dad to try to pay him back somehow.

"So what's ahead for you now?" Clara asks, bundled in a fitted powder-blue jacket. I have a white woolen coat on, and pink mittens, the result of intense debate among the wardrobe team. They wanted me in red, but I wasn't about to fall for that again. I insisted on the white, worn over a knee-length skirt and a pale pastel sweater. The colors of innocence.

"I'm taking some time," I reply. "Spending time with my family, and friends. It's good just to be home again for now; I missed it so much. Then I'm thinking about college. I'd like to study law, eventually," I add. "This whole experience has shown me how important it is to have people who believe in you, and who fight for what's right."

"Inspirational." Clara nods. "Just wonderful. Now, I know

so many of our viewers were rooting for you," she coos, "send-ing their thoughts and prayers all through your detention and trial. Do you have any message for them?"

"Just thank you." I clasp my hand to my chest, looking directly into the camera. "The people who never gave up on me . . . It means more than you could ever know."

"And thank you, Anna, for sharing your story with us." Clara smiles. "I know that everyone here, across the country, wishes you all the best in what's to come."

"Thank you, Clara," I tell her warmly.

"And, cut!"

"You get that?" Clara yells across to the producer.

He gives the thumbs-up. "Can we set up the graveside shots now? Maybe some more powder on Anna?"

I take my microphone off and let the makeup woman dab at my face as they dismantle the lights and rigging from around Elise's grave. The headstone is fresh, gleaming marble, and there's a flickering tea light set on top.

"Here." A production assistant hands me a bunch of flowers to set on the grave. "Peonies, right?"

I nod. They're out of season, but they were always her favorite. Something about this should be real, at the very least.

"Good work," Clara chats, checking her cell phone. "We'll start running the previews tonight. Have you finalized your book deal yet?"

380

"We're still talking to people," I answer coolly. "I haven't picked a publisher yet."

"Well, let me know when it's coming out. I'd love to have you back."

Of course she would. "Sure," I reply, with a fake smile. "I'll have my agent set it up."

They finally clear the area, then walk me through the staging of the final scene. It's a long-distance shot, wide-angle from across the graveyard. They want me standing at her graveside, then kneeling to place the flowers down, preferably with a single teardrop sliding down my well-powdered cheek. I follow their directions obediently, take after take, as they struggle against the wind. I don't mind it so much. After everything, I know how important a single shot can be, the story that can replace facts and hard evidence with just a single perfect frame.

"One more time?" The producer calls. I nod, and walk slowly back to the grave.

Elise Judith Warren

Loving daughter, beloved friend

Always in our hearts

I lean down, and gently place the flowers on the damp grass. I trace the letters of the headstone, tears stinging the corners of my eyes. I still miss her, every day. When they call it a tragedy, they're right. We could have still been together, if only she'd been true to me. If she'd only known what she was bringing on herself, maybe she would have thought twice.

Instead, she had to go and break my heart.

"And, cut!"

They tell me it's a wrap, and slowly the crew dismantles, packing up the vans and heading out. But I stay, right by her grave, until the last car winds its way out toward the main gates, and I'm finally alone. The skies are gray and overcast, the graveyard totally empty.

I reach into my coat pocket and pull it out: the necklace. The chipped metal of the pentagram pendant, the chain broken, still stained with her blood.

I close my fist around it and lean in close to whisper.

"I win."

BEFORE

"Babe, can you pass me that soda?"

There's no reply.

"Tate?"

I reluctantly sit up, squinting through the dark glass of my shades. The gentle curve of the beach stretches in front of me: sparkling white sand leading down to the crystal-blue waters lapping gently against the shore. The sun is hot in a cloudless sky, warming my bare skin. It's perfection.

I look over at Tate. He's sitting up with his bare back to me, bent over his cell phone, so I toss my magazine at him.

He looks around. "What? Oh, sorry." He passes a soda can from the cooler, glancing again at his phone.

"Are they having fun?" I ask.

"Oh yeah. They're out on the boat," he adds. "AK's taking tons of photos—you know he won't shut up about that new camera of his."

I laugh. "Let me guess, we're going to get fifty-seven million shots of some fish underwater?"

"Pretty much." Tate grins.

I lie back, letting the sun melt through my bones, taking with it all my tension and stress. Right now, Boston feels like a thousand miles away; college application drama and all my dad's business worries like something from another life. I let my mind go blank, soothed by the sounds of the waves, and the occasional burst of chatting and laughter from the other beachgoers set up around us on the sand.

Time slips past. Tate's phone sounds with another text, and then a moment later, I hear his voice. "Shit, I left my sunglasses back at the house."

"Here, take mine." I hold them out to him, resting my other elbow over my face to block the sun.

"No, it's cool. I need to go charge my phone anyway." Tate gets to his feet and grabs his wallet from the blanket. "I won't be long."

"You remember the security code?"

"Yeah, but Elise is still back there, right?"

"She could still be sleeping." I check my phone, but there

are no new messages. "Check on her for me, okay?" I tell him. "She's still not replying to my texts."

"Sure. She's probably just hungover, though."

I make a face. "She's not the only one."

Tate slips his feet into his flip-flops and makes to leave, but I reach up toward him. He pauses, leaning down to quickly kiss my lips. "Tell her to get her ass down here." I yawn. "She can lie around in bed any day back home. This is vacation she's missing here!"

Tate smiles, then sets off back across the sand.

I find the bottle of lotion, and start to reapply. My skin is pale and always burns easily, but the only alternative is this thick, white goop, sticky and smelling like coconut. I cover myself as best I can, but there's a wide swathe across my back I can't reach, so I set the bottle aside and turn back to my magazine, waiting for Tate to return.

The minutes pass. I finish the magazine and dig in the beach tote for my lip balm, bored. I'm getting hungry now, so I grab my beach bag and quickly slip into my shorts and sandals, then head up the beach.

The back doors of the beach house are open when I reach it: the glass slid aside. I climb up the stairs from the beach, and step inside. "Hello?"

The house is quiet, nobody in sight. Then I hear laughter coming from deeper inside. Elise's voice. And Tate. I can't hear what they're saying, only the tone of their voices.

Teasing. Affectionate.

I freeze.

And suddenly, I remember the necklace: the one Tate had in his pocket, the one Elise claimed as her own.

I had put all of that aside. After all, there were a dozen ways for us to have mixed them up: I probably took it by mistake, long before the trip. We sat here on the beach together, just the night before. Elise said it was the two of us. Always.

Their laughter comes again, echoing in the expanse of white and tile and bright sunshine. My heartbeat quickens. I feel a faint wave of nausea spread through me. I think of the way she was teasing him the first day, when we arrived. There was something pointed about it, taunting. And Tate, being so protective about Niklas . . .

I take a long, shaky breath. Part of me wants to turn back around—go lie out in the sun until Tate gets back, and spend the rest of the afternoon playing in the water—but now that the idea is in my head, I know I can't stop, not until I can prove to myself I'm wrong. I take a slow step, deeper into the house, toward their voices.

"Hey, hands!" Elise's voice exclaims. She giggles flirtatiously. "I'm trying to give you a show here."

"Aww, come on . . ." Tate groans.

"What do you think? I got it right before we left."

"I think you look fucking sexy."

"And . . . ?"

"And what?"

Elise's voice drops, seductive. "What are you going to do about it?"

There's no more talking.

I'm at the end of the hallway now, beside Elise's empty room. They're in our room, I realize. Our bed.

Bile rises in my throat, but I force myself to keep walking. It could be a game, I tell myself. Just, messing around. Something, some other explanation. It has to be.

I see them a split-second before I hear Elise moan, like lightning, flashing sharp ahead of the slow rumble of thunder. They're framed through the open door of the bedroom, tangled up in each other on the bed. Naked. Tate rolls her underneath him, groaning as he thrusts; Elise's legs are wrapped around him, pale against the golden tan of his back as she whimpers and arches up against him.

I can't look away.

They tumble over again, and this time, Elise is on top. She sinks deeply against him, her eyes closed, her arms drifting above her head. She looks the way she always does when she's dancing, lost in something bigger than herself. Swept up. Blissful.

Then her eyes open, and she looks directly at me.

I don't move. Our gaze is caught across Tate's oblivious body, and for a moment, it's like I'm there beneath her; her skin against mine. Then her face begins to change—she's caught up, too far gone to stop. I watch the orgasm rush through her; I feel it in my bones. Like an awakening. Like a death. And all the while, our eyes stay locked on each other's.

How much do you love me?

ABOUT THE AUTHOR

ABIGAIL HAAS

has written two adult novels and four young adult contemporary novels under the name Abby McDonald. She grew up in Sussex, England, and studied politics, philosophy, and economics at Oxford University. This is her first young adult thriller. She lives in Los Angeles.